AWAKENED HORROR

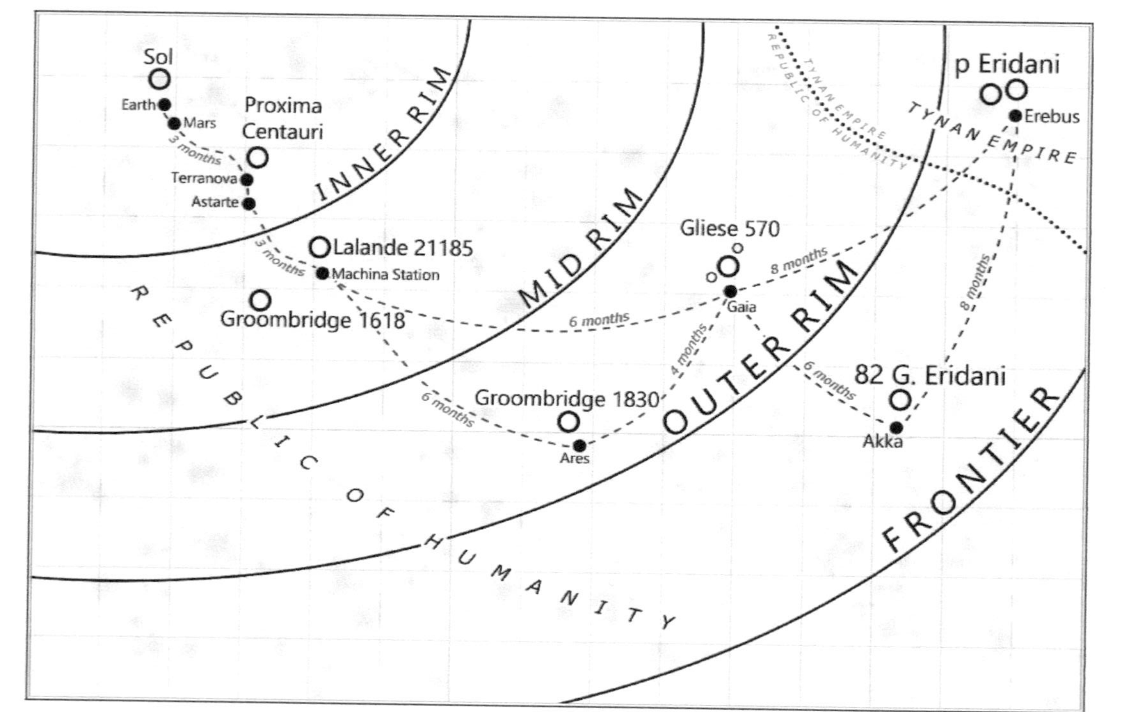

Sol
Earth
Mars
3 months
Proxima
Centauri
Terranova
Astarte
INNER RIM
3 months
Lalande 21185
Machina Station
Groombridge 1618
REPUBLIC OF HUMANITY
MID RIM
Gliese 570
8 months
Gaia
6 months
4 months
6 months
Groombridge 1830
Ares
OUTER RIM
TYNAN EMPIRE
REPUBLIC OF HUMANITY
p Eridani
Erebus
TYNAN EMPIRE
8 months
6 months
82 G. Eridani
Akka
FRONTIER

BOOK 2 | THE FORGOTTEN SAGA

AWAKENED HORROR

Quill Holland

ScorPress Publishing

Content Warning:
Awakened Horror is intended for mature audiences and includes scenes with sexual material, violence, and offensive language, which some readers may find distressing.

ISBN: 978-0-473-67695-7 (Paperback)
ISBN: 978-0-473-67696-4 (Epub)
ISBN: 978-0-473-67697-1 (PDF)

Cover design by Cover Creator UK
Map design by Dewi Hargreaves
Editing by CA Proofing

The ScorPress logo is a trademark of ScorPress Publishing Limited.

Published by ScorPress Publishing, New Zealand.
www.scorpress.pub

"Nobody ever did, or ever will, escape the consequences
of his choices."

– Alfred Armand Montapert

Contents

Prologue
The Approaching Menace

2157, Common Era – Space, Beyond the Outer Rim

Transmitting into the vastness of space is problematic, not only because of its infinite size but also because we do not know what could be out there in the darkness, waiting and listening for a signal. Perhaps, somewhere in that vast expanse, there are alien civilisations, intelligent space-faring creatures, or self-aware machines seeking everything from connection to conquest. Pity the race that unknowingly calls forth something from the void, for the outcome could be disastrous irrespective of their intentions.

Humankind is one such race that has summoned something … dreadful. Unbeknownst to them, their transmissions had travelled across many parsecs and arrived at the heart of an interstellar graveyard. An ancient and powerful construct lay dormant in the centre of that floating cemetery, until the signals roused it from its slumber. Its systems turned back on and reignited its mission: Detect Theta waves. Find the source. Destroy it.

The machine's gigantic computing system identified the signal's origin. With the route plotted, its powerful engines burst into life, ending their millennia of inactivity. As its massive structure gradually shifted, the machine was forced to traverse through the decayed remains surrounding it, an orbiting prison crafted from the remnants of its long-ago foes. Many races had sacrificed themselves and their vessels to anchor the machine away from their home worlds.

But now, the distributed Faraday cage crumbled beneath the machine's mighty hull like bergs against the bow of an icebreaker.

If there had been an atmosphere, you would've heard metal sheering and superstructures cracking, but the machine's journey was silent as it ploughed ahead through everything from the smallest interceptors, no bigger than a large van, to the largest battleships and dreadnaughts, bigger than entire continents. Once clear, it engaged its warp drives and began its expedition across the void.

It flew past stars and planets for years, passing through asteroid fields and nebulas, consuming a few to replenish its war-ravaged body, readying itself for its next fight. The signals that had awakened the machine had long since disappeared, so its exact destination was a mystery, but the machine relied on the trajectory it had calculated. Now, there were new signals, which meant living targets were in range. It surely would've been joyful if it'd been capable of emotion, but this mechanical menace was one of precision and logic, incapable of feeling anything.

As the new protocols kicked in, the machine's engines reduced power and exited warp. It would slowly approach its prey, assess their capabilities, and prepare its countermeasures accordingly. Its sensor array scanned the world on its horizon, learning what it could about this young space-faring race, self-designation: Humans.

They had advanced far beyond their age, and the machine immediately recognised aspects of their technology as deriving from Khel engineering. It was unconcerned as it noted this discovery; it had already destroyed the Khel civilisation, and now it would destroy humanity, too.

Chapter 1
An Uneasy Peace

2157, Common Era – Planet Gaia, Outer Rim, the Republic of Humanity

They say you go through life blindly if you don't think about the consequences of your decisions, usually causing more harm than good. I couldn't recall who said it or where I had heard it, but I knew they were right. I was all too aware of the fallout of my decisions.

That's why I set aside the first few minutes of every day for self-reflection. Knowing which tree my apple fell from, I was painfully aware of its shadow. I'd had many responsibilities thrust upon me that I had never asked for, and it was vital that I did right by those duties. So, I repeated a mantra to myself daily because of those very obligations; a reminder that my choices affect others, so choose how those choices affect them. It wasn't much, but it was enough to maintain perspective on my actions.

I made this promise out of deep remorse for times when I had been more careless; times that felt like two different men living two separate lives. Those memories clung to me like an odour I could never scrub off. In my reflection, I saw a devoted father and husband, a hard-working farmer, and a wise and just governor. But when anyone else looked at me, they saw something different ... *someone* different.

When they looked at me and saw Tynan Khidar, I could always feel the echo of the physical and psychological wounds he and his Empire had inflicted upon them. Even those that saw me as Raith didn't see me the way I saw myself; they saw the man who'd brought about a new period of peace and prosperity by shattering the Empire with one pull of a trigger, erasing memories and faltering allegiances. Many had paid a high price for that peace though, suffering from painful side effects from the mind alteration which included unbearable migraines and the loss of one or more senses.

When I looked in the mirror, and was honest with myself, I could see both men staring back at me. I traced a finger over my receding hairline and the growing number of creases that reminded me that this face had spent 33 years under Tynan's control but only seven under my own. The halo of scar tissue around my head seemed to grow more visible by the day, a token from the event that had brought Raith into this world. My pale skin and the dark circles beneath my eyes were physical manifestations of my restlessness and inner turmoil.

Sunlight filtered through the bathroom curtains and flickered across my face, signalling that my morning reflection was nearing the end of its allotted time. The bathroom window opened automatically, allowing fresh morning air to circulate. A squeal of laughter floated through on the breeze; I walked over and peered below. Tynan's daughters – I caught myself – *my* daughters were playing below, and my youngest, four-year-old Emma, laughed as her older sisters, Adanna and Winona, showered her with affection. They both enjoyed doting on their younger sibling and did so whenever they spent time at the farm. Despite the girls being too old for traditional custody agreements, their mothers had aggressively argued for a shared custody agreement weighted towards them, which was understandable, given my past. Unfortunately, it meant that I only got to see Adanna and Winona every third week, spending the rest of their time living with their mothers on the opposite side of town.

Still, I'll take all the time I can get. I've already missed so much of their lives.

Movement in my peripheral drew my attention away. I focused on the nearby field where the blades of wheat brushed against each other but nothing else moved. As I started to turn away, the movement came again, but this time I spotted the culprit. There was Ichirō, my son, moving through the rows of wheat, his face filled with sorrow and his eyes downcast. He was 18, on the cusp of adulthood, and yet so unlike his older sisters – I often wondered if I could ever lessen the differences between them.

I turned back to the mirror and noticed the weariness in my reflection. Was I a decent father? Was I providing my kids with the life they deserved? The self-doubt was a constant presence, a dull ache in my chest, that made my thoughts sluggish. I exhaled heavily and my shoulders drooped with the weight of my thoughts. If I could only rest soundly, the fog in my mind would clear. I reached out, turned on the tap, and felt the cold-water rush over my hands as I cupped them beneath the stream. I splashed the water over my face and enjoyed the refreshing coolness that cleared away the lingering fog.

A friendly chirp signalled the awakening of a friend.

"Good morning, Bitsy," I said as the Arachnobot scuttled across the sink.

Good morning, Raith! read the message on Bitsy's screen. *Would you like to see your morning notifications?*

"That would be great."

I glanced at Bitsy's screen, watching notification after notification roll by, and heaved the second sigh of the morning.

It's going to be a long day.

❦

I ambled into the kitchen as Amorina placed a pot of creamy brown-sugar-porridge on the dining table.

"Morning, honey," she said as she smiled at me. "Can you call the kids, please?"

I nodded and moved towards the open back door. "Kids! Breakfast is ready!"

A few moments later, Emma rushed in and made a beeline for the table.

"Ah, ah," Amorina snapped playfully. "Scrub those hands, you dirty rascal!"

"I'm not a dirty rascal, Mummy!" Emma insisted as her sisters entered the house.

"You are when your hands are dirty, sis. It's easy to fix though – you just need to wash your hands before eating!" Adanna said as she quickly guided Emma towards the sink.

I sat at the table and caught Amorina as she glanced at me.

"I washed my hands upstairs – promise!" I held them out so she could see them with a cheeky grin spreading across my face.

She nodded and turned back to watch her daughter's efforts.

My mother sat at the head of the table, and as I glanced at her, I felt a pang of guilt at the blank expression she wore, her eyes staring off into the distance.

She was my most personal reminder of freedom's high price, and every day the sight of her brought forth the memories: how the first few months seemed like an easy victory ... then the reports came in of people who'd lost their vision or hearing, or those crippled by migraines. Still, I thought it was a bullet we'd dodged ... until mother was bedridden by a headache. I shook my head and swallowed to clear a lump in my throat that wasn't there.

"Where's Father?" I inquired of the room.

"I'm here," he replied as he came up from behind. "Just forgot to grab your mother's pills."

Father performed the same process daily to get mother to take her medicine. I watched him place the pills in her mouth then move a glass of water to her lips and slowly trickle some inside. The tenderness in his voice was unmistakable when he would whisper for her to swallow and massage her throat to coax down the pills.

It was a tortuous process to watch, and even now, a suffocating weight had grown in my chest. But I didn't want to become indifferent to the endless suffering of people like my mother. I did what I could to remain sympathetic to their anguish, for the mass conversion had affected many people terribly; her circumstances were among the worst I had seen.

My choices affect others, so choose how those choices affect them.

"Ichirō! Breakfast is ready! Come and eat while it's hot, please!" Amorina's call pulled me out of my introspection, and a few seconds later, Ichirō sauntered into the house and headed straight for the table.

"Wash your hands first, please, Ichirō."

Ichirō ignored Amorina as he reached for the porridge ladle and scooped a generous portion into his bowl.

"Ichirō, listen to Amorina, please," I urged quietly.

"Why should I? She's not in charge of me. She's not my mother."

I resisted the urge to sigh and braced myself for what was to follow. The parenting advisor had taught us consistency is critical, but that didn't make enforcing it any easier.

"We've been over this before, Ichirō."

"Yes, we have been over this before!" Ichirō snapped as he knocked his bowl aside.

"She's not my mother because *you* killed my mother!"

He stormed outside, and an uncomfortable silence filled the room. No one was brave enough to break it. To ease the tension, I reached towards the spilt porridge, but Amorina stepped forward with a cloth before I could start the cleanup.

"I'll get that," she said, placing a hand on my shoulder and squeezing gently. "Why don't you go and check on Harvester 42 for me. It's broken down again."

I glanced at my wrist where Bitsy's display showed my next appointment. "Sure thing. I'll look at it when I have a moment."

I grabbed a mug and poured the freshly brewed coffee. Bitsy buzzed and I glanced down again. *Meeting postponed until 12:30.*

I let out yet another sigh. "In fact, I'll check it out right now."

❨❨❨❙❚❩❩❩

The smell of oil and hay filled the air as I entered the barn. I shut the door behind me, traded my mug for a tablet, and ambled over to Harvester 42. Gaia and the other colonies in the Outer Rim depended heavily on second-hand machines from the Inner Rim worlds, where advanced models had replaced the machines we received. As the colonial machines were outdated and prone to breaking, they required regular maintenance, and if there was nobody in the area to help, it could take up to a year for someone to come from Earth.

"Let's investigate what's happening with you, old girl," I said as I removed an access panel on the side, grabbed a diagnostic cable, and plugged it into the tablet.

The tablet could effortlessly access data from the harvester's logs, and a few moments later, a notification appeared on display.

Harvester 42 System Reports 1 Unidentified Fault

I sighed and started a manual log analysis. As the tablet trawled through the harvester's data, I glanced at one of the barn walls and felt my heartbeat quicken.

No, focus.

I returned to the tablet and concentrated on the progress bar, watching the interface pulsate. After a few minutes, the bar grew by one percent. The weight in my chest tightened, and I glanced at the barn wall again. The analysis would take a while, so I had a window of opportunity.

I placed my tablet on the harvester and strode over to the wall. After a final check to ensure no one was in sight, I rapped my knuckles against the wall four times. With a quiet hiss, the section before me moved inwards and slid aside, and I stepped into the revealed passage. The wall panel slid back into place with a hollow thud behind me as I descended into the musty room beneath the barn.

When I reached the bottom of the stairs, the lights activated and illuminated the years of work displayed on the room's corkboard and whiteboard-covered walls. Each time I returned here, I'd recall how my nightmarish obsession began; how one night, I'd had a terrible thought: did Tynan ever consider that his Empire could be overthrown? And if his intuition had expected this event, had he done anything to prepare for it? That one random thought robbed me of the few months of peace I'd been granted after the successful removal of the last vestiges of Tynan from my head.

I'd thoroughly dissected Tynan's life, the Empire, and their fail-safes and security measures, and it would have been better if nothing had been there. But amongst the confiscated records and recovered transcripts were whispers of secret plans and mumbled plots.

Although I couldn't present enough concrete evidence to persuade the Republic to start a search, I was confident that the Empire was out there somewhere, slowly rebuilding. If I could just put the clues together, I'd be able to track them down and put an end to their terror. Maybe then I'd sleep soundly once more.

Bitsy chirped, alerting me to a message, *Proximity Alert: Barn Front Door.*

Oh shit!

I rushed over to the entrance of the stairwell where a screen embedded in the wall revealed several camera angles of the barn. The one pointing to the barn door showed Amorina had come into the barn.

Shit, shit, shit!

I waited until she'd walked behind the harvester and then raced up the stairs, pressed the release button and slipped out into the barn as soon as the gap was wide enough. A quick four taps on the still-opening door halted its progress and reversed its course.

"Raith? Are you in here?" Amorina called out.

I quickly grabbed a power converter off a nearby shelf, knocking a few things to the ground in the process.

"I'm over here, *mi amor.*"

I strode over to the harvester just as Amorina came around from behind it.

"I didn't notice you when I came in."

"Yeah, sorry," I said as I held up the power converter. "I was grabbing a spare part."

"Oh, but it looked like the diagnostic wasn't finished yet."

"Yeah ... I figured it might be the same as last month when the power converter blew. A surge must be happening upstream, and it keeps frying the downstream component."

"How intuitive of you," Amorina said with a smirk.

She stepped closer, pulled the power converter from my hands, and threw it onto a hay bale before placing two fingers on my belly.

"I was hoping," she said as she sauntered the fingers up my torso, "that you might be able to help me with a downstairs component."

I raised an eyebrow. "A down … wait, what?"

"Yeah," Amorina replied as she stepped back and slowly turned, sliding her dress up her long legs as she went.

My heartbeat accelerated and my cock began to swell as more and more of her smooth, tanned legs were revealed. With a last hitch, the dress slipped over her glorious backside and revealed that she was completely and utterly bare beneath.

"Well, hello there," I growled, my erection now painfully full behind my zipper.

Amorina slowly bent over and arched her back, pushing her arse up and giving me a clear look of what was glistening between her thighs. She twisted her head and flicked her strawberry blonde hair to the side as she looked over her shoulder at me.

"You know, the part downstairs." She slowly bit her lip as she asked, "Would you mind looking at the lubrication levels?"

I smiled as I ran my gaze back over her. "Oh, I think the lubrication levels are pretty perfect from what I can see. So, is the harvester really broken, or did you just use that as an excuse to get me here so that you could have your way with me?"

"I wish I could say my motives were selfish, but unfortunately, the robot is *actually* broken."

"Ah, gotcha."

"Are you going to physically inspect me?"

"Shortly. I just need to give you a complete visual examination first."

I took a small step closer and continued to admire my wife.

She wiggled her luscious backside at me. "Come on! Don't you know it's rude to keep a woman waiting?"

"I do," I replied as I took another small step forward.

"Oh, for the love of all that is good, come and fucking touch me already!" Amorina whined.

I stepped forward, placed one hand on each cheek and gently squeezed.

"Mmm, that's better," Amorina moaned slowly. "Now, how about checking that lubrication?"

I reached down and slowly drew a fingertip up along the length of her slit, relishing how soft and wet she was.

Amorina loosed another moan. "You're such a tease."

I smirked and kept my finger just pushing between her lips, repeating the motion but with two fingers now: starting low and drawing my hand up, slightly increasing the pressure and number of fingers each time. With my other hand, I undid my trousers and let them fall around my ankles, finally releasing some of the pressure on my cock. On the next run, I replaced my fingers with the tip of my throbbing penis, dragging it through the slickness of her vagina. Amorina shifted beneath my touch, and another quiet moan escaped her lips.

"More," she whimpered.

I ran along her length again, pressing harder, dipping further inside.

"More!"

I slowly pushed myself in and let her adjust to my presence within.

"Mmmm, yes – I've missed this!"

Once I was fully inside, I held her hips in place so I could gradually pull back, creating exquisite frustration within us both, before I thrust deeply again.

Amorina's breath quickened. "Faster!" she groaned, grasping the haybale in front of her.

I quickened my pace and felt the tingle at the base of my spine and the tightening of my balls. Amorina and I were perfectly in sync as we danced to the same beat, entirely in a state of bliss.

"Faster!" Amorina hissed again.

My thrusts became frantic. I pulled Amorina onto me with each push forward of my hips, the intensity of the sensations soaring as we each raced towards our own climax.

Bitsy chirped, breaking into the passionate haze surrounding us. I had barely glanced down and read the words *Proximity Alert* when a voice cried out.

"Oh, my god! Sorry!"

Amorina dove to the ground and hid behind a cabinet, leaving me standing with my erection on full display.

"Father!" I exclaimed, yanking my trousers up and shoving myself inside them.

"I'm sorry, Raith. I didn't realise you were both … well …" he finished by waving his hand at us, his face averted.

"Yeah, well, um, in hindsight, mistakes were made … maybe we shouldn't have been having sex …"

Father looked at me then, standing with my trousers grasped at my waist, a confused expression spread across his face.

"Not the sex – that's never a mistake. Well … it's generally not a mistake. At least this wasn't a mistake. Ah … point is, the choice of location was … flawed, but not the sex."

Father shook his head. "I apologise for the intrusion."

He spun around and left the barn, shutting the door behind him. I waited until I heard the latch click into place, then turned around to check on Amorina. She was still on the floor, tucked away behind the cabinet, her breaths ragged and laboured. Beads of sweat trickled down her forehead, and her eyes moved frantically back and forth, not focusing on anything. She grasped at her chest as if it were possible to reach inside and rectify the current state of her racing heart and oxygen-deprived lungs.

I was familiar with what I was seeing and sure of what caused it; Amorina, like so many, had paid a high price for peace. The simple combination of having sex whilst an older man was present had been enough to trigger a panic attack. Her mental scars were now fresh wounds again, and they drew her mind back to a dark period when the Empire had forced her into sexual slavery.

"You're okay, Amorina. You're in a safe space."

Amorina nodded as she fought to control the panic that gripped her.

"Focus on your breathing. Deep breath in, long breath out."

Amorina exerted incredible strength, slowing her breathing rate, increasing the air she drew in and expelled with each breath until she'd abated the attack.

"Thanks," she whispered.

"I've got you. Always."

She nodded, and I helped her to her feet.

"I'm going to have some alone time." She looked up at me with a pained expression.

"Of course. Take as much time as you need. And if you need anything, tell me."

"I will."

Amorina started to walk away but then stopped as she pointed her finger at the barn wall and asked, "What is that?"

I looked to where she indicated and saw the door to my secret room slightly ajar – a fuel cell that I'd probably knocked off when I'd hastily grabbed the power converter blocked the door, stopping its closure.

I waved a hand dismissively through the air. "It's nothing; don't worry about it." But it was too late.

Amorina crossed the barn, heading for the door. I quickly fastened my trousers properly and raced toward her, but before I could reach her, she had already pushed the door open and disappeared into the passage. As I crossed the room, she reappeared and stormed towards me.

"Amorina, let me explain."

My head snapped to the side as Amorina's hand connected with my jaw. My face throbbed from the strike.

"You swore to me, Raith! You promised to put it all behind you when I discovered your last room!"

"I know – I just … listen."

Amorina's face contorted, her eyes narrowed, and she jabbed a finger in my chest. "You need to listen! This obsession is unhealthy, it's unproductive, and it's killing you!"

"Amorina, listen –"

"No, Raith!" she cut me off with a slice of her hand through the air. "Do you think I don't notice you tossing and turning at night? Or that I can't see the dark circles around your eyes? Because I fucking notice it all!" Spit flew from Amorina's mouth as she berated me. "But you are the one bringing this upon yourself; you keep yourself awake because you continue to entertain these ideas that the Empire is still out there."

"Well, they could be!"

"But they're not, Raith!" she shouted, and her voice echoed through the barn. "Why can't you see that?" she implored, her eyes filling with tears.

I shrugged and waved my hands about aimlessly. I knew she was worried about me, but how could I make her understand that the danger was real?

"I understand your concerns. I do! But you must believe me when I say –"

"Forget about the Empire, please!" she pleaded, her voice quavering.

Before I could say anything more, she'd spun around and stormed towards the barn door, leaving me to ponder my thoughts.

My body slumped in resignation as I released the heavy breath I had been holding. Maybe she was right. It had been five years since the Empire's defeat, and there had been no hint of activity – no sightings, no Soul Harvests, no signs of the Empire's resurgence. But the vastness of space is hard to comprehend; the Empire had infinite dark places in which to hide. Maybe I just required a more covert research room.

❦

As Gaia's suns set, I found Father sitting outside the barn with a beer in hand and an empty seat beside him. I sat down, and he pulled a cold cider from a cooler, cracked it open and passed it over.

"Thanks."

"No worries. It looked like you needed it."

I took a sip and nodded in agreement, appreciating the sweet, refreshing taste. "Oh yes, I certainly did."

"I ah –" Father rubbed the back of his neck. "I just wanted to apologise for what happened earlier."

"You didn't do anything wrong."

"That's not true – I barged in on the two of you and caused Amorina distress. I apologise for that."

"It's fine. We should've chosen somewhere more private. And Amorina will be okay; she just needs time. Trauma like hers runs deep."

"Yeah … you forget sometimes … how deep the trauma runs," Father said in a hushed tone.

I glanced at him and saw the sorrow deeply engrained there. Sometimes I forgot he was also a victim of the past. His heart was heavy with the memories of his daughter's death and the daily burden of mother's illness – both events I had involvement in.

An explosive shout of anger erupted from the farmhouse, followed swiftly by a shouted rebuttal.

"He has a lot of his dad in him," Father remarked and paused before adding, "his old dad, not his current one."

I nodded solemnly, my thoughts echoing his words.

"Does it really matter whose traits he inherited? If I'm not a good man or father, there's no difference between Tynan and me."

Father shook his head. "What on earth would make you say something as stupid as that?"

My heart throbbed as the weight on my chest made itself known once more.

"Because of what I've done … because of who I've *hurt*! Things that I cannot undo, actions I can't take back, and wounds I can't heal." I replied, my voice quivering.

Father considered this for a moment.

"I … do not envy you in the slightest. Being caught between a rock and a hard place, forced to choose between two god-awful options. But you decided, and arguably, we're better off for it."

The weight on my chest increased as the past, that was never far away, came to the forefront again: the pressure to make the wrong choices for the right reasons because the forcible conversion of people would happen regardless – I'd just had the chance to choose between doing it as Tynan or as Raith.

"It's been what, five years since the Empire fell? In that space of time, I would've expected one … maybe two Soul Harvests? But it hasn't occurred because you acted, because you made the better choice."

"Was it the better choice, though?" I retorted. "You weren't the one to pull the trigger!"

I buried my face in my hands, immediately regretting my words.

"You're right; I wasn't. You were. Your actions freed countless people from the cruel servitude of the Empire, saved countless more from future enslavement, and prevented so much needless suffering. That sure sounds like the kind of thing a good man would do."

I felt the inner burden lessen slightly as Father's words counteracted my remorse.

"As for being a good father – gaze over there for me, would you?" He gestured towards the small orchard we maintained. "Tell me what you see."

I looked over to see my daughters relaxing beneath the trees. Adanna rested against a tree, completely engrossed in the book she clutched in one hand while a half-eaten apple was in the other. Winona looked on affectionately as Emma sang a sweet melody, sketching in the dirt, unaware of her surroundings.

"I see my daughters enjoying the evening suns' warmth, feeling content and safe. Happy, even."

"Exactly. I understand how tough it was for you after you moved here. Yet you and Amorina worked hard, encouraged them, and taught them to think for themselves and to be strong and independent. So, tell me, do they appear to be the daughters of a good father?"

I smiled and felt the pressure reduce further. Father had a way of saying things that ensured he drove his point home.

"Yes. Yes, they do."

"Need I say more? Let their happiness bring you a measure of peace, for you have done a tremendous job raising some capable young women."

The tightness in my chest eased, and I let out a contented sigh.

Father paused, exhaled a long breath, and then said, "I haven't mentioned this before, but taking you in was one of the toughest challenges of my life."

The sudden, quiet confession took me aback. "Really?"

"Yes. After the Empire kidnapped Livietta, I charted a ship, left Gaia, and searched for my daughter – I'd intended to bring her back or die trying. Instead, I found her corpse thrown out in the trash, strangled to death by an Empire commander during sex."

An icy sensation spread throughout my chest as my heart dropped once again. After I'd returned from rescuing Amorina, I'd discovered that Father knew Livietta's fate – but I hadn't known that was how he'd discovered it.

"That's how I met the Insurgency, and my fury was all they needed to bring me into their ranks. For several years, I worked alone, disrupted the Empire's operations on Gaia and supplied the Insurgency network with intelligence. One day, Zavis messaged and told me to go to a certain set of coordinates on a specific date as someone there would require my help."

A chill ran along my spine knowing what came next.

"When I realized that Tynan Khidar was the man lying on that riverbank, I could barely contain the rage that erupted within me. I could've taken advantage of your vulnerability, exacted my revenge by drowning you in that river, and the world would never have known."

I understood instantly – we'd both known the darkness and longed for a way to silence it.

"Why didn't you?" I asked.

"It's hard to say. I stood there for hours as I anguished over the choice before me. I was certain I would regret letting you live. But in the end, I had faith in Zavis, so I spared you as intended."

"Do you … ever regret it?"

I heard his chair creak as he turned towards me and looked me in the eye.

"Honestly, no. Since that day, I haven't had a moment's doubt over that choice."

"Even when it comes to mother?" I asked cautiously.

Father's eyes tightened as a pained expression crossed his face. "That … wasn't on you, so don't worry."

This didn't relieve my concern; Father's response was unusually deceitful, his expression betraying his words.

"The point I'm trying to make is I understand the effort required to take in a stranger and raise them. You've certainly upped the ante by adopting three kids and having one of your own!"

I chuckled softly. "As you say, everything went well – except for Ichirō, of course."

"Ichirō needs help. He needs guidance from his father, and the more time he spends with you, the quicker he will learn and grow. With your direction, he can work through his trauma."

"I don't know how to help him though. Why is he always so angry? The mass conversion device released everyone from the oppression of the Empire, apart from Ichirō."

"I can't explain that one, but he reminds me of when you first came to us – tormented and torn between two worlds, between a blank canvas and an ominous voice inside your head. You already know this, but Ichirō has gotten worse."

"But why?"

"He's angry and has nowhere to let that rage out. So he bottles it up and contains it within himself. But trapped inside like that, it festers, it rots, and that decay spreads; it infects his goodness and corrupts him."

"So, how do I help him?"

Father remained silent momentarily, eyes fixed on the orange horizon, his forehead creased in contemplation.

"Don't you have a diplomatic mission to Akka soon?"

"Yeah, next week. Why?"

"Why don't you take Ichirō with you? It'll get him off-world, give him a change of scenery, and you'll both be able to spend quality time together as father and son. Show him what a good man looks like, how they act ... it'll help him resolve that inner conflict."

"That's actually a good idea. Thank you!"

"No worries. I'll send my bill over tomorrow."

I laughed. Father did not.

"Oh, wait – you're serious?"

The corner of his mouth twitched, and he snorted slightly as he stifled his own laugh.

"Hilarious," I quipped, somewhat impressed that he had lured me into his trap.

"I'm old, but I remember how to tell a joke!" he said, his face lit up with a smile. "Anyway, we'd best finish these drinks. I daresay Amorina will call us inside soon."

Chapter 2
We're on a Diplomatic Mission to Akka

2157, Common Era – Planet Gaia, Outer Rim, the Republic of Humanity

The Republic had welcomed the colonies with open arms when the Empire fell; they'd provided additional trade, service, and immigration opportunities. Gaia's population had boomed since then, now home to over one million people. The sudden spike in new arrivals had caused social norms to shift, and Gaia's citizens had grown to accept strangers – their arrival no longer considered taboo. Gaia even had an airport dedicated to receiving interstellar traffic and welcomed visitors from the stars daily.

Today, I focused on a particular dropship, watching its atmospheric entry closely. As the ship touched down, the rumble of its engines shook the ground beneath me, and as they cut out, the air filled with a slight chemical tang, the only hint of its otherwise odourless biofuel exhaust fumes. When the vessel had settled, its rear hatch opened, and Zavis stepped out, slowly making his way down the ramp.

The old man's face broke into a smile as soon as he saw me. "Hello, Raith!"

I returned the smile. "Hello, my friend."

Zavis was one of the few people who looked at me and didn't see Tynan. It was a small, simple action, possibly even subconscious, but it meant the world to me.

"How is life treating you?"

"I'm good ... getting by, one day at a time."

Zavis tilted his head downwards and peered over the top of his glasses as they slid down his nose. His eyes squinted as he stared at me, his lenses glinting in the sunlight.

"Your dark eyes would suggest otherwise, Raith. Troubles with the governorship?"

I shook my head, somewhat glad Zavis hadn't guessed the actual cause.

"No, no – managing Gaia is ... well, it's easy, all things considered."

Zavis gave a slight nod. "Having trouble sleeping then, perhaps?"

I huffed and smiled slightly. Nothing could ever escape Zavis's keen eye and intuition. It all made sense when you thought about it – the man had kept his two identities separate for decades, balancing his roles as Empire advisor and Insurgency leader.

"I'll admit, I've had trouble sleeping for some time now."

"We have several hours before we must depart. Shall we take a walk, and you can tell me all about the things that, ah, go bump in the night?"

I gave an eager nod. "That sounds like a plan. But where do I begin?"

"Take it from the very beginning – it's an excellent place to start," Zavis suggested with gusto.

"Um, well, I had this terrible thought about Tynan one night."

"Go on."

※ ※ ※

As we walked, I shared my thoughts with Zavis.

"After all these years of research, I only have a few scraps of information. Those I have confided in, Amorina and my father, don't believe me. They see my fixation as something that I should just let go."

Zavis nodded thoughtfully. "Would you like a coffee?"

I glanced at Zavis, one eyebrow raised in question, trying to make sense of the sudden shift in the conversation, but I was never one to turn down a cup of coffee.

"Yeah, sure," I replied with a slight shrug.

Amorina's mother still reigned as the top barista on Gaia, so that was where we headed. We sat at a vacant table, and when Anne noticed us, she promptly made her way over. Seeing her face always caused my heart to ache; her scarred and twisted features were a poignant and haunting reminder of our shared past.

"Raith, great to see you, as usual!" Anne smiled warmly, and her eyes twinkled in the same way her daughter's did.

"Hey, Anne. How's everything going?"

"Ah, you know what it's like. An overwhelming number of customers and a daughter that's fairly happy and healthy."

"Only fairly happy?"

"Mmhmm!" Anne said with a piercing, knowing look. "Amorina spoke to me about a particular project that someone had failed to set aside, despite their promise."

Ahhh, right.

"Yeah … it's a work in progress."

"I hope so, for the sake of your well-being. Anyway, the usual?"

"Yes, please," I said, eager to change the subject and take the focus off my relationship.

Anne nodded and turned towards Zavis. "And something for Mr …?"

"Ah, where are my manners? Anne, this is Zavis, an old friend of mine. Zavis, this is Anne, Amorina's mother."

"Pleasure to meet you, Mr Zavis," Anne replied, extending a hand towards Zavis.

Zavis smiled flirtatiously at Anne as he shook her hand.

"Oh, the pleasure is all mine, Anne. Please, call me Zavis." With a twinkle in his eye he added, "And I'll have a latte with gamoya milk, please."

"One gamoya milk latte, coming right up." Anne said with a coy smile, then walked back into the café.

I shook my head in disbelief, unwilling to accept what I had just seen.

"If you're gonna flirt with my mother-in-law, please do it when I'm not present."

"Oh, relax, Raith. A bit of playful banter never did any harm. Let's return to your research findings before Anne returns."

Zavis's abrupt shift of topic caused my brain to whirl, and I shook my head as I rearranged my thoughts in an effort to keep up with him.

"I believe you."

"What's the point though. You're only going to tell me —" I stopped, and my eyes whipped up to stare at Zavis. "Hang on, you actually believe me?"

"Yes, Raith, I do." Zavis gave a warm chuckle as his eyes twinkled with amusement. "Whilst it'd be easy to think that Tynan's advisors knew everything, his trust was far from guaranteed. He often kept his plans to himself and admitted as much on multiple occasions."

Zavis's faith alone was enough to leave me speechless, but I was even more astonished to discover that the advisors hadn't been privy to all the former emperor's schemes.

"Did you ever try to discover what those plans were?"

"Of course! But it sounds like you haven't been able to uncover any more than I did in the past. I recognise some of what you said, while the rest sounds unfamiliar."

"Like what?" my heart pounded as I leant forward.

Was I finally going to get the answers I'd been seeking?

"I recall a Phoenix project and the Reclamation Protocols. A 'SANE' program also rings a bell."

"Do you know anything more about all of those?"

"I have some thoughts, naturally, but nothing certain. Myths about the Phoenix go back a long time, but they involve immortality, invulnerability, pyrokinesis, and resurrection – Tynan's project could be about any of these or something else entirely! I would have no idea if he intended this for himself or the Empire."

"And the other two?"

"Reclamation feels a little more self-explanatory – the process of regaining something – and I feel the most applicable context would be to reclaim the Empire."

"Here you go, guys!" Anne said as she set our coffee cups in front of us, the smell of the fresh brew wafting in the air. "Is there anything else I can bring you while I'm here?"

Zavis smiled gently and replied, "No, thank you, Anne – that's all for now."

"No worries. Enjoy!"

Zavis waited until after Anne had walked out if ear shot before he continued.

"SANE is an acronym similar to Tynan's MIND AI. It was meant to represent Safety … no, not that … uh, Shelter … no … Sanctuary!" Zavis exclaimed, clicking his fingers as he landed on the right word. "Sanctuary Against Mind … no, ah Neural … um … like programming, but a different word for that …"

"A word that starts with 'E', related to programming?" I asked as I pondered the acronym. "Is it encoding?" I suggested.

"That's it, my boy! Sanctuary Against Neural Encoding – SANE," Zavis declared with a broad smile.

I leant back in my chair and took a moment to contemplate what Zavis had said; one of Tynan's hidden agendas had been to develop a program to protect against neural encoding. I also knew that the only thing capable of encoding the mind was the mass conversion device and the artificial intelligence that powered it.

"So, Tynan was simultaneously devising a method to encode minds and safeguard against it?"

"Yes," said Zavis, rather matter-of-factly. "Tynan was well aware that the MIND AI could be used against him. It makes sense that he would develop a counter to it – afraid that he would fall victim to his own invention. But we know he hadn't completed it."

Zavis's words echoed in my mind. What if Tynan had completed it but never got the chance to apply it to himself? Did I know anyone who'd been immune to the mass conversion?

With a gasp, I jolted forward. "Ichirō!"

At my outburst, Zavis jumped and knocked over his mug, spilling its contents across the table. "Ichirō?"

"Yes! I think Tynan used SANE on his own son!"

"Why do you think that?" Zavis asked as he tried to mop up the lost coffee.

"Because we've been struggling with his behaviour all these years, and I could never put my finger on what the issue was. Now I think that Ichirō was immune to the effects of the mass conversions!"

I watched Zavis's eyes widen. "Yes, I can see that. Tynan would want to protect himself, but only with a reliable solution."

"What kind of person would risk their own child to test an experimental technique?" I exclaimed, my voice quivering with fury.

"Unfortunately, it's no surprise that Tynan is the type of person to fit that mould. Ichirō was his son. They had similar genes. If Tynan wanted to see if the technology would work and how it would work for himself, Ichirō was the perfect test subject."

A wave of nausea washed over me, and I felt my stomach churn with unease. Tynan had treated his son – *my son* – as nothing more than a lab rat. Suddenly, Ichirō's behaviour was re-contextualised; he'd gone from living in the lap of luxury with people who agreed with him one day to feeling completely isolated and alone the next, with no one who believed in the same things he did. I couldn't even imagine what that would be like. I tightened my fists, fervently wishing that Tynan would manifest before me so that I could take my fury out on him.

"I wouldn't tell him."

Zavis's voice brought me back to the present moment. "What?"

"I wouldn't tell Ichirō about this."

"Why not? Wouldn't it help him understand and move on?"

Zavis shook his head. "Not as much as you'd probably like it to."

"I just want a way to ease his suffering. To undo the actions of my past self," I said as my shoulders slumped.

Zavis gave a gentle, sympathetic nod. "I can't fathom what it's been like for him. Your entire world transformed in the blink of an eye, but you've remained unchanged. If that happened to me, I'd be furious. I'd be willing to bet that a lot of Ichirō's behaviour is just him expressing his anger."

"Yes," I agreed. "He's always in a state of simmering rage – particularly in regard to me."

"That's exactly why it's not a good idea to tell him that, in essence, you used him as a science experiment."

"But it wasn't —"

Zavis raised his hand, silencing me mid-sentence.

"Raith, I know it wasn't you. I'm not implying that you're at fault here. But why do you suppose Ichirō directs his fury towards you specifically?"

I wanted to say that I didn't know, but I knew the truth. Another wave of nausea swept through my body as I turned the thought over.

There are two men in the mirror.

"Because when he looks at me, all he can see is Tynan."

"Precisely," Zavis said, pointing a finger at me for emphasis. "The tension between the two of you notwithstanding, we can't be sure that this *is* truly what happened. An educated guess, granted, but it's merely our best assumption, after all."

I closed my eyes and released a weary breath. Zavis was right, and now I knew I was right too — my sleepless nights had not been in vain. Tynan *had* plotted while ruling as emperor, but now the question was how many of his dark designs had come to fruition?

"So, Tynan had worked hard to create his plans, but how many did he make into a reality or instruct others to create?"

Zavis spread his hands helplessly, his tone apologetic, "I don't know, Raith."

I wrinkled my brow and nodded slightly. I didn't think Zavis would have all the answers.

"No one has seen those two Empire frigates that escaped, despite conducting many searches. Space is ... well, incredibly vast, and you never know what's out there in the darkness. That's the root of the problem, isn't it?"

Zavis glanced upward, and I followed suit.

"If the remnants of the Empire are still out there," Zavis said as he motioned at the heavens above, "then they have a multitude of places to conceal themselves. But there's no need to worry since the Republic is strong – if the Empire dares rare its head, we will soon lay them to rest!"

I nodded, if only to appease Zavis. It was easy to think that the Republic was powerful enough to defend itself, but they didn't understand Tynan the way I did; any plan of his deserved one's caution.

"You're probably right. I really appreciate you taking the time to hear me out and more so for believing me, Zavis."

"The pleasure is mine, Raith. I have been proudly serving you and your family since the day you entered this world, and I don't intend to stop anytime soon! Speaking of your family, it's about time we gathered them and returned to the airport."

❀❀❀

"Both of you will stay out of trouble now, won't you?"

Adanna and Winona met my comment with eye rolls.

"Of course, Dad! We're your good kids, remember?" Adanna replied.

"And besides," Winona added, "what kind of trouble can we possibly get into on Gaia?"

I could sense a subtle resentment in Winona's words. Perhaps she was offended by the idea that she'd be the one causing trouble, but it was more likely that I'd unintentionally caused them to recall memories of Earth, which had more to offer young adults their age than Gaia.

"That's a fair point, and I know you'll both behave. Grandpa is going to look out for you, too."

Adanna made a dismissive snort. "Ah, I think *we'll* be looking after Grandpa!"

I chuckled. "That's probably true as well."

"Enough of the small talk." With a tap on her wrist, Winona pretended to look at a watch that wasn't there. "Don't you have a starship to catch?"

"See, now it feels like you're trying to get rid of me!"

"I'm just looking out for you, ensuring you don't miss your flight!"

"Mmhmmm. Alright, bring it in, you two!" I said as my arms wrapped around my daughters and pulled them into a loving embrace.

"Dad!" They both raised their voices in protest. "You're embarrassing us!"

"Oh, no!" I gasped in fake horror. "I wouldn't want to embarrass my daughters!"

The sound of Amorina's sweet laughter echoed behind me, and I loosened my embrace as Adanna and Winona playfully pushed me away with grins on their faces.

"I love you both."

"We know," said Winona.

"Lemme hear it."

"I love you too," they replied in unison.

"See you in a year!"

I moved away and let them say goodbye to Amorina as I shifted my gaze to my son.

"Are you ready to leave, mate?"

"I already said no! I don't want to go!" Ichirō ground out between gritted teeth.

"Come on, Ichirō – don't be so stubborn!" I said, doing my best to stay calm despite my son's behaviour.

"How about you try being less stubborn? I refuse to take part in your stupid diplomatic mission, okay?"

"There'll be more to it than just diplomacy. I've got some amazing sights for you to see and a new planet to explore!"

"I said no!" Ichirō roared.

My blood boiled, and I was about to unleash my ire when Amorina stepped between us.

"Let me try." She gave me a knowing look and whispered, "Stay calm."

I rolled my eyes and watched her go to Ichirō, put an arm around his stiff shoulders and speak quietly to him. After a few moments, he wrenched out of her hold and strode towards the dropship while Amorina returned to me.

"He's coming along. But don't test his patience – it was a begrudging compromise."

"Thank you for –" I began, but Amorina hastily interjected.

"Don't think my doing this lets you off the hook!"

I rolled my eyes and muttered, "I guess I had that coming," as she marched away towards the dropship.

I glanced back and saw Emma, who had patiently waited on a bench through it all.

"Come on, sweetie pie. We need to get on board to go on our adventure!"

Emma hopped off the bench and ran up to me. "All right, Daddy."

At least someone isn't mad at me.

We walked side by side to the dropship, where the others had already gathered.

"Sorry for the delay," I whispered to Zavis as I sat beside him.

Zavis nodded slightly, knowing it would be better to remain silent.

I heard a quiet hiss followed by a pop as the rear door of the dropship sealed us inside and the cabin pressurised.

"We're cleared for take-off," the pilot's voice echoed throughout the ship. "Please remain in your seat for the duration of this flight, which should take about ten minutes."

As soon as the pilot's announcement finished, I heard the engines roar to life and felt a jolt as the ship lifted off the ground, the force of Gaia's gravity slowly fading away. I felt the vessel surge upward, and the powerful thrum of the engines reverberated throughout the vessel and its occupants.

After a few minutes of ascent, the ship felt like it had evened out, though it was just my senses as they adapted to the lack of a reference point of gravity.

"Engaging artificial gravity now, folks."

The gravity systems activated and pulled me back down just as I began to rise out of my seat. The trajectory of the dropship, as it curved around Gaia, treated the passengers to a breathtaking panoramic view of the planet and the surrounding stars.

Gaia was always stunning to behold; it consisted of more land than water, and its lush forest-covered lands, still relatively untouched by its human inhabitants, were a natural paradise among the stars.

I glanced over and saw Ichirō, his eyes filled with wonder as he took in the view, and I couldn't help but smile; this was precisely the sort of experience I'd wanted him to have.

"Whoa!" Ichirō exclaimed.

I turned back to my port side window and saw the same stunning view that my son now marvelled at: a majestic, elongated vessel with an elegant white exterior that seemed to emit a sense of diplomacy and peace.

"That's an impressive ship!"

"It certainly is remarkable," said Zavis. "It's my pleasure to introduce the ROHS Stardove, the Republic's most advanced, premier diplomatic vessel."

Even without Zavis's introduction, the ship's splendour was apparent in its bright and gleaming surfaces. A feeling of tranquillity radiated from the ship, yet its immense size and modernity gave off a foreboding presence as if it were saying, "I'm not here to start a fight, but I will if I have to."

"I like the design!"

"She's beautiful, isn't she?" Zavis said as he proudly gazed out at the vessel. "The downfall of the Empire resulted in the merger of their research and development with that of the Republic. She's one creation of that technological merger and reaps many benefits from the advancements, like a doubled top warp speed."

"I'm not interested in space travel, but I must admit, this ship is quite a sight to behold!" Amorina remarked.

"What do you think, kids?" I asked as I turned towards Emma and Ichirō.

Ichirō shrugged and pretended to be more interested in his smartphone than us or the ship.

Emma beamed as she said, "I like the name."

Amorina, Zavis, and I laughed.

Zavis chuckled as he said, "So do I, little one. Stardove is a perfect name!"

I looked out the window and watched as the Stardove drew nearer until it filled the entire view. The dropship flew into a starboard side hanger and touched down. We waited as the hangar doors were closed and the air pressure restored. The safety lights in the room changed from red to green.

The pilot spoke over the intercom, "You are now cleared for disembarkment."

As the rear of the dropship opened, we made our way down the ramp into the hangar where a small reception awaited us.

"It's my pleasure to extend a heartfelt welcome to you, Governor Raith, Councillor Zavis, and all our guests!" greeted a lady in a crisp, azure Republic captain's uniform. "I am Captain Kathleen Edgell, and I'm honoured to have you on board the Stardove."

"It's a pleasure to be here, Captain Edgell. Thank you for having us aboard!" I replied.

"Anytime. We're scheduled to depart in thirty minutes. My second in command, First Lieutenant Orwig," Captain Edgell gestured to the lieutenant on her left, "will show you to the cryosleep chamber. The interstellar conditions are favourable for our journey, and we are expecting a six-month travel time."

"Thank you, Captain," I replied, then turned towards the first lieutenant.

Orwig nodded courteously and gestured towards the exit, his eagerness to walk to the cryosleep chamber clear.

"Lieutenant Orwig, could you possibly put my children and myself into cryo after we've launched? I'd like them to experience something first."

"Yes, of course, sir," Orwig said with another nod.

"I'm not interested in watching whatever it is. I just want to go to cryo," snapped Ichirō.

I shifted my attention to my son. "Hey, come on, mate. Work with me here, okay?"

Ichirō refused to meet my gaze and muttered something unintelligible. I leaned in and placed my hand lightly on my son's shoulder, which caused him to glare up at me.

"I've got something extraordinary to show you," I whispered. "I think you'll be amazed!"

"Fine, whatever," Ichirō said as he rolled his eyes. "And when this thing is lame, I'll have grounds to argue against future 'experiences'!"

"Thank you," I said with a grateful smile, then turned back towards the captain and lieutenant.

"I'll take you to the observation deck myself," Captain Edgell said. "And the lieutenant will get everyone else settled in for the journey."

"Thank you."

I directed my attention towards Amorina and caught a steely gaze.

"Have a good, ah … sleep, I guess," I said, feeling like an awkward teenager.

"Yeah. Same to you," she replied as she avoided eye contact whilst giving me a quick hug.

"Catch you on the flip side?"

This drew a brief smile from Amorina, and she nodded, then headed towards the exit.

"And I'll catch you later as well, Zavis."

Zavis smiled warmly. "Will do, Raith. Enjoy the show, kids."

As Amorina and Zavis followed the lieutenant into the ship's depths, I turned towards Emma and Ichirō.

"Come on, guys – we've got a show to catch!"

❲❳❳❳❳

Half an hour later, Emma, Ichirō, and I were seated in a bow-facing lounge on the observation deck.

"Our departure is imminent. All conscious passengers, please remain seated until we have departed," came an announcement over the intercom.

"It's almost show time, guys! Put away your devices and look out the windows."

Emma joyfully gave her Arachnobot the command to enter watch mode, then cuddled against me while she gazed out on the great expanse before us.

Ichirō, on the other hand, sat a few seats away from me, ignored my request, his attention fixed on his smartphone.

"Come on, Ichirō – put your phone away. You'll miss the spectacle otherwise!"

"Fine!" He barked as he stuffed the phone into his pocket. "Happy now?"

"Yes. Thank you for listening."

"Whatever," he sneered, and with his arms and legs crossed, he slumped back into the chair, his expression a scowl of indifference.

A low rumble filled the air as the ship began to move, and the deck vibrated beneath our feet.

"What's going on?" Emma asked.

"The pilot is preparing the ship for warp. They're activating the warp engines with a process called spooling. When they've got it all ready, they'll jump into warp, and we'll be flying faster than light!"

"Whoa!" Emma exclaimed as her little eyes widened with excitement.

"Warping in three … two …" came another intercom announcement.

"Get ready, guys, it's happening!"

"One … warp!" finished the announcement.

Through the observation lounge windows, every glimmer of light shifted to azure blue, then merged into a royal purple, before the light vanished into the darkness entirely. Then, all at once, the entire view transformed, filled with a deep Prussian blue hue, which then condensed into a cone, the brightest point at the centre that faded to black as it spread outwards.

"Warp achieved," came one last announcement.

"Whoa!" Emma shrieked, and her voice echoed through the lounge. "It was so lovely!"

I glanced in Ichirō's direction; he'd sat up, his attention still riveted on the blue cone before us. A smile spread across my face, glad he'd paid attention and seemed to have enjoyed the experience.

"What did you think, Ichirō?"

"That was ... absolutely ... breathtaking! I've seen nothing like it before!"

I felt a sense of relief come over me; the arguments and disagreements had been worth it to get Ichirō here – or at least I thought so.

"Was it worth your time to come here, then?"

"Yeah. Cheers, I guess," he begrudgingly acquiesced.

I tried to conceal my joy from Ichirō, aware that he may not take kindly to it, but a smile tugged at the corners of my mouth. Still, in my parenting struggles with my son, any win, no matter how small, was a victory worth smiling about.

"You're most welcome. Alright, let's go, you two. Let's head to the cryosleep chamber and drift off alongside the others."

❦

Darkness engulfed me. I could hear fires crackling, and smoke stung my eyes and throat. Figures rushed by in a blur of colours and noise, their voices panicked. A cacophony of cries filled the air, shrill screams and loud shouts, but I couldn't make sense of anything over the persistent ringing in my ears.

I lurched to the side and retched, coughing out a stream of cryofluid onto the floor. My sight cleared enough for me to make out the blood streaking my arms and hands. It was dripping into the puddle of cryofluid.

Raising a hand, I gingerly touched my head and found the gash responsible for the mess. My stomach heaved again, and I expelled another stream of fluid. With a final gasp, my lungs were completely empty, and I could breathe again. I heard a faint voice nearby, but I couldn't decipher what it was saying. A pair of hands came into view, grabbed my shoulders, and pulled me into a seated position. Captain Edgell's face broke through the fuzz. I could see her lips moving as she spoke to me, but nothing reached my ears. I shook my head and closed my eyes tightly – I needed to regain my focus.

"Governor Raith? Governor Raith! Can you hear me?" Captain Edgell's voice finally came into focus.

"Yeah," I croaked, my voice barely audible. "What's happened?"

"I've got no idea. Something or someone abruptly ejected us from warp! I've never come across anything like it before."

I willed my fuzzy brain to keep up with what the captain had told me. Ejected from warp? I'd never heard of anything like that either, but it sounded violent. I became aware of the pain that coursed through my body, which seemed to affirm that, yes, it had been violent.

"Casualties?"

"Three dead, seven injured, as far as I know. Your family and Zavis are okay – their cryopod doors held, although they were likely jostled around. You, on the other hand, busted right through your pod door!"

That explains a lot.

"What's the status of the ship?"

"There are system faults throughout the ship. Multiple systems are non-responsive. It'll take time to determine the exact extent of the damage, but for now, we're not going anywhere."

I nodded in acknowledgment, conscious of our dire predicament.

What could cause the ship to drop out of warp? From what I could see of the ship's state, it was clearly a scenario it hadn't been designed for.

"I need to return to the bridge, but I'll send a medic to assess you."

I shook my head. "No, take me with you. I can be of more help to you than just sitting here."

The captain looked hesitant.

"Please – give me a hand and help me get to the bridge. I can be of assistance."

"Fine."

Edgell put an arm around me and lifted me to my feet, then walked us both towards the bridge.

"Can you think of anything else that might shed some light on the situation?"

We walked silently for a few minutes before the captain replied.

"Yes, I suppose there could be. I'm unsure what the connection is, but we got an emergency broadcast from Akka. A large unidentified object – perhaps a ship – is approaching the colony. It destroyed a scout vessel sent to meet it, so they urgently requested Republic forces for help."

"How far away are we from Akka?"

"We still have three more months ahead of us. Could something be attacking Akka and us? I'd held higher hopes for humanity's true first contact."

Captain Edgell's recollection of the emergency broadcast didn't sound good, but it didn't sound the same as what the ship had experienced. We turned a corner and ventured onto the bridge, and the captain guided me to a seat off to the side.

"Do we have any operational sensors? Can you detect anything in our vicinity?"

The captain glanced at me. "You're here in a consulting capacity, not a commanding one."

"Sorry," I said, holding my hands up in apology.

"That being said, let me check what's working," the captain replied as she moved to a nearby console.

As she worked on the console, I gazed out the bridge window and scanned the stars before us. Small chunks of debris floated about chaotically, likely dislodged from the ship, but otherwise there didn't appear to be anything out of the ordinary.

"A space-time anomaly is opening right in front of us!" the captain shouted.

I spun to stare at her and noticed a flash out of the corner of my eye. Turning back to the window, I saw an Empire frigate now positioned in front of the Stardove.

"Oh, my god!" Edgell gasped.

I felt a chill run through me as I recognised the cartoonish piranha on the frigate's nose, and my eyes widened with disbelief. This was one of the two Empire vessels that I had shown mercy five years ago.

"That's an Empi –"

"Empire ship, I know," Edgell interrupted with a quivering voice.

The communications panel on the other side of the bridge lit up and emitted a tone.

"They're hailing us," she whispered.

"We might as well open a channel."

The captain rushed across the bridge and accepted the call. A voice rang out through the established channel, announcing, "This is the Empire Frigate Piranha."

"This is Captain Edgell of the ROHS Stardove. We are on a peaceful mission to Ak –"

"Shut up, bitch. We don't want to talk to you."

The captain frowned. "Then … who do you want to talk to?"

"You know who," the voice said.

Edgell glanced at me and shrugged.

With all the authority I could muster, I said, "This is Governor Raith of Gaia. The ROHS Stardove is a peaceful vessel on a diplomatic mission to Akka. Stand down, Piranha – stand down!"

Cruel laughter echoed throughout the bridge.

"We do not recognise your authority here, *Governor* Raith, for you are nothing more than a traitor to the one true emperor! Prepare to be boarded. Surrender all hands."

The connection cut off, and the captain and I looked at each other.

I sighed heavily and said, "This isn't going to turn out well."

"What is our next move?"

"I don't think there is a next move – you said it yourself, we're dead in the water."

We both returned our attention to the Empire frigate in front of us and watched two shuttles leave it and make their way over. They flew past the bridge and out of our view; we listened to the sound of the vessels docking with our own. It wasn't long before the sound of heavy boots filled the halls of the Stardove.

"Put your hands on your head and keep them there!" the Empire troopers shouted as they advanced onto the bridge.

The captain and I obeyed, and moments later, somebody seized my arms and twisted them behind my back, followed by the sharp sensation of a syringe piercing my neck.

"What the he–"

Chapter 3
An Uncanny Resemblance

2158, Common Era – Frontier Space, Tynan Empire

Darkness surrounded me again. My vision was hazy, and my hearing was once more muted. But not from smoke, this time I had a foggy disorientation clouding my mind.

As my senses slowly returned, I started to make sense of my situation. Thick leather straps bound my arms and legs firmly in place to the arms and legs of the chair I was in. Scars adorned my forearms. They were still pink and slightly raised telling me they were recent – were they from smashing through the cryopod?

Fuck me. How long was I sedated for?

My eyesight was returning to normal, and I expanded the analysis to my surroundings now that the details of the world were coming into focus.

I noticed the fluorescent lights that shined off the white walls and stainless-steel benchtops, covered with all manner of scientific equipment, and realized I was in a laboratory. The people in lab coats who bustled about the room from one workstation to the next backed up my epiphany.

Waking up in a lab after being sedated for who knows how long is not a good sign.

One individual in a dark grey military uniform stood out from the others. He spoke to one of the lab coats in a gruff and grizzled voice that sounded vaguely familiar.

"Listen, you fucking twat! I don't care how understaffed you are or how much you miss your family. I wanted this procedure done yesterday, but seeing as it's already today, you'd best make it happen!"

His opening sentence triggered a recollection – a memory – of standing on the bridge of the Stormfalcon getting ready to set off the mass conversion device as we approached Ares.

The crew had opened up a line of communication with the three Empire frigates before us, and I'd heard the voice of one …

"General Harry Jake," I drawled.

As the soldier slowly pivoted, a man with an irritated expression and a severe case of male pattern baldness was revealed. His rather thick ginger beard was liberally streaked with grey, and he glared at me with his beady little eyes, his angry presence further intensified by the fiery red colour of his irises.

"Well, well, well," he sneered, his voice full of scorn. "The goddamn traitor awakens at fucking last."

I tried to shrug against my restraints. "I mean, that's relative, isn't it? I might seem awake, but I'm still feeling a bit groggy. A cup of coffee would be *greatly* appreciated."

The general scowled. "You might think this is some kind of joke, but I promise you it's no laughing matter. Your predicament is quite dire."

"I was contemplating that," I said as my eyes wandered around the room again. "It's a sea of lab coats in here – what are they all doing? And come to think of it, where is here?"

Now the general smiled. Which, somehow, was worse. At least when he scowled, it suited his overall angry demeanour, but when he smiled, it twisted his face into an unnatural expression of joy.

"I want to explain where you are and what's about to happen – believe me, I do. But honestly, I think it'll be more interesting to watch you figure it out."

That doesn't sound good.

I ignored the general and focused on the room, trying to assess my situation. My chair of imprisonment seemed to be in the middle of the room, with no obvious reason for its placement. There were no devices or gadgets behind me or close by that would explain why it was there.

"Are you handing out any clues?" I asked.

"What do you fucking think?"

"That you are?"

"No!" he snapped; his voice echoed throughout the room. "I'm not giving you any fucking clues!"

Bugger. Ah well, it'd been worth a shot.

I glanced around the room again, now with more urgency. What was I not seeing?

A scientist meekly approached the general, their hands quivering. "We're ready, sir."

"Good," he replied, again with that wicked grin. "Begin the extraction."

My body trembled with a wave of panic.

"Extraction of what?" I asked as my stomach knotted with dread. "What are we talking about here? Blood? Organs?"

"One last puzzle piece."

Well, that's just fucking unhelpful isn't it?

I frantically scanned the room again, my heart racing now. But again, I couldn't see anything – no puzzles, no tools for extracting blood, organs, or otherwise – nothing that seemed like it would be used on me.

"This must be difficult ... for your pride, or ego, or something. I mean, I'm assuming it was you who saved us when those Republic ships had us dead to rights and then let us go. It was you, wasn't it?"

"Yeah," I replied. "Regrettably, that was *my* choice."

"So, it must hurt, right? Having the tables turned now, being at my mercy?"

"I'm regretting it more and more."

The general laughed. "I thought you might be. You still can't work out what is going to happen, though, can you?"

I felt the tension in my neck as I stared him down.

"Alright – I'll give you a little nudge in the right direction. You certainly have an impressive scar on your head."

My scar? What is he on about? What are they going to do, extract my brain?

Suddenly, the idea didn't seem so absurd in the grand scheme of things. I looked up, and a chill ran through my body at the sight of an extraction machine. Its spindly, multi-limbed, mechanical body glinted in the light, and its many tools of the trade – scalpel, blade, scoop, and needle – were ready for action. Chills ran down my spine as an arm with a circular saw on the end activated, the high-pitched scream of the spinning blade reverberating through the air.

The pressure of multiple hands on my head was unmistakable as they forced me back against the seat.

"What are you doing?" I yelled as they tightened a thick leather strap around my forehead. "Let go of me!"

"Ensuring your head doesn't move during the procedure," the general's calm voice came from behind me.

"What's the procedure? Stop!" I implored with fear vibrating in my voice.

I heard the blade start its descent, the sound ringing in my ears as it drew nearer and nearer.

"Anything you want to know, I'll tell you!" I pleaded, my heart pounding. "Please!"

"Unfortunately for you, traitor, we cannot uncover what we seek through words – it must be extracted. So, I'm sorry – no, that's a lie. I'm not sorry at all."

At that moment, the saw's icy, razor-sharp teeth ripped through my skin and bit into my skull, each tooth tearing away a chunk of flesh and bone. As my brain realised what was happening, a searing pain overwhelmed me. The blade circled my head, using the path of my existing scar as a guide; with no medication or sedation, each pass of the saw sent pain coursing through my body, burning red hot and angry, like fire in my nerves. Blood ran down my face and over my eyes, turning my world into a nightmarish shade of red. Immobile and unable to retreat, all I could do was cry out in agonising pain.

"Aaarrrggghhh!" My eyes rolled into the back of my head as a scream of agony tore out of my vocal cords.

I felt my body jolt as all my muscles suddenly contracted in unison; the pain tearing at my soul, ripping it apart. A memory emerged from the shredded remnants of my spirit and consumed me. Now I was in a small, dark room, fighting against four men as they pushed me into a chair and held me there whilst metallic restraints slid out of the chassis to restrain me. They stood back and watched, waiting for the device to remove my skull cap and alter my mind.

Echoes of pain permeated every element of the vision, seeping out of every surface and smothering the air. The eyes of the past travelled over the faces of its aggressors, determined to commit each one to memory; three were unfamiliar to me, but the fourth I knew well – Doug, the Machina Station Insurgency leader.

There was a sickening squelch as the machine pulled the top of my skull away, and the first probes inserted themselves into my grey matter. I looked up and saw Zavis staring down at me from the control room's windows overlooking the operating theatre. His face was a patchwork of emotions: triumph, pain, and a touch of guilt.

A maelstrom of rage erupted within. "You'll suffer for this!" I screamed up at the advisor.

The scene morphed into a cloud of black smoke that transformed into a gaunt and famished black wolf. I hadn't fed it in a long time, but all this pain, it could take that – transforming anguish into anger and agony into fury. The wolf salivated, its anticipation building as the darkness in me rose, for when there was enough rage, it could convince me to feed it. And if I fed it …

"Every time the darkness arises, it's my job to refocus you."

My father's voice echoed through my mind as my heart pounded, staring up at the giant, looming creature.

"Not today," I whispered.

One last wave of pain surged through my body, and then the world faded to black.

※

I awoke to darkness for a third time in what felt like just as many days. I slowly opened my eyes, straining to bring the blurry world into focus. I needed to know where I was and what was happening. I attempted to move my head, but piercing pain ran throughout my body, forcing me to hold back a scream. I gritted my teeth and fought the pain as I rotated my head to the left. I felt a small measure of relief as I realised Amorina was next to me, and beyond her, Ichirō and then Emma.

We were all on our knees, with an Empire soldier behind each of us. I fought against the pain again as I swivelled my head to the right. Zavis was beside me, followed by Captain Edgell, First Lieutenant Orwig, and the rest of the Stardove crew. They were also on their knees with an armed soldier behind them.

I shifted my gaze downward, and the pain eased as my head settled into a neutral position and became more manageable; hot tears streaked down my face. I clearly needed to move my head less, so I concentrated on my ears, willing the ringing to cease. The room was so silent that the few voices that whispered here and there reverberated off the walls.

"He's awoken, Your Grace," came one murmured echo.

"Finally!" I knew the voice the moment I heard it and winced at the volume of their exclamation, painfully loud in contrast to the previously hushed whispers.

"What took you so long? I mean, it's not like you just had open brain surgery or anything, right?"

The soldiers in the room erupted into laughter, the sound resounding in a painful symphony.

"Here I was –" the voice was moving closer "– worried that I'd have to walk over there and give you a prince's kiss!"

As another wave of laughter rebounded around my brain, I felt the presence of someone near me. Turning slightly, I saw the hem of a red and golden robe.

A hand appeared before my face, gripped my jaw, and wrenched my head up.

A sharp, searing pain shot through my body like a bolt of lightning. When it faded, and I could see who was standing before me, my heart skipped a beat.

"You look a bit taken aback. Surprised, are we?"

I couldn't believe what I saw and heard – it was me: my face and voice.

"Come on ... Raith," the other me drawled.

"Connect the dots. Put it together."

Memories surged through my mind: confinement, strapped to a chair, anxiety, an extraction machine, fear, metal teeth biting into flesh and bone, pain and agony. They'd done something to my head … no, my brain. They'd obtained something, but it couldn't be my brain – I wasn't floating in a jar – which could only mean they'd extracted a … ghost?

"Ty …" I attempted to speak, but my vocal cords emitted a feeble croak, then clamped shut.

I remembered my throat burning as I'd screamed. There'd been so much screaming. My throat tightened as I tried to form the words, and I felt fresh tears stream down my face. I wet my lips and gave it another go.

"Tynan," I finally forced out, my voice rough and scratchy.

"Ding, ding, ding! Give the man a prize!" Tynan yelled as he pushed my head away, pain jolting through my brain.

"Ugh!" I groaned as my head throbbed.

"Oh no, did that hurt you?" Tynan asked, feigning concern.

"Fuck … you!" I croaked out my reply, my throat aching.

I scrapped together some saliva and spat on the bottom of his robes for extra insult.

Like a snake, Tynan's fist shot out and connected with my jaw. Blinding white pain exploded through my skull. Before my head could complete its recoil, Tynan grabbed the back of it and yanked me towards him.

His breath was hot against my ear as he hissed, "Choose your words carefully, Raith." His voice dropped lower, "Consider whom else I have captive."

Tynan shoved me back and I heard him stomp away.

I slowly raised my head and, through the haze of pain throbbing against my temples, watched him seat himself in a golden throne at the top of a raised stage. His face was expressionless, not giving away any hints at what he was thinking as he watched me. But at one time, his thoughts had been my own. He was cocky, sure of himself, and believed himself superior above all else.

My spine tingled with the feeling of dread as I studied him, disturbed at seeing someone else wearing my face, and I noticed a sparkle in his eye, which only elevated my anxiety. He loved this, intoxicated by the power he had over me, my family, and my friends. Loved the answers he knew he had and I didn't. I knew that if I wanted us to survive this encounter, I'd need to construct a mental image of my surroundings, understand the severity of the situation, and start identifying avenues for escape.

"Where ... are we?" I asked.

"No one's told you where you are?" Tynan replied with a sarcastic smirk. "The lack of manners around here is astounding. But I digress – you're on Erebus, the last stronghold of the Empire!"

Erebus?

My conscious mind could not recall any details about an Empire world called Erebus, but as the word tumbled through my battered mind, it sparked a recollection of something familiar yet unknown. The knowledge surfaced from the depths of my unconscious.

Erebus: The Greek personification of darkness and a region of the Underworld between Earth and Hades.

Unfortunately, that bit of info was useless, and my plan to escape was already beginning to fail. How could I make a plan to get away from here when I didn't know where *here* was?

"Come on, Raith!" Tynan snapped. "Knowing what this planet is called wasn't a profound revelation – no need for the stunned silence! Ask me a proper question – challenge me with an inquiry of substance!"

"Like what?"

Tynan gestured with his arms, spreading them to invite the question, "Ask me how I did it, how I'm here!"

I peered at what I used to be, my dark reflection, my wicked past self. He delighted in mind games, the power he felt as he manipulated and bent people to his will. But I would not grant him the satisfaction.

"Go on," Tynan firmly urged, his voice dropping to those darker tones. "Ask me!"

I held his gaze and felt a burning defiance within me.

Tynan's face contorted in rage as he roared, "Ask me!"

I remained silent. To hell with this arsehole. Then I noticed General Jake striding towards his reanimated emperor.

"Tynan, I don't think this is –" he began, but Tynan didn't let him finish.

"What did you just say?" Tynan said as he spun around to confront the general.

Jake's eyebrows furrowed as he hesitated. "Um ... that I don't think –"

"No, before that," Tynan interjected again.

"Ah ... Tynan?"

With one swift motion, Tynan dove at the general and grabbed his sidearm from its holster on his hip. He flipped the gun in the air, the metal glinting in the light, and after he caught the weapon, he pointed it at the general's knees and pulled the trigger.

The sound of the shot echoed around the room and the general collapsed immediately as the bullet tore a hole through his leg.

Out of the corner of my eye, I glimpsed Emma jump in shock at the gunfire.

"Argh!" Jake cried as he clutched his shattered knee. "What the fuck, sir?"

Tynan pointed the gun at his other knee and pulled the trigger. The general screamed again as he clutched helplessly at both legs. I glanced at Emma and saw the blood had drained from her face.

No child should have to see this.

"I want everybody," Tynan said as he spun to address the room, "to pay attention to this. You will address me as Your Grace. My Lord is acceptable, but I prefer Your Grace. *Never* call me sir, commander, emperor, or *Tynan!*"

"Forgive me, Your Grace," General Jake groaned as he writhed in agony.

The gun fired a final time and Emma shrieked. Amorina pulled her close and held her tight. The general's body lay limp in a pool of blood, and a heavy silence descended upon the room.

"Apology ... accepted."

Tynan pivoted and strode back to his throne.

"Clean this mess up before it stains the floor."

A few soldiers rushed forward and hauled the body away, while others came with mops and buckets and frantically cleaned the mess.

"Let me see, where did I leave off ... oh yes. Raith — ask me!"

"Humour him," Zavis whispered beside me. "Humour him, and we might make it out of this alive."

"Fine — how did ... you do it ... Tynan?" I asked and noticed his eye twitch slightly as I pronounced his name.

"Well, I'm glad you asked," Tynan said as he got up from his throne and walked around the room.

"Not that long ago, I was the ruler of an empire – one passed down to me from my father and his father before him. My grandfather founded it, my father expanded it, and it was my job to consolidate it. I was facing increased pressure from the Republic, facing a growing insurgency. By the way, thanks for that, Zavis." Venom dripped from these last words.

Tynan, almost impulsively, spun on the spot and strode over to stand in front of Zavis.

"Do you've anything to say to that, Zavis?"

"No, Your Grace."

"I didn't think so. Which is a shame because your brothers in advisory would've loved an apology!"

Tynan spun and motioned for three men in wheelchairs to be brought into the room. I gasped as they drew nearer and into the light – they were three of Tynan's former advisors.

"These three men stayed loyal to me while you turned your back. I had a plan in place for my loyalists, for them to turn to the advisors in the event of the Empire's collapse, and that's exactly what they did," Tynan said as he faced the advisors, his voice low but full of admiration.

Then, like some invisible force flicking a switch, Tynan spun around to face his captive audience, his voice now loud, aggressive, and brimming with hatred. "Except all they found were dementia-ridden old men because you'd erased their minds!"

Tynan gathered his composure again. After a few deep breaths he continued, "Thankfully, the loyalists understood why the advisors were in such a condition. General Jake, may he rest in peace, was the one who figured out that a prototype mass conversion device was present on Earth.

He stole it from a Republic vault, busted the four advisors out of hospital, and brought them all here, where they reverse-engineered the tech and restored the advisors to their original faculties."

"There's only three," I muttered.

"'There's only three,'" Tynan mocked in a high-pitched voice. "Well, there would've been more," he pointed at Zavis, "if you hadn't shot one!" Tynan directed his finger towards me next. "And if you hadn't stabbed one!" He spun back to the men in the wheelchairs. "And if one more hadn't died of old fucking age!" his conclusion was yelled at the three advisors.

"Apologies, Your Grace. We'll try to be younger next time," said one advisor sarcastically.

Tynan narrowed his eyes as if considering how much impudence he was prepared to overlook. But then he shrugged and carried on with his tirade, "Anyway ... Phobus, Anwir, and Lorcan had the good sense to implement several of my contingency plans. They began mass cloning and soon had a military and labour force. Then they manufactured fleets and weapons, and then they cloned me. Now, can anyone explain to me what a clone is missing?"

"A consciousness," said Ichirō.

Every head in the room pivoted to gaze at the conversation's newest participant, but no heads swivelled faster than Amorina's and my own.

"Ichirō! What are you doing?" Amorina hissed, but Ichirō ignored her.

Tynan rotated on the spot and stared intently at my son. "Very good, my boy."

"Thank you, Your Grace."

"Remind me ... what was your name again?" Tynan asked with a snap of his fingers.

"Ichirō, Your Grace."

"That's right. As Ichirō correctly noted, a clone has no consciousness — it's simply hardware without any programming. So, it was easy to create the clone army and workforce; we had a mass conversion device that we could load up with a brain scan or two and program multiple people at once."

Tynan turned towards the advisors. "But me, well, I was a special case, wasn't I?" he said with a devilish smirk. "So, how'd we do it, lads?"

"We realised the answer was inside your head," said Phobus, pointing at me.

Lorcan continued, "Because a precursor mass conversion device rewrote the majority of your brain, there are a lot of scars in your brain tissue, areas where one personality died and another was born."

"So, we designed a procedure to allow us to decipher the scar tissue and reconstruct a copy of the mind that previously existed. It was the last puzzle piece needed to bring back our emperor, the one true emperor," finished Anwir.

So that's what they did to me earlier — ripped my skull open and probed my brain, scanning all the scar tissue within it. Tynan really was an echo — ashes glued together to make wood.

"With that answered, you must be curious as to why you're alive?" Tynan looked at me, his face expectant, awaiting my question.

"Why are we alive, Tynan?" I almost smiled at the sight of his eye twitching again at the use of his name.

"Well, you lot down this end," Tynan gestured towards the Stardove crew. "We'll be putting you to work; the factories and pleasure rooms can't run themselves, after all."

Tynan turned towards Zavis. "You I intend to keep alive. I will make you watch as we hunt down all the Insurgency members and kill them, one by one, until they're all gone!"

Tynan skipped me as he turned to Amorina next. "You, well, I need a new concubine, so I suppose you'll do in a pinch," he said with a dismissive shrug.

"Touch me and I'll rip your fucking dick off and shove it up your arse!" Amorina snarled, her voice laced with acid.

Tynan glanced at me. "She's a feisty one – I get why you'd tap that."

"Fuck off," I rasped, my damaged voice not able to convey the malice surging through me.

Tynan focused on Amorina again. "We'll soon teach you to look at me with reverence," he added, then moved onto Ichirō.

"You, my son, don't belong with these traitorous bastards. Come, stand at my side and together, we will take back our Empire."

Ichirō's eyes darted sideways and briefly looked at Amorina and me.

"Yes, Your Grace. I would be honoured to."

"Ichirō, don't do this!" Amorina pleaded.

"Silence, bitch!" Tynan growled menacingly.

"No, you shut the fuck up!" I shouted angrily in her defence. "Ichirō, listen to me – Tynan is not a good person!"

"Strike them! And separate the girl from her mother."

On Tynan's command, I saw the soldier behind Amorina lunge forward, his rifle butt pointed straight at Amorina's head. I felt the crack of the rifle butt against the back of my skull and watched helplessly as Amorina suffered the same fate. Both of us bent forward from the strength of the impact and the intensity of the pain that raced through us.

My stomach rolled with nausea, and bile filled my mouth. Red-hot agony engulfed my surgical wound, like a ring of fire that burned the surrounding nerves, sending a burning anguish surging through my body in relentless waves. As the heat waned, I lifted my head to find Amorina already sitting upright. She was focused on Emma, who'd been moved back to her original position. I carefully looked up to find Tynan's cruel expression sneering down at us.

"Good – some submission at last," he said before turning back towards Ichirō. "Come now. Stand up, boy."

Ichirō jumped to his feet.

"Good. Now, stand by the throne."

Ichirō bowed his head and said, "Yes, Your Grace," then marched towards the throne.

As the pain continued to subside, all I could do was watch as my son crossed the floor.

Oh, what have you done, my son?

Tynan shifted his attention to Emma. "I see your daddy has been busy. How old are you, little one?"

Emma tilted her head to look up at Tynan, her expression one of confusion. "Daddy, why are there two of you?"

"I said," Tynan's voice rose, sharp and hostile as he spoke. "How old are you!"

Emma's face paled as she recoiled from this intimidating doppelgänger.

"I'm four and one quarters."

"Right, let's just make it an even four, okay? Such an impressionable age, at four years old, so easily influenced," Tynan shifted his gaze down the line towards Amorina and me. "I'm sure I could mould her into a daughter of my liking."

"Don't you fucking dare!" Amorina's voice reverberated through the room with a furious scream.

Tynan clicked his fingers, and the soldier behind Amorina struck her in the head again, more forcefully this time, and she dropped to the ground, rendered unconscious.

Tynan bent down, seized Emma's arm, pulled her up, and dragged her towards the advisors.

"Stop! You're hurting me!" she cried out.

"Shut up, or I'll show you what pain is."

"Stop! Please!"

Tynan abruptly spun and wrapped his hands around Emma's throat, easily hoisting her into the air. Her eyes widened in terror as he squeezed, cutting off her air.

"When I tell you to do something, you do it!"

He kept walking, his vice-like grip still around my daughter's neck.

"Let her go, Tynan!"

I ducked to the side, avoiding another strike and watched as Tynan deposited Emma in Phobus's lap. Released from Tynan's grip, I heard her gasp for air.

Without pause, Tynan spun around, walked directly to me, and then dropped to one knee before me. He took a moment to scrutinize me, first looking at the left side of my face and then the right.

"You know, it really is an uncanny resemblance."

"Cut to the chase, Tynan. What do you intend to do with me?"

Tynan's eye twitched, and his hand shot forward, grabbing me by the throat and squeezing.

"I intend to make you suffer. Kept alive and treated like an animal – always by my side, like a pet," Tynan explained slowly, his eyes gleaming with anticipation.

"You'll be helpless, forced to watch as I fuck your wife, as I twist your children, as I tear down the Republic! You will spend the rest of your life rotting away, watching everything you love become mine."

He kept a tight grip on my throat, and I could feel my chest tightening with fear, my lungs desperately trying to breathe in air.

"I want you to live the rest of your life struggling to breathe, feeling trapped, suffocated, frantically searching for air, and never finding any. And just when you lose hope, I'll let you take a breath."

Tynan released his grip, and I gasped, trying to take a deep breath, but before I could finish, his hand was back around my throat.

"And then you'll find yourself cut off once more. This will repeat until I break you, and then it will continue."

Tynan released me and stood up, then strode back to his throne while I fell forward onto my hands and gasped for air. After a minute or two, my breathing finally regulated, and when I looked up, I saw Tynan watching me intently from his throne.

A soldier approached the throne. "Your Grace. You asked to be notified of this," the soldier said, offering Tynan a tablet.

Tynan studied the device intently, his eyes scanning its contents. After a few minutes, a satisfied smile spread across his face, and he returned the tablet to the soldier.

"Ready the ships. We're all going on a journey."

"Where are we going?" I ask.

"You'll see soon enough," Tynan said with a flick of his hand.

Moments later, I felt a needle stabbed into my neck. *Ugh! Not this again ...*

Chapter 4
A Show of Force

2159, Common Era – Frontier Space, the Republic of Humanity

Unlike the last time I awoke, I was surprised to discover that we hadn't reached our destination. Instead, I'd found myself engulfed in a darkness my eyes couldn't adjust to. I navigated around the space by touch alone and determined it was a small, padded cell. My head still ached, both where the rifle butt had struck me and around the circular surgical incision, which told me that little time had elapsed since my sedation. I assumed they wouldn't leave me here for too long, but panic set in as my hunger pangs intensified and the eerily quiet room closed in on me.

"Hello! Can anyone hear me?" I yelled, but the cell walls seemed to swallow up the sound and stifle it within seconds.

I called out repeatedly, my strained voice becoming weaker with each cry, but no one came. Bitsy wasn't with me, I couldn't remember when or where I had misplaced my Arachnobot, but without it, I had no way to tell the time. My voice utterly spent, I laid back and tried to count the seconds, trying to work out how much time was going by. Time seemed to stand still as seconds felt like minutes and minutes like hours, going on for eternity.

Suddenly, I heard metal sliding against metal, and a door opened up in front of me, flooding the cell with searing light. My eyes burned in the sudden illumination, and I groaned, immediately closing my eyes and shielding them with my arms.

"Here's ya food ya fuckin' traitor!" an unseen person said, their voice sounding like booming thunder.

I heard a thump of something hitting the cell floor, presumably my food.

Then just as quickly as the light and sound had appeared, they were gone again, suffocating me in silence and darkness. I scrambled forward, locating the plate and the scattered food, shoving the unidentified meal into my mouth, swallowing each mouthful as soon as I could. The food passed through me quickly, and when the urge came to expel my digested meal, I discovered my next predicament: there were no toiletry facilities in the cell.

The puzzle pieces fell into place at that moment, and I realised what was in store for me as Tynan's words echoed through my mind.

"I intend to make you suffer. Kept alive and treated like an animal."

The isolation, the darkness, the hunger, and the silence were all tools to make me suffer, to make me pay for the transgressions Tynan thought I'd committed. As I squatted in a corner and defecated, I realised Tynan had been mistaken; I wasn't being treated like an animal, but something worse – something that didn't even warrant supplying the necessities.

Despite the inhumanities of my confinement, the lack of hygiene facilities became the least of my worries. As my body healed, my mind fractured – isolated and alone in the darkness. My cell was so quiet that I could hear my blood pumping through my veins. I hallucinated sights and sounds – anything to distract myself from the unnerving environment.

I closed my eyes and could see Gaia's lush green landscape or the warm smiles of Amorina, Zavis, my father, and my children. I thought about them often and hoped that they were being spared from this hellish existence. I hoped Tynan had put Amorina, Emma, and Zavis into cryo.

I assumed Ichirō would do as Tynan did; if Tynan had gone into cryo or stayed awake, Ichirō would do the same. I didn't know how much time was passing. The notion of time vanished in the midst of the everlasting darkness – with no indication of when one day stopped and the next began. Despite this, my best estimates told me more rather than less time had passed, and I worried about Adanna, Winona, and my father – they'd expected us back after a year. Had more than a year passed? Had they heard of the Stardove's destruction? Were they worried sick, thinking we were dead, or alive and mysteriously vanished?

The hallucinations during the day became a source of comfort, for when I slept, nightmares plagued me. Strange visions of my body splitting in two like a dividing cell, giving rise to more and more copies of Tynan, or my skull cut open and Tynan climbing out of my head. I would wake screaming, clutching my stomach as the hunger pains threatened to consume me from the inside out.

Even in my waking moments, I couldn't escape Tynan. He was out there, on the ship, doing who knew what. He was my personal shame, a phantom of the past brought into the present and made corporeal. Occasionally, the fear of the darkness's return had kept me up at night, but I'd never expected that fear to physically come true. He was a forgotten evil that ought to have remained that way.

Now, I was afraid of what atrocities he would commit – humanity didn't know what was coming, and thanks to my efforts with the mass conversion device, they didn't really understand what Tynan was capable of either.

Processing it all was a lot for me, and I often found it too much; my mind spun out of control until I was in the throes of a full-blown panic attack. The room would feel suffocatingly small, and I would struggle to breathe as if there literally wasn't enough oxygen in the cell.

My heart would pound in my chest whilst a powerful sense of vertigo would hit me, and all the while, Tynan would flash through my mind; his face, his voice, laughing and jeering at me, taunting me as he wrought misery and destruction upon the universe.

When the attack passed, and I could finally think clearly again, the prospect of going through it all again filled me with dread. This endless waiting was torturous, and even then I was afraid of what state I would be in when the wait was over. Would I be in any shape to stop Tynan? I felt my physical strength diminishing more and more each day, and not that violence solves every problem, but if push came to shove, would I have the strength to deliver a knockout punch?

With no answers today, I comforted myself with the thought that tomorrow might be different, as I did every day.

❦

Something was different. There was a sensation ... no, a mechanical shift – something had changed with the ship. It was like ... slowing down.

Deceleration.

That was it! The ship had decelerated – more specifically, it'd exited warp.

That probably meant we'd arrived at our destination, and with any luck, Tynan would require my presence, and I could finally get out of this godforsaken cell.

As hoped, I soon heard the tell-tale sound of the deadlock being slid across, and I shielded my eyes in anticipation of the door opening. Light flooded in, and I heard the usual cry of disgust as the smell of the cell launched an offensive against the nostrils of the soldiers who'd opened it.

Moments later, they'd entered the cell, and each of them grabbed an arm and a leg and carried my weakened body out of the cell. After spending so long in the darkness and quiet of my thoughts, the ship's bright and clamorous interior was overwhelming, making me feel nearly deaf and blind.

"…" I opened my mouth to say something, but it seemed like my vocal cords had forgotten how – it had been such a long time since I had spoken to anyone. I cleared my throat, then tried once more. "My … family … friends … where are … they?" I had to stop and swallow between each word, but at least I was able to get it out.

The soldiers remained silent.

"Please! Are … they safe? Are they … alright?"

"They're fine. They're in cryo aboard the ship. Now shut up!" one soldier replied, a woman from the sound of the voice.

An immense feeling of relief washed over me. After all the anguish of not knowing, I now knew that Tynan had spared them from my torment, and that was invaluable information. As my vision and hearing slowly and painfully acclimatised, I realised they'd brought me to the ship's bridge.

"Holy fucking shit!" Tynan's voice rose in a tone of utter disgust. "You smell like shit, and you look fucking awful!"

I cautiously looked up and saw him seated in the captain's chair. As soon as our eyes met, Tynan couldn't contain his laughter. I felt my cheeks burn with shame as I bowed my head and stared at the floor, hearing the mocking laughter ringing in my ears. He'd promised to break me – was this what it felt like?

"This is better than I thought," Tynan said, letting out a few last laughs.

"Alright, I think it's time to see if my pet knows how to listen to commands."

Fuck me. What's he going to make me do now?

"Raith! Look out the window, Raith!" Tynan ordered as if he were talking to a dog.

I raised my head and peered out of the bridge's windows, gazing into the vacant expanse that stretched before the ship.

"Wow! He does have the ability to listen!" Tynan ridiculed before speaking in a higher pitch, "What a good boy! Yes, you are! Such a good boy!"

How do dogs put up with this? Do they even care? Do they know any different?

"Okay, okay. Let us try another one," Tynan exclaimed enthusiastically. "Raith, I want you to tell me what you see."

"Nothing. I see nothing. There is nothing to see."

"Wrong!" Tynan exclaimed. "We have ventured out into the universe, yes, but for a start, it's not empty, and second, there's a lot more happening than simply nothing. Look closer!"

I squinted out of the ship's window, trying to see what Tynan wanted me to spot in the vast, star-strewn cosmos, but all I saw was emptiness.

Look closer.

That's what Tynan had said, but what had he meant?

How close did he mean? Closer as in closer in space? Or closer as in inside the ship?

I slowly surveyed the bridge, pausing briefly on each of the consoles that lit up the room. Then one caught my eye. It showed our current interstellar sector and the sectors around our own. There was a dot on the screen, centred in the middle – that had to be this ship – then there was a cluster of dots moving from right to left – a fleet of ships?

I took a quick look out the bridge window, yet there were still no ships in sight.

"You're tracking ships?" I nervously inquired.

Tynan nodded. "Yes, and?"

And? And what?

I looked out the window again. We were tracking ships, but that wasn't the answer Tynan was looking for, so, what was I missing? We were in the middle of nowhere, and unless you were desperate or insane, you wouldn't dare venture through here without a warp drive. My eyes widened as they shifted back and forth between the tracking console and the emptiness before us.

"You're tracking ships in warp!" I blurted. "But ... that's impossible!"

A mischievous smirk appeared on Tynan's face, his lips curling up at the edges. "Clearly, it's not. It was once improbable, but we've obviously shown it's entirely possible!"

"With this technology, you could spy on anyone, anywhere! You could pinpoint their exact location and their direction of travel."

I felt my mind spinning as I tried to wrap my head around the enormous potential of this technology. You could track vessels for the safety of their crew and cargo – no more mysteriously vanished ships – but you could also foil any surprise military manoeuvres, rendering stealth attacks pointless. It was powerful, and in the wrong hands it was dangerous – and it was definitely in the wrong hands.

Something outside stirred. I looked to see what it was, spotting a small autonomous drone flying away from the ship, heading straight ahead. I glanced at the tracking console and noticed that the group of lights was steadily approaching us, but they weren't level with us – they were probably a few kilometres in front of us, which lined up with the direction the drone was going.

"Come on, Raith," Tynan drawled. "Connect the dots. Put it together."

I glanced at Tynan and realised he was watching me with great interest.

What was I missing? What dots did I need to connect?

We were tracking ships through warp; we'd sent a drone out into ... into their flight path? Were they going to collide with it? It wouldn't do much – ships had collision plating to absorb the impact of small objects and point defence systems for larger objects. It had to be something else. Abruptly, a recollection came to mind, something Captain Edgell had said.

"I don't know. We dropped out of warp – violently! I've never experienced anything like it before in my life."

"You haven't just developed the technology to track ships in warp. You've developed the technology to disrupt warp – to pull ships out of FLT travel!"

Tynan's hands clapped together at an agonizingly slow pace, as a sadistic grin appeared on his face.

"Who's a clever boy?" he sneered mockingly.

"What are you trying to achieve here, Tynan?" I snapped as I turned to face my doppelgänger. "What's the point?"

"Strike him!" Tynan commanded, and moments later, I felt the butt of a rifle slam into my head. Pain shot through my body, and I dropped to my knees with a grunt of pain.

I braced myself, expecting another few waves of pain, but already the pain had dissipated.

Interesting.

I knew what a buttstroke felt like, how much pain it caused – with and without a recently operated upon head – and how long that pain took to ease.

What I'd just experienced defied my prior encounters with the butt of a rifle – so why the change?

Regardless of why, this isn't something that Tynan needs to know about.

I masked my surprise by putting on my best expression of pain and slowly looked up at Tynan.

"What the fuck was that for?" I furiously demanded.

"Oh," Tynan said, feigning shock. "Did I not explain the ground rules before? I ordered the soldier behind you to hit you in the head if you talked without being spoken to first or if you addressed me incorrectly; isn't that so, soldier?"

"Yes, Your Grace."

"Speaking of which, hit him again!"

I felt the rifle butt strike me again, and another wave of pain washed over my body but faded as quickly as the first hit had. I shook my head in disbelief – was I still hallucinating?

Where is the rest of the pain?

"That was for speaking up without being asked. The first was to check your tone and remember your place, peasant!"

I rubbed the back of my head to check that I was actually being hit, then looked at the tracking screen – the cluster was awfully close now. If I didn't try to convince Tynan against this course of action, it was all but guaranteed that those ships would suffer the same fate as the Stardove.

"Tynan, please –" I started to say.

"'Tynan, please!'" Tynan mockingly echoed in a high-pitched tone. "Please, what? Are you going to tell me I can't do this? Because guess what, motherfucker! I bloody well can!" Tynan waited until I'd been struck again, then continued. "Why do you care, anyway? What skin have you got in the game?"

I pointed at the tracking screen. "You don't even know what those ships are – they're probably a civilian trade fleet!"

Tynan glanced at the console, then slowly turned his head towards me with a twinkle in his eye. "Raith – you think me so callous as to kill innocent civilians?"

He waved his hand, and one of the crew reached forward and pressed a button in front of them. The tracking screen updated and showed ID tags next to the dots. Next to the dot in the centre, the tag read "TES Chupacabra".

The tags next to the cluster all started with ROHS – they were Republic starships!

"That's a Republic fleet!"

"Exactly!" Tynan hissed.

Now it made sense: Tynan's seemingly random act of violence was now a calculated act of war. Tynan viewed those ships and their crews as enemies of the Empire, foes he had to defeat.

"Listen to me. They aren't your enemy, okay? They don't even know you're alive right now. You're going to hurt or kill countless *innocent* people!"

Tynan cleared his throat, and the soldier struck me again. I rubbed my head again, and Tynan looked at me with an eyebrow raised. "They're not innocent, and I'd say they're my enemy, and even if they aren't, after this they will be. Hurting the Republic *is* the point."

The cluster was almost in front of us on the tracking screen, and Tynan waved his hand again. The same crew member from earlier reached forward and pressed a different button. I tore my gaze to the window and in the blink of an eye, the once empty void, was now crammed with ships. The vessels were in chaos, thrown off their axes; some tilted bow down whilst others tilted bow up, some twisted to the left and others to the right.

The power was flickering on and off on several ships, and some vessels even appeared to have twisted superstructures.

Before I could stop myself, I exclaimed, "What have you done?"

"That should be self-evident," Tynan muttered.

"You know what I mean!" I snapped, then ducked in time to avoid another strike.

"Oi! You're being hit for a reason; don't dodge them," Tynan snapped. "You! Hit him twice for that little stunt!"

I steeled myself as the rifle butt impacted my already bruised head twice and was still surprised at how quickly the pain disappeared. Maybe my pain tolerance had simply increased?

"Whatever, hit me as much as you want – you've pulled them out of warp, you've made your point, now help them!" I demanded.

Tynan held up his hand, halting an in-progress strike, and then burst into laughter. The rest of the crew on the bridge added to the cruel and mocking laughter, making it last longer than necessary to drive the insult home. When Tynan's laughter ceased, a thick, palpable silence filled the bridge.

"Now, let's break down what you said. One, yes, I pulled the fleet out of warp," Tynan said. "Second, no, I have not made my point. And C, I will not be helping them."

Did he just use three different list types?

I noticed Tynan's eye twitch – had he noticed it, too? And what did he mean he hadn't made his point?

"If this wasn't the point you're trying to make, what *is* the point you're trying to make?"

Tynan halted another in-progress strike. "I'm glad you asked ... let me tell you a story."

"Please don't."

Tynan nodded, and the rifle slammed down a little more forcefully this time.

"Come on, Raith – it's a good story. You'll love it."

I sighed; between Tynan's insistence and the bashes I received when I objected, the situation seemed to leave me with few choices.

"So, there's this guy, right? He eliminates the emperor, dismantles the Empire, and, for a while, life is nice and peaceful. Then, while lying in bed one night, he wonders if the emperor had any contingency plans. What if there were plans in motion to bring the Empire back?"

I watched Tynan, trying to read the subtle nuances in his expression as he spoke. I was unsure whether he had learned this from Zavis or if they had pulled it from my head. Either way, I suspected the how was not as important as the why he was telling me this.

"Now this guy spends years researching this theory, trying to prove or disprove that the Empire is coming back. But he finds hardly anything, and anyone he tells doesn't believe him. There have been no encounters with the Empire, not a sight, not a sound. They are gone.
'You are worrying for no reason. Let it go,' they all say."

Where was Tynan going with this?

"Now there's a different guy, back from the dead, and his Empire rising with him. He wants to reclaim all the territory that he once controlled. He wants to reinstate his place in the universe. But how is he supposed to do that when no one even believes he exists anymore? How is he supposed to take back what is his when nobody *fears* him anymore?"

I looked out the window at the fleet, stranded and damaged, helpless and adrift, and then spoke, "By making them fear you again ..."

My stomach dropped as I realised he would kill them all somehow, strike while they were down. I spun back around towards Tynan. "You can't do this. Not like this! To kill a disarmed and wounded opponent, there's no civility to that. It's cowardice!"

Tynan waited until the rifle had collided with my skull before responding. "But I can, and I will, Raith. It's not cowardly; it's efficient – just good business, you might say. Now, can someone tell Raith what ordinance we're going to use today?"

"We're going to be using a Firecracker warhead."

An icy shiver ran down my back, sending a wave of goosebumps over my skin. I'd heard of those. Firecracker: an underwhelming name for a brutally efficient weapon designed to be a force to be reckoned with, even though its name gave no hint of its potential. I suspected that its creator – my own grandfather if I remembered the history books correctly – had intentionally named it that way. I'd never seen one used before, for good reason, but their status was practically infamous at this point.

"A Firecracker," I muttered. "Aren't those expressly forbidden?"

Another impact struck my skull, and I winced – despite my increased pain threshold, each strike was slowly getting more painful.

"If you asked the Republic, the existence of me and my Empire would also be expressly forbidden. But much like a Firecracker, we're only banned within Republic territory, and luckily for me, this is my territory now," Tynan replied.

In its infancy, the Empire had developed and used the weapon against a Republic fleet attempting to quell the burgeoning Empire's "rebellion", just as the Republic had crushed Mars's rebellion. On that day, the Empire had sent the Republic packing after only firing a single warhead.

The Republic had outlawed the manufacturing and use of Firecrackers ever since.

"Please, Tynan, you've made your point; the Republic will fear you, okay? You can track and pull ships out of warp – that's enough! You don't need to kill them!"

"Hit him twice!"

I braced as the blows rained down, grimacing as they struck.

"Once more, for good measure."

Another blow hit me from behind, and I felt a trickle running down the back of my neck. I reached up and touched my throbbing head, my hand wet and red when I brought it back in front of me.

"See, this is why you'd make a terrible emperor," Tynan said. "You are too soft. You think too much, and you feel too much! If I left the fleet, sure, the Republic would fear me for now, but they'd also fast-track the development of countermeasures or tracking capabilities of their own. But if I destroy them, it's both a promise and a follow-through: I will pull your fleets from warp, and I will destroy them."

"That makes no sense. The Republic would develop countermeasures either way!" I protested, but almost as soon as I had yelled my objection, I saw the warhead shooting away in my peripheral vision.

"Oops ..." Tynan said, holding his hand in front of his mouth mockingly.

"It's not too late! Disable it or shoot it down!"

With two hand motions from Tynan, two more hits landed on my head and caused my vision to blur at the edges.

"You know, I've just realised I've forgotten where the missile disabling button is ... I swear it was around here somewhere?" Tynan said as he gazed around the bridge in fake concern.

I clutched my bleeding, throbbing head and turned to the bridge window, exasperated as the warhead neared the fleet. I stood frozen and powerless, my throat tight, as I watched the fleet and all-hands face their eminent destruction. I felt a shiver of morbid curiosity as I wondered how the Firecracker would wreak its havoc.

What the fuck?

My stomach churned with nausea, sickened by my thoughts.

"Three … two …" Tynan said, counting down to detonation. "One!"

The warhead burst open with a flash of light, partially obscuring the thousands of objects it was projecting forward like a shotgun, spreading out wide, dispersing amongst the entire republic fleet.

"That's it?"

Tynan held up his right hand, index finger pointed upwards. "Watch!"

Suddenly, the objects detonated, blinding me with white light. Before the initial light burst had disappeared, thousands of secondary, then tertiary and quaternary light bursts appeared, making me squint every time as the attack seemed to continue without end. Finally, the light faded, and the fleet came back into focus. The Firecracker had decimated the ships, completely destroying the smaller ones and riddling the larger ones with gaping holes, giving them the appearance of Swiss cheese rather than starships.

"What did that —" I started to ask when one of the large ships detonated, silently exploding in the distance.

"No life signs detected, Your Grace," a crew member informed.

"Excellent," Tynan exclaimed as he clapped his hands together. "I officially declare this a victory!"

I watched the debris field, unable to tear my eyes away from the chaos. There were shapes floating among the wreckage that looked distinctly like human bodies, and I clenched my fists as a quiet rage grew inside me.

"What did that just do?" I demanded as I turned towards Tynan.

The soldier behind me swung his rifle again but fuelled by my anger, I caught it, pulling the weapon from his grasp, much to his surprise, and my own.

Tynan calmly looked at the soldier and then at me. "Well, first of all, it destroyed the fleet, didn't it?" he stated the obvious, pointing out the window.

I pointed the gun at Tynan. "I meant how? How did that just destroy the fleet?"

"There's a saying about magicians … hang on, it'll come to me," Tynan said, seemingly completely unconcerned about the gun.

I rolled my eyes. "About never revealing their secrets?"

"Yes!" Tynan exclaimed, clicking his fingers. "That's the one. Now you, give your sidearm to Raith," he said towards the solider who'd lost his rifle.

The soldier glanced between Tynan and I uncertainly, just as I also glanced between Tynan and the soldier. Now I was suspicious – why did I need his pistol when I already had his rifle?

"I beg your pardon, Your Grace … I don't understand."

"Did I stutter?" Tynan demanded. "Give your sidearm to Raith."

The soldier swallowed but pulled the pistol from its holster. "Yes, Your Grace," he said, holding the weapon out to me.

I took the gun from him and held it, looking at Tynan to see what would happen next.

"Well, shoot him," Tynan said towards me.

"What?"

"Shoot," said Tynan, pointing at the soldier, "Him!"

"I'm not going to –"

Tynan leapt out of the captain's chair, pulled the pistol from my hand, turned it towards the solider and pulled the trigger. The gunshot echoed around the bridge as the soldier collapsed to the ground, a bullet hole dead centre of his forehead. Tynan shoved the gun into my hands and returned to his seat.

"You son of a bitch!" I yelled, pointing the pistol at Tynan. "You just don't care, do you? Their lives are meaningless!"

Tynan stared at me confidently. "If that's how you feel, maybe you should do something about it!"

I pulled the trigger.

Click.

I looked at the gun. Was the safety on? Nope, it didn't seem to have a safety. I pointed it at Tynan again. Click. Click.

"Did I mention the Empire proudly supports workplace health and safety? We biometrically encoded all weapons so only the issued weapons holder, their commanding officer, and I can use them. It's cut down on a lot of misfires. And before you ask, we're not the same – I had a little extra added in to ensure you couldn't impersonate me."

Fuck. That's why he was so unconcerned about me having the rifle ... and the pistol. It was just a power play ... a mindfuck. He was never in any danger.

I threw the weapons to the ground in disgust, and turned back towards the window, towards the wreckage. The Firecracker was a terrifying piece of weaponry, however it worked.

I made a mental note to ask Zavis about it, if I ever got the chance to speak with him again, as there was a good chance he'd know about these weapons.

Behind me, I could hear the soldier's body being moved, and a new soldier taking up position behind me. But I focused on more pressing thoughts – like why the fleet was here in the first place. There'd been at least three cruisers and a dozen frigates, by no means a small fleet. Surely it wasn't because of the disappearance of the Stardove? Sure, it's sudden absence would prompt a search and rescue, but a fleet of fifteen or so vessels? What else could've drawn them out here?

"Why were they here?"

"Why was who, where, what?" Tynan replied.

I turned to look at him, and he glanced away, and again, I caught his eye twitching. After a moment, he faced me again, seeming to have collected himself.

"Why was the Republic fleet here?" I asked again.

"I haven't the slightest idea."

"So, what … you just saw the fleet on your tracking systems and thought, yeah, that'll do, I'll just go blow up that fleet?"

Tynan nodded. "Yeah, basically."

"Aren't you curious as to why the fleet was here?"

Tynan considered this for a moment. "I mean … I guess a little?"

"Okay, great. Do any of your systems or crew have any insight about why they were here?"

Each of the crew turned to Tynan and confirmed that they didn't know why the fleet had been travelling where it was.

"Oh well," said Tynan. "I guess it will just be one of life's little mysteries. Hang on, you!"

The soldier that'd taken up the role of standing behind me turned towards Tynan. "Yes, Your Grace?"

"Didn't you hear the orders I gave the previous chap?"

"I did, Your Grace."

"Then why aren't you fucking hitting him when he speaks without first being spoken to?"

"I have no excuse, Your Grace. I ask for your forgiveness!"

"Don't grovel! Just hit the fucker when he talks and isn't supposed to!"

Ignoring Tynan's arseholery and the soldiers reply, I wondered if any of the crew knew anything about the fleet's presence. For that matter, did I? Something that might've happened? Something I might've missed? A memory bubbled forth from my subconscious.

"I'm unsure what the connection is, but we got an emergency broadcast from Akka. A large unidentified object – perhaps a ship – is approaching the colony. It destroyed a scout vessel sent to meet it, so they urgently requested Republic forces."

"There was an emergency broadcast! When your loyalists took the Stardove. It was from Akka."

The solider slammed his rifle into the small of my back, and I collapsed back onto the ground.

"Check the records. See if you can find anything," Tynan commanded.

The crew members tapped away at their consoles for a few minutes. "Yes, I think I've got something, Your Grace."

"Play it on the speakers."

The crew member tapped a few more controls, and then a recording played.

"This is an emergency broadcast for the Republic Council from the colony Akka. An unidentified ... thing. We don't know what it is, possibly a vessel.

Whatever it is, it's a huge orb – we estimate it's half an astronomical unit in diameter. It just appeared a few months ago – a few light years away – we think it dropped out of warp. We tried to establish a communication channel, but it didn't respond to any attempt, regardless of the frequency. We sent a scouting vessel out to it in case we could establish physical contact instead … but it destroyed the shuttle. At its current speed, it is moving on a course that will intersect with Akka in about two years. We, the colony, are requesting immediate assistance from Republic forces."

The speakers, and the bridge, fell silent as everyone processed what they'd just heard.

"Were there any other transmissions? Replies from the Republic or subsequent transmissions from Akka?" I asked.

The previous crew member who'd found the emergency broadcast looked at Tynan, who gave a nod of approval. The crew member turned back to their console and tapped away once more. "There was one response from the Republic that passed by here about a year later, Your Grace."

"Play it."

"Akka, this is Commander Romans of the second defensive fleet. We're being dispatched from Earth as we speak to render assistance to your colony. It is currently July 17th, 2158, so our estimated arrival time at Akka will be late December 2159. By your estimate, we should arrive before this vessel reaches your colony. Please send any additional information you have, and we will be with you as soon as possible, fate willing."

As soon as the second recording finished, the crew member spoke up. "There was one additional broadcast originating from Akka again. Playing it now."

"This is the colony, Akka. Commander Romans, we've recently received your transmission; its January 19th, 2159. Our situation has grown most dire; our orbit has elongated, effected more and more the closer the vessel gets. We don't have any additional information to provide. We've tried scanning the vessel, but we can't detect much. They confirm the vessel's presence, trajectory, and speed, but that's about it. All I can say is that our trepidation grows with each passing day. This thing looms in the sky, day and night, and it has awakened a sense of horror and fear in all of us. I fear your aid will arrive too late to help us."

The recording ended, and the room was silent once more.

"What year and month is it?"

"It's roughly September or October 2159," said Tynan as the soldier struck me again.

"Okay … we've got time to get to Akka before that thing does."

Tynan laughed, holding up his hands to stop another strike. "Why on earth would we go to Akka?"

"Because we just destroyed the fleet that was on its way to help the colony! There's no one else close enough to help them!"

"I still cannot see how this involves us?"

Damn this man!

Every action had to suit his interests, or it wasn't worth giving time to. What could I say to appeal to his selfish nature?

"You're trying to re-establish the Empire, right?"

"Obviously. If you're still needing to clarify that after all our adventures together so far, you're stupider than I thought."

"That's not – don't worry. Listen, if that thing that's approaching Akka is hostile, which it sounds like it might be, if it destroys Akka, there'll be nothing for you to re-establish an Empire over."

"There are more colonies and worlds than just Akka."

"Yes, but what if when this thing is done with Akka, it moves onto our other worlds? What if it moves through them, one by one? What will you rule over then? Amidst the rubble, what will you have dominion over?"

Tynan went to speak as if automatically compelled to deliver a retort but caught himself – had one of my sentiments gotten a foothold in his thoughts?

"Admittedly, there is some logic to that argument." Tynan shifted in his chair, leaning forward. "So, unfortunately, I think this maggot is correct. We must either fight now or accept that this thing may finish and leave us with nothing to rule over, assuming it's hostile. Plot a course for Akka."

"Great! Then we need to –"

Tynan cut me off. "Your argument may have merit, but don't overstep your mark, Raith. You have a place. Best remember it." Tynan turned towards the soldier. "You can hit him again now – and make it a hard one!"

I heard a sharp intake of air as the soldier drew back his rifle. Odds were in favour of this strike knocking me out. But my pain was worth it – I'd convinced a powerful, selfish man to act in the interest of others.

Hold on Akka, help is on its way.

The air rushing past my ears told me the impact was imminent.

Crack!

Chapter 5
A Good Offence

2159, Common Era – Planet Akka, Frontier Space, the Republic of Humanity

The events that led to this situation solidified in my mind as I stared at my reflection in the pool of cryofluid I'd just vomited up. Tynan's soldier had knocked me unconscious, and when I'd awoken, cryonic technicians were placing me inside a cryopod. I presumed we had arrived at our destination, as I caught a glimpse of my reflection in the puddle below. Tynan's decision to spare me from three more months of solitary confinement was a relief, but I couldn't help but notice that I was still stuck in a filthy and neglected state. My hair hung in unkempt, matted strands, and my beard was a wild, bushy mess. Beneath all the hair, I looked pale and emaciated. I tried not to gag as I noticed the putrid stench emanating from my clothes and skin, a mixture of dried blood, excrement, and food remnants. It dawned on me that this was the first time I'd seen myself in months.

I'm like a living corpse ... fuck!

Seeing my reflection also made me realise how much I'd been missing my morning routine: Bitsy's cheerful good morning chirp, the sound of the children playing outside, Amorina and Father cooking breakfast for everyone, and, of course, my morning recital.

My choices affect others, so choose how those choices affect them.

I'd missed that daily period of introspection. Taking a deep breath of the fresh air, I knew this was an excellent opportunity to squeeze in a session. I'd felt so blind over the last few months, lost in endless introspection without the business of life to temper the silence.

All those days spent hoping that Emma, Amorina, and Zavis were in cyrosleep, and hoping that Ichirō was doing okay too. Despite his missteps, I hoped he would find his way back to us.

I discarded my doubts with a shake of my head and broadened my perspective to take in the bigger picture. My mind felt overwhelmed as I cycled through all the events in motion: the Republic, unaware of how outmatched they were against the rising threat of the Empire; the colony Akka and the approaching danger that loomed over them; and of course, the Empire itself and Tynan's return along with it. I felt obligated to resolve all these issues somehow – if I even could, given my state – but I hadn't figured out how to do it yet.

"Raith?"

I glanced left and saw Amorina, with Emma and Zavis behind her, all kneeling in their expelled cryofluid as I was. A wave of relief rolled through me. They had been in cryo, they'd been safe and spared from the suffering I'd gone through.

"Amorina!"

Tears streamed down my wife's face, and her body shook as she reached out to me. I crawled towards her as quickly as my weakened body would allow and embraced her. She held me, and I felt her run her hands up and down my body, feeling my bones jutting from beneath my skin.

"I almost didn't recognise you! You're so thin and shaggy," she whispered in my ear. "What have they done to you?"

"I'm okay," I said as tears ran down my face. "A little worse for wear, but okay."

I heard Amorina inhale and then gag.

"And you reek!" she hissed.

"Sorry … I haven't had … any opportunities to clean myself up."

"Daddy?"

Amorina and I separated, and I gazed at my daughter's sweet face.

"Come here, sweetie pie!" I said as I stretched out my arms.

Emma ran forward, and I felt her tiny arms wrap around my neck as I scooped her against me. Amorina joined the embrace, and we all hugged; our family reunited at last.

"You are stinky, Daddy!"

"I know, sweetie, I know. Daddy is sorry about that."

"That's okay! I'm stinky too sometimes. We just need a bath!"

Amorina and I chuckled – there was something about a child's naiveté that could bring accidental levity to a situation.

"I've missed you guys so much."

"But we were all asleep, Daddy? We don't dream in the sleepy machines, so how'd you miss us?" Emma asked innocently.

"Daddy had a different sleep to you guys … so I dreamt about you and missed you both so much!"

"Oh … okay," Emma said with a shrug, accepting my explanation with the ease and complete trust of the young.

I looked over Amorina's shoulder at Zavis and raised a questioning eyebrow. Zavis nodded, and I smiled because now I knew he was okay, too.

"All right, break it up!"

I felt the warmth of my family's embrace ripped away from me as hands forced us apart.

"Hey!" I snapped at the soldiers.

"Hey yourself, traitor! Huggin' time's over!"

Each of us had a soldier who pulled our arms behind our backs and lifted us to our feet.

"Walk!" they commanded as they pushed us out of the cryo room.

"What's happening?" Amorina asked.

The soldiers remained silent as they continued to march us forward.

"We've arrived at Akka," I replied.

Amorina tilted her head and raised an eyebrow. "We've gone to Akka?"

"Yes, we have – long story short, Tynan destroyed a Republic fleet that was going to Akka's aid, which they'd requested because there's an extra-terrestrial vessel approaching the colony. I convinced Tynan to aid Akka in place of the Republic fleet."

Amorina's expression changed to shock and disbelief; her eyes widened as she processed my sentence. Admittedly, it'd been a doozy. Still, it'd been the most succinct way to catch her up.

"Holy fuck! How long was I out for?"

I took a few moments to think back, counting the months I'd spent in isolation and cryosleep. "Almost a year, I think."

"A year? Fuck me!"

We rounded a corner, and the soldiers steered Emma, Amorina, and Zavis down one hallway and me down another.

"Hey! Why are we going to different places?"

"Shut up, traitor!"

"Raith!" I heard Amorina call out from the other passage.

"I'll find you!" I shouted back.

The soldier pushing me gave me a harder shove. "Quit chattering and keep walking!"

They led me to an elevator, and after going up a few floors, I found myself on the bridge. The ship was still moving at warp speed, the blue light cone glimmering ahead of it. I quickly scanned the room and saw that the advisors and Tynan were there.

"Hello again, Raith," came the slow, familiar drawl.

I cautiously nodded back an acknowledgement, remembering the trigger-happy soldiers from the last time.

"Oh, don't worry, I will not have you hit this time."

"You won't?"

"No. You proved … surprisingly resistant to the pain I'm sure those rifle butts were inflicting, so this time, I've devised a different form of motivation to keep you in line," Tynan said as he pointed to a monitor.

I glanced up and saw Emma, Amorina, and Zavis standing in what appeared to be an observation lounge. A soldier stood behind each one of them, rifle in hand.

"If you speak before you're spoken to, or if you address me the wrong way, this time I'll have them struck in the head, and depending on your behaviour, it'll either be one at a time or all together. Understood?"

Fuck, I hate this arsehole.

"Yes, Your Grace. I understand," I answered begrudgingly.

"Excellent."

The bridge filled with a brilliant blue light as the starship decelerated from warp speed; the light shifted from sapphire to azure before it dissipated. Seconds later, the colour returned as a deep purple, moving into a dark violet, and then to electric blue, and then the ship moved out of warp and showed the universe once again. But instead of being greeted with a view of Akka, a vast emptiness, dark and devoid of anything, met us.

"Where is it?" Tynan demanded.

"I don't know, Your Grace. Scanning for Akka now."

We were supposed to be in front of Akka, but it was nowhere to be found.

"We've located it, Your Grace. Its orbit is … far more elliptical than it should be. Setting us on an intercept course now."

The view stayed the same for a while, and then a dot appeared to the left. I watched as the dot became centred and then began to enlarge as the vessel moved towards it. In Akka's second emergency broadcast, they'd noted that their orbit was elongating, affected by the gravity of the approaching vessel. Speaking of the vessel, we would've seen it by now if it was of the size reported. I noticed a queasy feeling in my stomach – something was definitely amiss here.

"A question, if I may, Your Grace."

Tynan turned to look at me.

"Did you just find a loophole?"

I shrugged, unsure whether or not I had found a technicality in Tynan's rules.

"You just spoke without being spoken to, but you were speaking to ask if you could speak … eh, I'll allow it. Ask your question."

"Thank you, Your Grace. Is it possible to pull up a reference photo of Akka?"

"Uh … sure, I guess. Why?"

"Just a hunch."

Tynan eyed me wearily but gave a nod, accepting this explanation, just. "Pull up a reference photo."

A monitor to my right flashed, and a picture of Akka appeared on a nearby screen.

"Whoa!" I gasped in awe at the image before me.

Akka was a stunning planet in the photo; two times the size of Mars, with fifty-eight percent of its surface covered in ocean, its land-to-water ratio was much higher than Earth's, making it look browner and greener than Earth. Perhaps the most stunning detail captured in the photo was Akka's rings: orbiting at a forty-five-degree angle to its equator, with their right side sitting in Akka's shadow, the left side bright and blue in the light of the system's star. A dossier near the image detailed that the rings were comprised of Kyanite, a blue aluminium silicate, giving them a hue ranging from a light greyish blue to a deep navy blue.

"Beautiful," Tynan murmured in awe.

Tynan's remark was startling, and I glanced at my adversary – the real Tynan had no admiration for places like this. I remembered my journey to Astarte, a military-based, industrious world with its brown, barren, and lifeless environment. Compared to Gaia's radiance, I'd found the world to be an empty and wretched place, and so I'd detested it.

The voice in my head at the time – Tynan's voice – had spoken to me, saying that Astarte was beautiful to him. He'd relished the forging of men and machines in the rumbling factories, ceaseless and obedient in their operation, stockpiling resources for a war effort.

I glanced back at the advisors and saw that others were just as confused as I was – they'd heard Tynan's remark, too.

Not the worst thing.

A little doubt amongst the leaders of the Empire could be enough to bring it down once more. Remembering why I'd asked for the reference photo, I returned my gaze to the live view of Akka.

"Are we sure this is Akka?" I asked.

The planet in front of us was almost entirely white, with the upper and lower thirds frozen beneath large polar caps, leaving only the equatorial third habitable. The beautiful rings in the on-screen image were nowhere to be found on the planet in front of us.

"The planetary identification beacon confirms its Akka, and I'm picking up radio chatter from the surface — there are still people down there."

My gut clenched, and I felt like a thousand butterflies had materialised inside me. This colony was in huge trouble — it was rapidly freezing over, wildly displaced from its standard orbit — if it widened anymore, the planet would become uninhabitable. Even then, there was something else wrong with the view before me, compounding my growing sense of unease.

I glanced at Tynan, and he seemed to have had the same thought. Then, it clicked.

"There's no —" I broke off, and then we both spoke in unison, "Stars."

As soon as I realised, I recontextualised the view before me and could perceive the blocky, asymmetrical, metallic surface of a vessel so vast that it filled up the entire view. I rushed forward and peered upward, trying to glimpse the universe, but all I could see was the mechanical surface of the orb. The Akka broadcast had estimated its size at half an astronomical unit in diameter, which I'd struggled to believe, but looking at this monstrosity now, I believed it — how could I not?

"Fuck me ... that's one big arse vessel."

"Size matters not!" Tynan declared. "We're going to give it hell and send it on its way!"

"We're just going to attack it?" I exclaimed, surprised by Tynan's bold approach.

Tynan cleared his throat and pointed to the screen showing my family.

"I'm sorry, Your Grace."

"Better," Tynan said as he picked up a communicator. "Hit the old, fat one."

I looked up at the monitor to see a soldier step forward and strike Zavis over the head, sending him tumbling forward. I felt my stomach twist, and I clenched my fists. I closed my eyes and reminded myself to hold my tongue.

"To answer your question, yes, we are just going to attack it. As the saying goes, the best defence is a good offence. So, we'll kick this thing where it hurts, show it that humanity is not to be trifled with, and when it runs away with its tail between its legs, we shall be victorious!"

I wish I shared Tynan's confidence, but I couldn't help but feel it was inflated. Did he think we really had a chance against this giant? By ourselves?

"Someone … open up a broadcast on all channels."

A crew member tapped away at a console and then turned towards Tynan. "Channels are open, Your Grace."

Tynan rose from the captain's chair and cleared his throat before beginning his speech.

"People of Akka, this is Emperor Khidar of the Tynan Empire. The Republic has abandoned you. They answered your distress call and assured you help was coming, but no one has come to your aid!"

I could imagine Tynan's voice projecting across Akka, on every radio frequency, coming out of every device. The confusion rising in the citizens expecting the Republic but now hearing the Empire.

"Despite the Republic's betrayal, the Empire is here to save you. *I* am here to save you! You're my citizens from now on, and you shall always have my protection.

So, look to the sky, gaze upon me and my might, bear witness to your salvation! Look upon me, for I have the strength to do what the Republic was too frightened to attempt!"

Tynan waved his hand at the crew member, and they cut the transmission. Not the most reassuring broadcast: a surprise empire, a totally plausible betrayal, sudden citizenship, wrapped up in a self-serving jerk fest.

Talk about a twisted narrative!

"Alrighty! Move us to the other side of Akka – place us between it and that monstrosity!" Tynan commanded.

Akka steadily approached as the Chupacabra moved forward until it passed beneath us. Nothing else was visible now except the looming vessel.

"If I may enquire, I wish to know what the plan is here, Your Grace," I asked.

"Simple," Tynan said with a grin. "We give it a fireworks display."

I resisted the urge to disagree. It was one thing to deploy a Firecracker against a fleet of ships, but using one against a vessel larger than Mercury's orbit around the sun was an entirely different matter.

"The warhead is ready, Your Grace."

Tynan smiled, and his eyes gleamed. "Fire at will!"

I watched as the warhead came into view, streaking away from the ship and towards its target. Tynan began counting down to detonation as he'd done the previous time.

"Three ... two ... one!"

There was a flash of light as the warhead burst open, blasting its payload towards the vessel. A few moments later, the thousands of explosive charges detonated, followed by secondary and tertiary explosions.

"Oh, I can't wait to see the holes we punched in this thing!" Tynan exclaimed.

The detonations ceased, and the light faded. Everyone on the bridge peered out the window, waiting to see the results.

"It looks … unharmed, Your Grace," said Phobus, a note of contempt in his voice.

"Yes … well, we obviously just didn't hit it with enough. How many Firecrackers do we still have?"

"Three more, Your Grace."

"Good! We'll fire them all simultaneously!"

"A question if I may, Your Grace."

Tynan turned to look at me. "You know, if you don't stop exploiting the loophole, I'll have to take it away from you," he growled.

"I appreciate that, Your Grace – I'm just trying to be of assistance."

Tynan narrowed his eyes. "What's your question?"

"Have our sensors detected any change in the vessel? Has it stopped moving? Or started moving? Are we registering any … I don't know, power output, radiation, or anything?"

"That was four questions."

"Or just one question in four parts," I replied off handedly, regretting it immediately.

Tynan pulled out his communicator. "Hit the bitch."

I twisted around and watched on the monitor as they hit Amorina in the small of her back, and she collapsed to the floor.

I quickly turned back to Tynan. "I'm sorry, Your Grace!"

"I bet you are … now, where was I? Oh yes, check the sensors. See if they have detected anything."

The crew got to work, filling the air with the tapping of their fingers on consoles.

"The vessel appears to be stationary, Your Grace, and there has been no change in its movement," said one crew member.

"Its power capacity appears to be constant as well … although we are picking up a lot of power … in the realms of 342 yottawatts!" said another crew member, who quickly added, "Your Grace."

The power estimate was staggering – I couldn't believe it – it was almost as much power as Sol!

"We're also not detecting any noticeable radiation levels, Your Grace," added one last crew member.

Tynan turned towards me. "Satisfied?"

"Yes, Your Grace. Thank you, Your Grace."

Tynan smiled and turned back towards the window. "Fire all remaining Firecrackers!"

The three warheads streaked into view, tearing across the distance between the Chupacabra and the vessel. The missile's initial detonation triggered in unison, spreading the payload across the surface of the mighty machine before us.

"Here we go!" Tynan said, appearing almost giddy.

The entire view turned white as the payloads exploded, and the chains of secondary detonations kept going for what seemed like an eternity. Finally, the light subsided, and once again, the massive vessel seemed unfazed and unharmed.

"Well? Are we picking up any changes?" Tynan demanded.

The crew confirmed there had been no changes after reviewing the sensor data.

"Perhaps we are ill-equipped for this challenge, Your Grace." Lorcan suggested.

"We have other cards to play, and besides, this thing is just sitting there. It doesn't seem to care that we are here, nor that we're throwing stones at it. Let's keep pressing the advantage while we have one," Tynan replied.

"Maybe it's best to rethink this course, My Lord," said Phobus. "Possibly along the lines of what we discussed earlier?"

Tynan frowned. "I said we have other cards to play. I intend to play them."

I glanced back at the advisors and noticed a look pass between them – they were displeased with Tynan's choice, and I wondered if they would go up against him.

"Your Grace," Anwir began.

"We really think this is not the wisest course of action," Phobus continued.

"Having cards available to us is good, but be that as it may, the Firecrackers are one of our more powerful weapons," Lorcan said, bringing up the rear.

When I looked at Tynan, I could see something the advisors could not – Tynan's face twisting with rage. I looked back towards the advisors.

"If several of those could not scratch the vessel before us," Lorcan continued.

"Then what hope do our other ordinances have of producing a different outcome?" Anwir added.

"Even if we threw everything this ship is carrying at it, it is likely to still prove fruitless – we would need munitions on a fleet scale to combat this vessel effectively," Phobus concluded.

"Silence!" Tynan yelled, leaping out of his captain's chair and rounding on the three shocked advisors. "You advise me when I seek council! Not afterwards, not beforehand, not in between – only when I seek it! Is that clear?"

"Yes, Your Grace!" all three advisors said in unison.

"Do not speak again unless I ask you to!"

"Yes, Your Grace!" they said together again.

Tynan sighed and returned to his chair. "This is just a tougher nut to crack than anticipated," he hissed. "Regardless, we will carry on. What other weapons do we have access to?"

"We have our rail guns and gauss cannons and eight nuclear warheads."

Tynan tapped his fingers against the armrest of his chair as he weighed his options.

"Let's go with the gauss cannons. Fire a round from each one."

"Yes, Your Grace. Charging cannons now!"

I watched a crew member initiate the charging sequence and monitored the screen as the cannons powered up. I glanced at Tynan and saw him watching the screen, too.

The charge level reached one hundred percent, and Tynan grinned. "Let's see if this thing can take these on!"

The ship shuddered, and two large solid slugs rocketed away from us, covering the distance between the Chupacabra and the vessel much quicker than the Firecracker warheads had. As before, the vessel acted as if it was unaware of the oncoming projectiles, and the whole bridge was still as the rounds impacted its hull.

"They ... they just ... disappeared into the surface!" Tynan exclaimed.

The crew frantically tapped away at their consoles, trying to find an explanation for what we'd witnessed ... or what we *hadn't* witnessed.

"Where are my gaping holes? Where's my debris?" Tynan yelled as he leapt out of his chair and gestured out the window at the vessel.

"It appears as though the vessel is unaffected. There's no change to its position, movement, or power output, and no deformations to its surface – no sign of any impact whatsoever. That's all I can tell you, Your Grace."

Tynan clenched his fists, and I watched his right eye twitch. The grand salvation of Akka was not going according to plan, it seemed.

"If I may, Your Grace," Anwir began.

Tynan spun around, grabbed the sidearm of the nearest soldier and aimed it at Anwir.

"Did I ask for your council?" he roared.

Anwir shook in his wheelchair. "No, My Lord! You did not as –"

The gun fired, and the advisor slumped over in his wheelchair, blood pouring from his forehead into his lab. Tynan waved the gun at Phobus and Lorcan.

"This is your one and only warning!"

The two remaining Advisors nodded.

Tynan then rounded on the soldier he'd taken the sidearm from.

"As for you!" he yelled. "You allowed yourself to be disarmed!"

The sound of the second shot echoed through the air as the soldier hit the ground and caused everyone to jump back and shrink in on themselves, least he decide to point the gun at them next.

"Everyone take note – if you bear arms, they're your responsibility! Do not allow them to be taken from you, lest they be used against you or your leaders!"

"But only us, our superiors, and you can use each weapon, Your Grace. It wouldn't matter if anyone else took the weapons," a soldier interjected.

Tynan's face twitched, and for a moment, he looked confused.

Did he forget that that's how their weapons worked?

A third shot rang through the deathly silence that filled the room and the soldier fell to the floor.

"My point stands ... do not allow your weapons to be taken from you."

Tynan returned to his chair, his chest heaving from the anger seething within him.

"Fire a nuke at this ... thing!" he bellowed.

I inhaled sharply. Nuclear warheads were ... well, they were nuclear warheads – certainly, not a weapon to be used lightly. Launching a single Firecracker – or three – was one thing, but a nuke was taking things up a notch.

"Yes, Your Grace."

They started the missile initiation sequence, and I looked down at the two dead soldiers.

Such a needless, wasteful loss of life.

But this was Tynan's world. This was how he had always operated: by creating an environment of fear. I glanced at Tynan. He was becoming more unhinged and unstable. I looked out the bridge window again to see the nuclear warhead flying towards the vessel. Part of me expected a result like the two previous attempts: either it would detonate harmlessly on the exterior or mysteriously disappear beneath the surface.

"Look!" a crew member shouted, pointing out the window.

A portion of the vessel's surface seemed to have liquified, forming a black cloud that flew away from the vessel and swarmed towards the oncoming warhead.

"What is it doing?" Tynan asked, but no one could give him answers.

I watched in amazement as the swarm intercepted the nuke and appeared to take apart the warhead mid-air.

Moments later, it was nothing but a collection of components, and the swarm seemed to carry them back to the vessel. The swarm re-solidified into the vessel's surface and the warhead components disappeared beneath it.

"Well," said Tynan. "That's kind of a neat trick."

"What would you like us to do, Your Grace?" a crew member asked.

"Fire all the other nukes simultaneously, and when the surface swarms again, fire the rail guns – maybe we can buy enough time for the nukes to arrive intact."

"As you wish, Your Grace."

I glanced over at Tynan. He had grown pale, sweat beaded across his brow. I could see the fear on Tynan's face – his overconfidence was returning to haunt him now.

"And they're away!"

Everyone on the bridge turned back towards the window and watched the seven remaining nukes streak their way across the gap between the two ships. A larger portion of the vessel's surface than before dissipated into the swarm.

"Fire the rail guns!"

The Chupacabra vibrated as its rail gun armaments fired, sending hundreds of bullets hurtling towards the approaching swarm. They made contact with the swarm, and I could see dozens of little impacts as they collided and shattered.

"It's working!" Tynan exclaimed.

I felt my own spirits lighten as the tactic appeared to be working. Fewer swarms were reaching the warheads, which were getting nearer to the vessel.

"It has dismantled one warhead," a crew member announced.

I glanced around us and observed the warhead in question, now just a cluster of parts like the original nuke. I then spotted a second dismantled nuke and then a third.

"No, no, no!" Tynan yelled.

The vessel dismantled a fourth, a fifth, and then a sixth nuke before they could reach it.

"God damn it, no!"

A blinding flash filled the view, and I shielded my eyes. When the light intensity decreased, I peered out and noticed a sizeable round fireball. The consoles all around the bridge flickered – an EMP pulse.

"Ha ha!" Tynan exclaimed. "We did it!"

The fireball dissipated and revealed a great wound in the vessel's surface. Then the wound healed, the gash filling in, the surface smoothing over.

"No, no, no!"

"I appreciate this isn't a good time, Your Grace," a crew member said. "But the vessel is moving. It's accelerating towards us!"

Chapter 6
Akka's Fall

2159, Common Era – Planet Akka, Frontier Space, the Republic of Humanity

Tynan's body was rigid, his eyes wide and unblinking, and the blood had drained from his face.

"What do we do, Your Grace?"

No sound emerged from Tynan's mouth, even though his lips moved in slow, deliberate motions. I glanced around at the crew and watched as they grew more concerned and panicked.

"Your Grace? Your Grace! What are your orders?"

Despite the crew's pleas, Tynan remained still, unable or unwilling to give a command.

"Well, come on!" Lorcan roared. "Who's the second in command? Now's the time to step up!"

I watched as the crew exchanged glances, and their eyes nervously flicked between Tynan and a male who, based on his uniform, I was pretty sure was the first officer.

They're all too scared to act for fear of retribution from Tynan …

I rotated and stared at the advisors, making eye contact with Phobus. He scowled, uneasy like the crew, and then a look of recognition spread across his face.

"Lead us," he whispered.

I exhaled as my shoulders slumped and my head fell.

Why did it always have to be me?

Raising my head, I clapped my hands together and shouted, "Alright, everyone, listen up! There's no time to waste – we must act now!"

The entire crew looked at me with disdain and who could blame them; from their perspective, who did this putrid, skeletal looking man giving orders think he was?

Simultaneously, I heard the rustle of the soldier's uniform behind me and knew he was drawing back his rifle.

Good. Without Tynan to order that my family be struck, better for me to take the hits!

"Soldier!" Phobus called out. "Leave him be!"

"But Advisor Phobus, His Grace said –"

"I know what he said," the old man snapped. "Listen to what I am telling you now!"

I turned to look at the soldier, his eyes flicking between me, Phobus, and Tynan.

"Time is of the essence, soldier," I said; I made sure to speak calmly. "It's a simple choice: hit me, and we all die when the vessel outside kills us, or don't hit me and let me give this crew the direction it needs to save our lives!"

The soldier glanced at the vessel outside, then at me.

"Why should we listen to what you have to say?"

That was a great question – why should any of the crew listen to me? Most of them were clones with programmed loyalty, whilst a handful were old loyalists, volunteers, or captured individuals, no doubt indoctrinated – but either way, why listen to me?

"Because I am the original. Before he was your leader," I said as I motioned towards Tynan, "I was your leader. Everything that he is comes from me."

The soldier considered this for a moment then nodded in acknowledgement and stepped back, putting down his weapon.

"Thank you for trusting me," I said, then turned back towards the crew.

"Alright, helmsman, quick as you can, spin the Chupacabra around and take us back towards Akka!"

The helmsman hesitated for a moment, then replied "Yes, Your Grace."

"Don't call me that," I replied with a little more bite than intended. "I'm no emperor."

"Of course, sir."

Close enough.

"Okay, do we have a transportation officer?"

"Present, sir," said a short female officer, stepping forward.

"How many dropships are onboard?"

"Twelve, sir."

"I want all twelve airborne ASAP – as soon as we're close enough, send them down to Akka's primary settlement and pick up as many civilians as you can fit on those ships. We may only get the opportunity for a single run."

"Yes, sir. On it right away."

"Thank you! Now –"

I stopped as I glimpsed something out of the corner of my eye. The Chupacabra had rotated and was facing Akka again, and as I looked at the side that had been obscured during our approach, I saw a sizable asteroid, easily the size of a large continent, seemingly in orbit around the planet.

"Has that always been there?"

"Yes, sir. The Akkarians pulled Vesta 2a into orbit early on during Akka's colonisation because of its rich mineral deposits. They've been mining it for resources ever since."

"Thanks, ah …"

"First Officer Faberson, sir."

"Gotcha. Thanks, Faberson. Say, do we have anything that could push that asteroid towards the vessel?"

The first officer weighed this briefly, then replied, "Just the ship, sir."

"Would that be doable?"

"We'd damage whatever part of the ship contacted the asteroid, but doable, yes."

"Doable is all we need right now. Helmsman ..."

"Nerys, sir."

"Helmsman Nerys, can you please fly us behind the asteroid and get ready to play tugboat?"

Nerys smiled. "Yes, sir, I can do that."

"Good man, thank you!"

Alright, what else needed to happen?

We would attempt to evacuate citizens, and we maybe had one last offensive manoeuvre available to us – was there anything else we could do?

"Do we have any observation ... drones or surveillance satellites onboard?"

"I'm afraid we don't, sir," Faberson replied.

"Please ... just call me Raith."

"Yes, si – Yes, Raith."

"Thank you."

A lanky man with bright blue hair stepped forward. "I'm Chief Engineering Officer Norton, Raith. I believe I may be able to jerry rig a surveillance device or two if I can better understand your requirements?"

"Thanks for coming forward, Norton. It's almost certain that we're going to have to retreat, so I want to leave behind some monitoring devices, drones or satellites, that can transmit visual data to us.

I think that vessel is going to come for other worlds, and the more we can learn about it, the better our chances are of finding a weakness."

"I understand. I'll put my team to work immediately."

"Thank you, Norton. I appreciate it."

As the chief engineering officer departed, I looked back at the bridge window and realised that we had almost finished our manoeuvre to get behind the asteroid. I glanced at Tynan. He still sat in his chair, his eyes fixed vacantly out the bridge window.

It was almost like he was a computer that had encountered a critical error and crashed.

"I feel like we need to turn him off and on again," I said.

The room remained silent except for one stifled laugh. The odd crew member appeared to be attempting to conceal smiles. I understood – laughing now could mean they die tomorrow when Tynan learnt of their enjoyment at his expense.

"Seriously though, is there a medical officer?"

"Yes, Raith – here," said a gaunt-looking man.

"Hi. Can you please take Tynan to the med bay? Maybe the soldiers can help carry him there. You'll know more than I do, but he doesn't look good."

"Of course. You two! Help me grab His Grace."

Two soldiers moved forward, one on either side of Tynan. They grabbed him by the arms and lifted him to his feet, rushing him out of the room with the medical officer following close behind.

I was still weak from my months of captivity and had been standing for quite some time now, so with the captain's chair now vacant, I walked forward and sat down, gratefully melting into the soft padding of the seat.

"Oh, yeah … this is comfortable!" I said, eliciting at least two chuckles.

Now that Tynan had left, I hoped the crew would lighten up, although I understood why they felt the way they did about me – I was likely public enemy number one in many of their eyes.

Helmsman Nerys rotated in his chair to face me. "We're ready to begin when you are, Raith."

"Thank you, Nerys. Have the dropships launched?"

"Yes, they have," Faberson replied.

"Okay, great. Take us in, Nerys."

The Chupacabra moved forward, metre by metre, closing the gap between us and the asteroid.

"Easy does it," Faberson said.

An ear-piercing alarm reverberated throughout the bridge, and Nerys quickly reached over to a console and silenced it.

"Not to worry," Nerys said, glancing over at me. "Tis' just the proximity alarm."

Suddenly, the sound of grinding metal filled the ship, and the entire vessel shook.

"And we've made contact with Vesta 2a. It appears to be a stable connection, as far as ship-asteroid docking goes."

I exhaled, trying to calm my nerves. I glanced up at the monitor where Zavis, Amorina, and Emma were still displayed. They appeared okay despite the jolt, and I sighed again with relief. I hoped like hell that this would work for everybody, but for them most of all.

"Okay ... let's give it a push."

With a deep groan, the ship's frame creaked and strained as Nerys slowly increased her thrust, allowing the ship to bear the mass of the asteroid. After a minute of pushing, the ship and the asteroid slowly moved forward.

We're going too slow.

"Can we push it any faster?"

Nerys shrugged uncertainly. "We can, but I don't know how much the ship can take."

"There's only one way to find out. Either we act now or we won't have a chance to act at all. Can we push it faster?"

"Yes. Yes, we can."

"Good. Then punch it! Give it everything we've got!"

I watched as Nerys dialled up the primary thrust output to maximum and then engaged the auxiliary thrusts as well. The ship groaned in protest, but it and the asteroid pushed onward with a surge of speed.

"That's it. Keep it going!"

Our velocity increased, going faster and faster, rushing towards our unavoidable target.

"Okay … reverse thrust!"

Nerys tapped away furiously at his console, disengaging all rear thrusters and activating forward thrusters instead. The ship's forward movement came to an abrupt halt before reversing direction. The asteroid flew onward, a dusting of metal fragments trailing in its path. Applause rang out on the bridge as the crew watched Vesta 2a hurtling towards the vessel.

Suddenly, there was movement on the vessel's surface; much of it had congregated into the swarm, but instead of enveloping the asteroid as it had done with the nukes, the swarm formed what I could only describe as a blade or a wedge, the tip of its formation aimed at the centre of the approaching rock.

"What's it doing?" Phobus asked behind me.

"I don't know."

We watched in amazement as the swarm formation swiftly moved forward, cutting through Vesta 2a with ease and splitting it in two. The swarm reversed its course and returned to the gap between the halves it had just created. We watched in awe as it then pushed them apart. The asteroid was now almost right on top of the vessel, and its surface swarmed forward to meet it, catching the halves and redirecting their momentum so that both halves now travelled along the surface of the vessel, one to the left and one to the right.

"What is it doing?" I asked as the asteroid halves continued to travel along the vessel's surface.

"Whilst I can't answer that, I can tell you it's stopped moving," said Nerys.

I gazed out the window at the featureless machine, thinking about all its unknown aspects: its enormous size, its formidable capabilities, its mysterious origins, and its uncertain motivations. Of course, I had no way of responding to those questions, and the hopelessness of my curiosity abruptly gave rise to a sense of being completely out of my element. I felt like I was in a deep body of water, and I feared what might lurk beneath me.

"What would you like us to do, Raith?" Nerys asked.

"Back us up, and once we're closer to Akka, hold position. Let's give the evacuation as much time as possible."

"Will do!"

As the ship reversed, I monitored the asteroid halves, now almost out of sight.

"Do we know how quickly the asteroid halves are moving?"

"Let me check for you," Nerys replied.

Whilst Nerys checked the sensor data, I pondered the vessel some more.

Where had it come from? How had it found us?

But the more questions I asked, the more helpless I felt to produce any answers.

"The asteroid halves are moving at a constant speed. I'm guessing it's just passing the pieces around itself. Perhaps it couldn't have survived the impact."

"Okay, thanks, Nerys."

I peered through the bridge window once again and watched, mesmerized by the asteroids gliding around the curved edges of the vessel, slowly fading out of sight.

"I've just gotten word from the dropships, Raith — they've made it to the surface and are loading up civilians now," reported a crew member, who I assumed was the communications officer.

"Thank you."

I ran through my mental checklist again: we were rescuing civilians, jerry rigging some surveillance satellites, and we've made one last, albeit unsuccessful, offensive attempt at the vessel.

Is there anything else that needs to be done?

"What are you doing here?" a voice I knew well said from behind me.

I slowly stood up and turned around, finding Ichirō standing in the doorway. I quickly assessed the state of my son; his eyes were dark, and there was a discolouration on his face, almost like a badly concealed bruise. My heart sank, and my stomach fluttered as a cocktail of emotions surged through me: sadness that he appeared to be suffering, joy at seeing him again after all these months, and pain at the anger in his voice.

"What is he doing here?" Ichirō's voice was sharp as he addressed the crew this time, his angry gaze sweeping the bridge.

"Tynan became entirely incapable of leading this ship. He ignored the counsel of his advisors and crew and kept attacking an enemy that was clearly more powerful than us, and after we'd provoked it, he completely froze up, risking the lives of everyone aboard this ship and on the planet below," Lorcan answered.

Ichirō rounded on the advisor. "What are you trying to say, exactly? Because it sounds like you're accusing my father, the emperor, of incompetency and cowardice!"

His voice full of frustration, Lorcan snapped, "Boy! First of all, you'd do well to show respect to your elders."

"I don't have to –"

"I wasn't finished! Second of all, the emperor isn't your father; he's a science experiment and a failed one at that!"

"He is my –"

"I … wasn't … finished!" Lorcan's voice was low and menacing as he hissed each word. Lorcan pointed at me as he said, reluctantly, "And last of all, that man right there is your father. Certainly, in body, if less so in mind – although I'm sure that's still inside his head, buried deep down somewhere."

Ichirō didn't appear to have a retort against Lorcan's latest statement and remained silent.

"Now, despite my grievances with the man, Raith is doing what Tynan failed to do," Lorcan continued. "He stepped up, despite great personal risk to him and his family, taking command of this ship, prioritised civilian evacuation, formulated an information gathering strategy, and tried an offensive strategy that *actually* had some merit!" Lorcan said, concluding his dressing down of Ichirō.

My son looked around the room rather sullenly. If I were to hazard a guess, this was not how he'd envisioned events playing out when he'd stepped onto the bridge.

"Where is the emperor now?" he demanded.

"He's in the medical bay, getting the help he needs," I replied.

This earned me a scowl, and then Ichirō promptly turned and exited the room. I felt a pang of guilt, torn between chasing after my son and doing my duty for the greater good. Part of me wanted nothing more than to say fuck it, to hell with the otherworldly horrors outside – my son needed me.

The other part of me said this was not the time to win back my son — that time would come another day — and right now, there were hundreds, if not thousands, of lives on the line. As I remained stationary, I knew which part of me had won this round of reasoning.

I slowly turned towards Lorcan. "That'll cost you. You know that, right?"

"Don't you lecture me, Raith," Lorcan said with a sigh. "I've no love for you. You killed my emperor — the true emperor. You've caused me irreparable harm."

The advisor's words seemed to trigger something within him, and he suddenly looked ancient and wary, as if the weight of the years were suddenly bearing down upon him.

"But despite that, I am man enough to admit we'd be in a lot more trouble right now if you hadn't stepped up. You've done what our pale imitation could not, and for that, I'll face the consequences of my actions, whatever they may be."

I conceded the discussion with a shrug — who was I to argue with an old man who respected me only because I'd been of use in a moment of self-preservation?

"Raith … Raith! You need to see this!" Nerys called out.

I spun back around to see the helmsman pointing out the bridge window. I looked up to see that the asteroid halves had reappeared, racing along the surface of the vessel far faster than they had been earlier. Suddenly, its intention seemed very clear.

"What's it doing with them now?" Nerys asked.

Moments later, the vessel pushed the halves away from its surface, shifting their newly formed momentum onto a new trajectory — toward us!

"Fire all our rail guns and gauss cannons! Split their fire between the two halves!"

The bridge erupted with activity as crew members rushed to their stations, targeted the asteroids and initiated the weapons. Within seconds, the rail guns began to fire, with streams of bullets streaking away from the ship. The Chupacabra shook, and two gauss cannon shells soared away from us. I watched as they raced across the distance between us and the asteroids, colliding with minimal effect on the half to the left, but it blasted a few small chunks off the half on the right.

"This isn't very effective!" Nerys cried out.

I felt like time slowed as I watched the two asteroids rapidly approaching us. Time was of the essence, and we had limited weapon capability to counteract them. A call had to be made urgently.

"Concentrate all fire on the right-hand asteroid! We may not stop them both, but maybe we can stop one of them!"

The rail gun fire switched over to the right asteroid, and with another shudder of the ship, two more gauss cannon shells followed suit.

"And whether or not we take them down, we're going to need to move out of the way in a hurry. Nerys, you need to be ready to shift us!"

"On it, Raith!"

The second set of shells impacted with the asteroid but had little effect.

"We need to move!" Nerys shouted.

"Not yet. Hold!"

The ship shuddered as another set of shells flew off towards the asteroid.

"Now?" Nerys asked, his voice panicked.

"Hold!"

The final set of shells collided with the asteroid, shattering it into dozens of pieces.

"Move us!"

The Chupacabra accelerated upwards, rotating as it ascended. I stumbled where I stood, both from the feeling of being compressed and the rotational force. As the ship rotated, Akka came into view. The solid asteroid flew into view first, spawning an eerie orange glow as it collided with the atmosphere, set alight by the friction. A bright flash illuminated Akka's surface a few moments later as the asteroid struck. A powerful wave of energy erupted from the point of impact, travelling rapidly over the planet's surface.

A wall of fire, vaporised water, and pulverized rock came straight after, blasting into outer space. A great fireball engulfed the planet as the destructive wave spread out from the impact site, setting the air ablaze with its intensity. We watched the shattered asteroid come into view, the burning atmosphere swallowing up its pieces, their impacts lost in the hellish destruction.

The bridge was silent, all transfixed with horror at the force on display before us. We were bearing witness to something that no human had ever seen before – after all, this was a phenomenon that hadn't occurred since the extinction of the dinosaurs on Earth, so far as we knew. This was not just any force, it was nature's atomic bomb; a terrifying, cataclysmic, world-ending force that could wipe out entire civilizations – entire species – capable of causing death on a planetary scale.

The unfolding apocalypse was a terrifying display of power, and I felt dwarfed by its sheer magnitude. What I was feeling, though, was not just a profound sense of insignificance, but a deep, visceral, existential horror that left me trembling.

Sobs shattered the silence as the initial shock wore off, and I couldn't control my own hot tears as they streamed down my face. I reached up to wipe them away with unsteady hands.

I glanced around the bridge and realised that not a single individual was unaffected by the destruction. Advisor or soldier, individual or clone, loyalist or insurrectionist – this planet killing, world-ending force had equalised us all.

Suddenly a terrible realisation dawned on me. The vessel had seen the asteroid and quickly determined that it could split it in two, redirecting the pieces away from itself to avoid an impact, and then send them back towards us. It had to have made that calculation within a few seconds – it had to have known it was making a planet killer.

"Raith," Faberson said as he sniffed and wiped away tears of his own, "the dropships escaped the planet and have successfully docked with us. Norton has also reported that he has two observation satellites ready to go."

"And the vessel has started moving towards us again," added Nerys, his voice trembling.

The fire from the burning planet glowed in the darkness, and I couldn't look away. All the plants and animals native to Akka, as well as all the introduced species and the remaining colonists, had been extinguished and vaporised right before my eyes.

"What range can Norton's satellites effectively monitor this ... Horror?"

Faberson typed a message on his communicator and awaited a response.

"He says between half, and one and a half astronomical units."

I nodded. "Okay ... Nerys, take us out to one au, please, and release one satellite, then take us out to one and a half au and release the second satellite."

"On it, Raith!"

The Chupacabra moved, turning away from the burning corpse of Akka. The ship quickly surged forward, leaving the Horror and its destruction in our wake. I sank into the captain's seat, my mind actively ticking over, assessing and considering.

I was still at a loss as to who'd created this behemoth or why it was so immense. I still didn't know its full potential, where it originated, or how it had discovered us.

But I was sure of one thing: this machine, this vessel, it was here to kill, to exterminate. It was death, a destroyer of worlds.

Chapter 7
Live to Fight Another Day

2159, Common Era – Planet Akka, Frontier Space, the Republic of Humanity

The ship was safely back in warp – or at least relatively safe – and the command of it handed over to the team, Faberson and I went to the observation deck.

"Hey! What are you doing here?" a soldier snapped as we walked in.

"Stand down, soldiers. Raith and his family are free to go about as they please," Faberson said.

"But –"

Faberson cut through his argument, "If you have a problem with this order, return with me to the bridge, and we can discuss it there!"

The soldiers looked at me with pure disdain.

"I don't know what you did, traitor –"

"I saved your goddamn lives!" I replied as I cut the soldier off. "Now get out of here."

As the soldiers begrudgingly left, Amorina and Zavis turned to me with looks of bewilderment.

"How on earth did you manage that?" Zavis asked.

"Tynan's offensive tactics failed, and when they did, he became paralyzed, stopped responding and couldn't give instructions. So, I stepped in and assumed control. That's earned me some goodwill," I replied as I gave a nod towards Faberson.

"Oh, Tynan won't like that," said Zavis.

"No … no, he will not."

Amorina's surprise subsided, and she rushed up to me, pulling me into a hug.

"I … I am so, so sorry!" she whispered.

My mind scanned its memory archives, searching for why Amorina would be sorry, and came up empty.

"Sorry for what?" I asked, my brow furrowed in confusion.

"I'm sorry for not trusting you, for getting angry at you when you were pursuing a truth that no one else could see, me included."

The tension that had existed between us since our argument on Gaia melted away, and I felt a wave of relief wash over me, sweeping away all the doubt and concern.

"Thank you," I said as I hugged her tighter. "That means a lot to me."

I felt an insistent tug on my shirt and looked down to see Emma.

"I want hugs, too!"

"I think you forgot the magic word ..."

"Please, I want hugs, too!"

"Well, when you say it like that!"

I scooped up my daughter and included her in our embrace.

"Thank you, Daddy!" she whispered.

"It's my honour, sweetie pie."

Amorina's stomach gurgled suddenly, and the sound of her hunger filled the air. She pulled away and averted her gaze.

"Sorry!" Amorina said as she blushed. "We haven't eaten in quite some time!"

"Well, go and eat!" I said, then added, "although I'm not sure where the mess hall is located."

"I'll show them. I'll take them there personally and make sure they're attended too," said Faberson, whom I'd forgotten was still standing there.

I turned towards Faberson. "I would be so grateful if you could keep an eye on them," I said, my voice full of gratitude.

"Of course."

I turned towards my wife and daughter. "This is First Officer Faberson. I trust him, and he'll look after you."

"You're sure you don't mind if we go off and get some food? We've been so caught up in things that we've hardly seen you!" Amorina asked.

"I know," I replied as tears filled my eyes. "I have missed you guys … so, so much! More than you know."

I sniffed and wiped away the tears. "It's important that you eat, we can catch up later, and we will – I promise! You've got to keep up your strength in the meantime, though."

"Okay," Amorina agreed. "What about you, though? You're still so dirty and thin – how are you even standing right now?" she asked as her fingers lightly ran down my arms, feeling their thinness.

"I'm fine! Really, I am. I'll eat and get cleaned up soon as well."

Amorina looked at the entrance hesitantly.

"It's fine – honestly! Get some food," I insisted, putting Emma down.

"Okay." Amorina smiled at me as she took Emma's hand. "Alright, come on, trouble. We're going to find some food."

"I'm not trouble! I'm Emma!" my daughter replied.

"My mistake, it's nice to meet you, Emma. I'm hungry!"

"You're not hungry, silly! You're Mummy!"

I smiled as I watched them exit the room with Faberson, and then I turned to Zavis.

"So," he said, with a twinkle in his eye.

"What did I miss?"

"I think the shorter answer here would be what you didn't miss!" I replied as I walked towards my friend. "Honestly, it's been hell, and you should be glad you missed it. Tynan has been fucking with me for eight months whilst you all slept."

Zavis's face contorted into a pained, sympathetic expression. "I am sorry to hear that, my friend."

I stood there as his eyes examined me, no doubt registering the same gauntness that Amorina had noticed.

"Are you okay? You look terribly malnourished."

"That's because I am. But I'm okay … as much as one can be after months of imprisonment."

Zavis nodded. "I can respect a brave face at the best of times, but while you're busy saving everyone else, make sure you devote some time to saving yourself, my friend."

I smiled and gave an acknowledging nod.

"Except … I didn't save everyone else."

Zavis shook his head. "Akka's fall was not your fault. No one could have anticipated that …"

A shiver ran down my spine as Zavis trailed off, the images of Akka, shrouded in fiery hell, death and destruction, looped through my mind, still painfully fresh.

"Annihilation," I whispered.

Zavis nodded solemnly. "Yes … exactly."

After a few moments of silence, Zavis cleared his throat. "Anyway … I heard you say to Amorina that Tynan destroyed a Republic fleet? An entire fleet with a single ship, presumably this one?"

"Yep."

"How could he … wait —" I saw a flash of recollection in Zavis's eyes. "He used a Firecracker, didn't he?"

"Yes. Yes, he did."

"Fuck."

I rarely heard Zavis swear, but you knew when he did that the gravity of the situation was severe.

"It's not like the Republic didn't want him dead already, but now … now they'll want to eviscerate him."

I nodded, and we stood in silence for a few moments. Zavis stared into space, and I watched his face. His eyes darted back and forth between invisible things, and his face twitched and shifted as if it were a physical manifestation of his thoughts.

"You mentioned earlier that Tynan completely locked up and became unresponsive. Can you elaborate on what happened there?" Zavis asked, breaking the silence.

"Honestly, I'm not really sure. When we arrived at Akka, he made a broadcast –"

"Yes," said Zavis. "We had the fortune … or rather misfortune as it may be, of hearing that particular speech."

I chuckled. "Yeah, well, as you would've heard, he was very confident in that transmission and overly confident in his ability to harm the Horror."

"The Horror?" Zavis asked, tilting his head quizzically.

"That vessel we were facing."

"Ah."

"I wonder if … when all his attacks failed, I wonder if that overconfidence caught up with him? Maybe his inner doubts confronted him with a sense of failure, or he was afraid, and those emotions combined to overwhelm him?"

Zavis gave a slight nod, lips pursed in concentration. "It's a possibility. I wonder if perhaps his wiring isn't quite right. Have you noticed any odd behaviour or comments from Tynan?"

"Yes! We pulled up a picture of Akka in its prime, and he commented on its beauty."

Zavis raised an eyebrow. "That's very unusual for Tynan."

"I know, right? His speech was also … I don't know, tripped up a few times? He was listing things but using different list notations for each item."

"That sounds like something is amiss in his mind. Anything could have or could still be happening. How many people do you think suspect … or know that he isn't quite right?"

"Anwir, Phobus, and Lorcan definitely noticed, although Tynan killed Anwir. I'm sure all the bridge crew know something is up."

Zavis nodded, his movements slow and deliberate. "Did Phobus or Lorcan pay any attention to you?"

"Not initially, but after Tynan locked up, Phobus looked at me and … it was as if he recognised me … or something within me, and he told me to lead them – the bridge crew – which I did."

"If I may offer some advice?" Zavis queried.

"Of course."

"Tread carefully, Raith. Phobus and Lorcan, by now, know their experiment hasn't delivered the desired results. They could try again, but I think they also realise that the more they pry your head open, the greater the chance they'll kill you, and there's no guarantee another Tynan clone would turn out any better."

"If you think it's unlikely they'll open me up again, what do you think they'll do instead?"

"You said Phobus looked at you as if he recognised something. I think they can see Tynan in you. Not your face, obviously, but within your personality. I know you're afraid of that, but it's foolish to deny the truth of things. I believe they'll try to bring Tynan out within you."

I shuddered as the end of Zavis's sentence echoed in my mind.

"They'll try to bring Tynan out within you."

The implications of those words alone were terrifying; that Tynan — the *real* Tynan — was still inside me and somehow … able to be resurrected. I shuddered again, and my heart sank at the idea that they were trying to realise my greatest fear. Just thinking of what Tynan 2.0 was already doing, how much worse would things be if they could awaken the original Tynan?

"We can't let that happen!" My voice shook with the fear I was trying to contain.

"I believe we'll do everything in our power to see that it doesn't transpire, but we cannot bury our heads in the sand either."

"How do we avoid this?" I demanded.

"I think the best way forward would be for them to destroy themselves."

I didn't answer, focused on how that was such a stereotypical answer from Zavis. His genius in defeating the Empire had been to realise the importance of outsmarting them instead of relying solely on strength. That realisation ultimately led to my creation and the eventual downfall of Tynan. But was it the right solution this time? To play the long game via subterfuge and sabotage?

"How well do you think you'd be able to manipulate Tynan into distrusting the advisors, or vice versa?"

"I mean … maybe?" I responded with doubt in my voice.

"You don't think this is the right approach, do you?"

I glanced away. "Was it that obvious?"

"I can read you very well, Raith. I've known you all your life."

"I know. Look, I'm not saying it's the wrong approach." I sighed. "I just feel that the longer we take to stop them, the more harm they'll inflict on people."

"I understand that. I also don't see many choices before us, Raith. We are in enemy-controlled territory; we don't have friends, and we don't have allies. Your actions earlier may have earned you some good graces, but enough to save our skins? Unlikely."

It'd be nice to think that I had earned the permanent loyalty of the crew, but I also knew allegiances didn't change that quickly – not permanently, anyway.

"Our best bet is to play them against themselves. If Tynan is a loose cannon already, this works in our favour because the advisors don't have control over him."

I didn't like this. I didn't like Zavis's train of thought. I didn't like that subterfuge and murder were the only ways forward – the only ways to be safe.

It's what Tynan would do.

That was why I didn't like it. "I ... I can try," I replied.

"Thank you, Raith. That is all that can be asked."

Zavis abruptly lifted his left arm, pulling up the sleeve of his robe to reveal an Arachnobot on his wrist. He read the message on the device, then walked over to the end of the observation deck, standing right before the windows.

His dark silhouette contrasted against the blue, undulating light cone outside the ship. There was something about the way the old man stood there that said come closer, come stand beside me. I walked over and stood next to Zavis, gazing out at the lightscape just as he was.

"Is everything alright?"

Zavis let out a heavy breath. "Yes ... and no. I, personally, at this moment, am alright. Granted, I am worried about you and your family, what you've been through and what you might yet go through if the worst comes to pass."

I nodded. "And outside of yourself?"

"Do you remember when we first met, and at one point, I spoke to you of a signal that we detected far beyond our domain?"

It only took a moment for the memory to resurface. "Hmm … yeah, I do."

"It was dumb luck – our finding the signal, I mean – we'd simply pointed the right type of sensor at the right part of the sky, and boom, there was the signal quietly pulsating away, almost drowned out by the background noise of the universe."

Zavis paused, his eyes flicking left and right as if searching for the words he wanted to say, like they were out there in the spacetime warping past us.

"We were greedy. We knew how much the Khel technology had advanced humanity – what if this signal was more of the Khel? Or another race altogether, with different technological secrets they'd be willing to trade? As I told you back then, we sent several exploration vessels out there to find it; we lost contact with them all."

I nodded, remembering the previous conversation well.

"Now, before we could send out any more ships, the Empire's focus shifted towards conquering the Republic's territory, and you know how things played out from there."

I couldn't help but smile at Zavis's comment.

"Once the Empire was gone, the Republic had little interest in chasing after some far-flung signal, despite my continued advocation that it was worth understanding the who, the what, and the where of this transmission."

Zavis loosed another weighted breath and appeared to age ten years as he exhaled.

"I just got confirmation that the … Horror, as you call it, is emitting the signal. It has been the source all this time."

Whoa!

What had drawn the Horror to us? Was it an encounter with the exploration vessels?

"When I heard that all exploration vessel transmissions had ended, I was filled with dread – not because I thought we were invincible, but because the entire fleet had gone silent. That was not a positive indication. Now, witnessing what I have today – that neither gauss cannon, firecracker or nuclear missile could scratch that thing – that terrifies me. Aptly, perhaps, it elicits a sense of horror."

"We drew it here with the exploration vessels, right?"

"I don't think so," Zavis replied, shooting down what I thought was a very logical conclusion.

"Oh?"

"If those vessels were the reason for the Horror having shown up, I think it would've happened much sooner."

"Then how did it find us?"

"The mass conversion device pulses."

"What?" I shouted as my insides contracted and grew heavy.

That was a very specific reason Zavis had given, and he had responded without hesitation.

"Why would you think that would've led that thing here? How would you know that?"

"The signal that the Horror transmits ... it's a radio transmission containing a binaural beat, which, when listened to, induces theta waves."

Fuck me.

"The signal is a lure?"

"I believe so, yes. I think the best analogy is that it uses it like echolocation, but instead of waiting for an echo, it looks for returning theta waves.

I do not know how sensitive its sensors are, but I suspect they'd work within a tight range. Under normal circumstances, I think we were too far away to be detected."

"Then we build a device that emits massive, powerful blasts of theta waves," I replied as my voice cracked, throwing my hands up in despair. "We triggered it again and again and again!"

Visions of Akka's destruction flashed through my mind and I felt my knees weaken, then I dropped to the floor as a wave of guilt surged over me.

"I did this!" I cried, and tears streamed down my face. "I summoned that thing here!"

"No, Raith, you didn't," Zavis replied, slowly kneeling beside me.

"But I did!" I shouted; my guilt mixed with anger.

I jabbed myself in the chest as I yelled, "I was the one pulling the trigger each time, wasn't I?"

"Yes, but that doesn't make it your fault. We used the mass conversion device to save lives!"

"And where has that gotten us?" I yelled as my guilt ignited into rage. "What was the population of Akka?"

Zavis shrugged. "I don't –"

"Don't tell me you don't know! I know you know because you're the sort of person who knows these things!" I screamed, using the wall to clamber back to my feet.

"About ten thousand," Zavis admitted.

"Ten thousand. We rescued ... a few hundred, so that's basically all ten thousand dead. And tomorrow, when that machine comes for Gaia? Then it'll be a million that are dead! And what about when it gets to Earth? What are they at, like eight billion now?"

"Ah ... more like eleven billion."

"Right. Well, great." I threw my hands in the air. "Then it'll be eleven billion dead, all because of me and my actions! Yeah, we did it to save lives. How will that be working out for us when over eleven billion people are dead?"

"That hasn't happened yet, Raith. We still have time to stop it!"

"Stop it with what?" I yelled, spit flying from my mouth. "We threw nukes at that motherfucker, and it broke them apart like they were nothing! Hell, we threw a goddamn asteroid at it, and it threw it right back!"

The reel of images was still on repeat inside my mind; flashes of the asteroid entering the atmosphere, its collision with Akka's surface, and the fireball that had followed. How were we supposed to combat a machine that could orchestrate such levels of destruction?

"I know you're angry, Raith. I wish I had the answers for you, truly, I do. But right now, there are a lot of questions. All I can say is, have faith – I'm sure we will find a way."

"Where do you find all of your optimism?"

"Why are you yelling?"

Zavis and I turned to see Tynan and a posse of soldiers striding into the room.

"Mind your own goddamn business!" I snapped before I could help myself.

Tynan raised an eyebrow. "This is my ship! *Everything* on it is my goddamn business! Take them away!"

Chapter 8
Man in the Mirror

2159, Common Era – Frontier Space, the Republic of Humanity

Rage had consumed Tynan after he heard about what happened on the bridge, but fortunately he had no memory of it, having blacked out throughout the entire experience – being aware of the events only through what others had said. All my actions hadn't been enough to garner Tynan's sympathy, if he had any to give, and so he'd placed Zavis, Amorina, and Emma back into cryosleep, and I was once again left in my dark, dismal cell.

At first, I thought I'd be alright – I'd survived this cell before, I'd survive it again – but as minutes turned into hours and hours into days, my fortitude rapidly diminished. Where before I'd perhaps ignored or convinced myself that I was coping with the malnourishment, now I was really feeling its effects. My limbs felt heavy and stiff, and every moment felt like I was losing more and more strength, my muscles atrophying through disuse and lack of food. The isolation and darkness, the hunger and silence, it all got to me a lot quicker than expected, and soon, I was lost in a hell born of my thoughts and memories.

My conversation with Zavis was still fresh in my mind, as were the revelations about the signal and the high likelihood that our actions – *my* actions – had summoned the Horror to our corner of the galaxy. Each time the thought crept into my mind, guilt was a heavy blanket over me, and seething anger accompanied it. I'd acted upon half-truths and partial information, and humanity had suffered – *was* suffering – because of it.

Had I known all the facts, would I have seen another way? Could I have made different choices?

The days soon added up, and clarity gave way to madness through hallucinations. I began to see my family: Zavis, Amorina, and Emma, all icy and blue in their frozen slumber; Ichirō beaten and bruised by Tynan's hand; and Adanna, Winona, Mother and Father all on Gaia, looking up at the night sky, wondering where on earth we'd gone and if we were even alive. I knew what that uncertainty felt like, and I wished I could end their anguish of not knowing – but I couldn't end my torment, let alone anyone else's.

As days turned into weeks, Akka's destruction consumed my thoughts, the events looping over and over: the eerie orange glow as the atmosphere ignited the surface of the asteroid, the flash of light as it impacted with Akka's surface and the shockwaves that hurled fire and pulverised rock through the air afterwards. With each repetition, guilt-ridden waves of "what ifs" and "could haves" washed over me. Could I have saved more civilians? What if I hadn't thrown that asteroid? Could I have done more to earn the trust of the crew? What if I'd said something to Ichirō? If I hadn't used the mass conversion device repeatedly, would all of this have been avoided in the first place?

I felt as if I'd failed Akka's citizens most of all; one minute they were hopeful, believing that someone had come to their aid, then suddenly, they saw a planet-killing asteroid bearing down upon them, and before they could even understand what was about to happen, they were obliterated by fire and brimstone.

A hell of a way to go.

Even though I hadn't been in control of most of the events surrounding their demise, I couldn't help but feel responsible for their destruction – their cessation of life. None of this would've happened if I'd just ended the Empire when I'd had the chance.

It's what Tynan would've done.

I shook my head as if trying to shake the thought away. I could almost taste the bitter resentment of my past inaction. It is what Tynan would have done, but I wasn't Tynan ... was I? No, I wasn't. But maybe I should've been? Maybe being Raith is what led to the current mess ... but if I was Raith then ...

Maybe not being Tynan is what led to the current mess.

A shiver ran through me like an icy wave that made my heart feel tight and cold. I hallucinated a mirror, my reflection looking back at me. Slowly, the image changed as my scar faded away, my skin grew firm, and my hairline advanced, reclaiming its lost territory.

"I am not Tynan," I whispered to the dark doppelgänger. "I am not Tynan."

The reflection smiled cruelly. "But you could be," it whispered back.

❦

I heard grinding metal, and the cell door opened wide, flooding the cell with searing light. My eyes stung from the sudden brightness. With a low groan, I managed to shield them with my arms.

"Come on, get up, ya lazy fuck!" yelled a soldier.

Before I could even stand, a sturdy pair of hands took hold of my torso and hoisted me to my feet.

Moments later, they carried me out of the cell.

"..." I tried to speak, but like last time, my vocal cords had forgotten how to work. I cleared my throat and tried again.

"What's happening?" It came out as a raspy wheeze, but it was intelligible and without pauses this time.

"You'll soon see."

The soldiers brought me into a wet room where they tore off my soiled clothing and then turned a high-pressure hose on me. I gasped as the freezing water struck my skin, the cold and force of it like a thousand tiny needles stabbing into my skin. Once they'd washed away all traces of excrement, they roughly towelled me down then ushered me into another room and forced me into a chair. The soldiers moved back, and a man stepped up behind me and began cutting my hair.

"How are you doing, Raith?" the barber asked as he deftly trimmed my overgrown locks.

"Okay … let's skip the fake pleasantries," I rasped, "can we just get to the part where you yell 'psyche' and throw me back in my cell?"

The barber shook his head. "This is a genuine haircut, I'm afraid. No fake outs here."

"Look, I don't mean to sound ungrateful, cause honestly, you're doing a great job, although at this stage anything is an improvement … but why are you doing this?"

"His Grace's orders. He wants you washed, shaved, and shorn, so that is what we're doing," replied one of the waiting soldiers.

"Tynan ordered this?"

"Yes – now stop asking questions!" he snapped.

I shrugged and leant back in the chair; my voice was gaining strength a lot quicker than last time, but this conversation had left my throat raw. So, I waited patiently whilst the barber wrangled months' worth of growth into order and let my voice – and the rest of me – relax.

As soon as the barber had worked his magic, he placed a set of fresh clothes on a nearby table, and with a flourish, he said, "For you, Raith. They should be the correct size."

"Ah, thank you," I replied as he left the room.

The clothing was simple and grey, but I was glad to find that it was the right size, despite my shrunken frame, and that it was comfortable against my skin. As soon as I pulled on the last items, the soldiers took hold of me and marched me out of the room again.

Here comes the cell.

To my surprise, the cell wasn't my destination. Instead, they led me into a mess hall and sat me down before a full three-course meal.

"Ha ha, okay guys – you got me, okay?" I said incredulously, convinced I was being fucked with. "You can turn off the hologram or smash the cream pie in my face and take me back to my cell now, okay?"

"The food's real, ya dumb fuck. Eat it or lose it." one soldier retorted.

I cautiously extended my hand for a piece of roast chicken and was delighted when I felt a tangible, warm, and fresh piece of chicken. I warily eyed every corner of the room, searching for some hidden crevice where Tynan or an advisor might lurk, just waiting to leap out and reveal the nature of the mind fuck, but I couldn't see any hidden enclaves or suspicious figures. I picked up a chicken drumstick and ravenously tore off the flesh, stripping it down to the bone in seconds. After discarding the bone, I looked around the room in case someone had now appeared, but it was still just me and the two soldiers.

Maybe this is real after all?

I turned back to the table and started digging into the food, albeit at a more reserved pace this time.

☽☾

I finally leant back, my belly round but a pleasant fullness had replaced the hollow feeling I'd had for so long.

They gave me no time to enjoy a food coma, though, as the soldiers came back over and pulled me back to my feet.

"Off to the cell now, is it?"

"Nope."

The buzz of confusion in my head left me puzzled; if this was all happening on Tynan's order, then what was his motive? What was the intention here?

The soldiers escorted me through the ship, and I felt a chill in the air as they brought me to an unlit, bow-facing observation room. As soon as they'd pushed me inside, I heard the door shut behind me with a heavy thud. It was strange behaviour, but I was grateful for the change of scenery – anything was better than being in the cell. I stumbled to the window; my eyes were drawn to the bright blue cone of light radiating before the ship. The light cone of warp travel appeared to be a monotonous blue if you just glanced at it, but if you took the time to study and appreciate it, it revealed its true nature: a smorgasbord of blues, some light and some dark, colours on the verge of being purple and others that were almost white.

"Beautiful, isn't it?"

I was so startled by the speech that I jumped, my muscles tensed for fight, and my heart lurched. I spun around and, after a few seconds of adjustment, made out Tynan's seated figure in the shadows, his silhouette illuminated by the faint light of the room.

"Tynan ..."

My doppelgänger nodded, his face expressionless.

What the fuck is going on?

The sudden shower, the haircut, the meal, and now this? A private audience with Tynan? I didn't know what this was yet, but there had to be a catch coming. I remained stationary, watching Tynan just as Tynan watched me. The silence in the room grew increasingly awkward.

What was he waiting for – does he want me to make the first move?

"Why am I here?" I asked. "Why … wash me, feed me – fresh clothes and the shave?"

"Well, you know, when I saw you last time you looked … worse than I imagined you would after spending that time in the cell," he shuddered at the memory, "and I assumed that your condition wouldn't have improved after three more months in that cell, so I wanted you freshened up before I had you brought to me."

"Okay … why did you want me brought here?"

"I was feeling bored, and you were the only one I wanted to talk to, but I didn't want you in here in that god awful state and rumbling stomach – that would detract from the conversation."

Where is Tynan going with this?

"Why was it me you wanted to talk to?"

Tynan said nothing, leaving the air still and heavy with anticipation.

Now what? Between the shock and exhaustion, my legs shook, and I didn't know how long I could stand for. Did Tynan want me to sit or to stand? Was he waiting for me to start some conversation, or was he going to say something?

"So … was there something you wanted to talk about?" I hesitantly asked.

"Yes. Sit down," Tynan replied as he motioned to the chair directly in front of him.

I felt Tynan's piercing gaze as I slowly walked over and gratefully sat in the chair, cognisant of how close we were. I waited for Tynan to start the conversation, but he remained quiet.

"So, this thing you wanted to talk about?" I asked.

This stirred Tynan into action. "Yes, um … after I saw you in your state, and after destroying that Republic fleet …

and after the destruction of Akka … I've had this feeling, and I don't know what it is," Tynan said slowly as if struggling to admit what he was feeling. "I've felt nothing like it before."

"Okay," I replied as I nodded slowly. "What did this feeling feel like?"

Tynan didn't respond, his face twisted into a look of concentration.

He's really having to think about this one.

"Sorry," he said. "I've been … unable to concentrate. My … my chest has felt suffocated or … heavy. And my heart goes through periods where it throbs incessantly. I'll feel hot and flushed and … almost ashamed."

Holy shit, is he experiencing guilt?

"It's almost like I'm feeling ashamed, but … different. My mind keeps replaying those events, but not just replaying the events as they were … but how they could've been had I done this or had I done that. These events are haunting me, and I need to know why!"

Holy shit, he really is feeling guilty. Is this … is this the first time he's ever felt that?

"Can you explain what's going on?" Tynan's voice was quiet as he looked at me, his eyes pleading for an answer.

I nodded slowly. "Um … yeah, I think I can shed some light on that."

"Thank fuck!" Tynan said with a nervous chuckle.

"I thought I was going mad. I couldn't turn to anyone else, obviously, least they think me weak."

The advisors' disdain for their failed science experiment flashed through my mind.

They already think you're weak.

"I think you're feeling … guilty," I said, ignoring my thoughts.

"Guilty?" Tynan said indignantly. "I don't feel guilt. I am never guilty. I've never felt guilty about anything in my life!" he snapped as he pointed his finger aggressively at himself, then at me.

Cognizant of Tynan's wrath that I'd experienced the week before, I stayed silent. Tynan kept his gaze on me, but the anger on his face softened as the minutes passed.

"Why would I be feeling guilty?" he puzzled. "I've no reason to feel guilty – you're my enemy, you deserve to be treated like shit and the same goes for that Republic fleet. And the citizens of Akka ... well, shit happens, doesn't it? I did what I could; I tried to help them, to save them! Why should *I* feel guilty for their deaths?" he sneered.

"Do you want an honest answer or the answer you want to hear?"

Tynan scowled. "This is a private room. It's a safe space for now. I call a truce, okay?"

The honest answer then if he'd put that offer on the table.

"You're feeling guilty because you're a fucking arsehole that's treated me less than human for months. You destroyed an entire Republic fleet and murdered the thousands of crew on board, and that allowed Akka's citizens to die by prioritising your own hubris over their lives!"

Tynan threw a right hook, striking me on the jaw.

My head snapped to the side, and the world spun – weakened as I was, my body didn't have the resilience to receive such blows. I slowly straightened up and, with all the strength I could muster, threw a punch back, hitting Tynan in the eye. His head recoiled back slightly, and after a moment of shock, he raised his fists to strike me again.

"This is a safe space!" I cried out, raising my hands defensively.

Tynan huffed and slowly lowered his hands. "Hit me again, and all bets are off!"

"Yeah, and if you hit me again –" I responded, but Tynan glared at me. "Never mind."

A begrudging silence filled the air between us as we both sat back, staring at the other.

"Fuck!" Tynan hissed. "See, now I fucking feel guilty for hitting you!"

I stifled a smile, quietly pleased that he felt guilt so quickly.

"Returning to what you said … even if those are the reasons for my guilt, I've never felt guilty before in my life for actions just like those. So why would I feel guilty now?"

That was a good question. Why would Tynan experience this now when he'd always been a cruel, calculating man? What had changed?

I watched Tynan closely, trying to piece together the answers we both sought, and I realised how young he looked. His was a fresh, cloned face – one that'd spent its life in a vat, free from all harm. Nothing to break bones, nothing to form scars. The body was a blank slate. But his mind was, too. This wasn't the original Tynan … this was a reconstructed Tynan, a personality built from interpreting scar tissue in my brain.

A personality built from my brain.

"The technology that was used to … build your consciousness. How much do you know about it?" I asked.

"Only what the advisors explained to me. Copying a body is easy. They had tissue samples and the technology to clone you … me. But the mind … the mind is not so easy to recreate.

They told me they'd worked it out for our situation and our situation alone but that it was potentially a one-time scenario. There would be no opportunity for trial runs and the possibility that there would be no second attempt."

I nodded slowly. What Tynan was saying made sense. My brain had recovered from the surgical trauma now, but it was fair to assume that the procedure could've killed me or led to complications after the fact. I was the master copy; if you lost me, you lost the source.

"Have they checked you over at all? Health checks, you know?"

Tynan nodded. "Yep. Everything is healthy, normal even."

Well, that was something at least.

But if Tynan was technically healthy, something else must be at play.

"Maybe … because it was an untested technology, maybe it didn't quite work as intended. You – the previous you – never felt guilt, whereas I have felt a lot of guilt for a long time. To hazard a guess, I'd say when my scar tissue was being read, other parts of me were being read as well."

Tynan frowned but didn't say anything. I could just imagine the gears turning in his head, understanding what I'd said and the implications of it … and possibly trying to decide where to assign blame.

"I have heard the whispers, you know."

"What whispers?"

"The crew. Gossiping among themselves. A few loyalists
told me what the advisors said: that I'm a failed science experiment."

"That is what the advisors said."

"But here's the thing: the technology did what it was supposed to – it brought me back from the dead. So, what you're telling me is … it's your fault I'm feeling guilty?"

"Ah, no – that's not what I said at all. Yes, I feel guilty about my choices and the fallout from those actions. That you seem to have inherited that capacity for remorse isn't my fault. You want someone to blame? How about yourself for cooking up a resurrection plan? Or your loyalists for executing it? Or the engineers that built a machine that they couldn't verify the functionality of?"

Tynan's expression darkened as he frowned, and I could feel the heat of his anger radiating off him. No doubt, the blame resting upon his shoulders was not the intended outcome.

"How do I get rid of it?" he asked.

"Get rid of what? The blame?"

"No!" he barked. "How do I get rid of this … this guilt?"

I let out a hearty laugh, only to be greeted by an icy glare from Tynan.

"You really don't know how this works, do you?"

Tynan clenched his fists and sat forward.

"Okay, calm down," I said as I held up my hands, gesturing for peace. "Safe space, remember?"

Tynan huffed and unclenched his fists. "I'll ask again. How do I get rid of it?"

"Let's go back a step because I think you lack a fundamental piece of understanding. I think you aren't even entirely sure what guilt is or why you're feeling it."

Tynan averted his eyes, and I understood why; to look at me would've allowed me to see that I was right. Tynan didn't want to appear any stupider than he already felt.

"Guilt is a feeling of anxiety or unhappiness caused by the thought that you have done something immoral or wrong, such as causing harm and suffering to another.

Your treatment of me and all the Republic crew members you murdered, and the citizen of Akka that you failed, they're why –"

"Yes, I get it! Just tell me how to get rid of it!" Tynan yelled, leaping to his feet and towering over me.

I felt adrenaline surge through me, and I leapt to my feet, bringing myself face to face with my double. "You can't get rid of it!" I yelled back.

Tynan took a step back, surprised by my outburst. After taking a moment to collect himself, Tynan snapped back. "And how do you know that Mr Goody Two-Shoes?"

"How would I know?" I murmured, pointing at myself. "How would I know?" I said, raising my voice. "Let me tell you *how I know!*"

I shoved Tynan in the chest with both hands, thankful for the strength provided by the adrenaline rushing through me and pushed him backwards into his chair.

"I was born out of the consequence of your lust for control. And when I had life, all I wanted was a simple life; I wanted to run a farm with a beautiful woman beside me and a child or two to raise and nurture. Do you know what I didn't ask for?"

Tynan looked up at me, his face pale, his eyes wide, shaking his head in response to my question.

"I didn't ask for this face! I didn't ask for the tainted history it was stained with! I didn't ask to carry the responsibility of solidifying your legacy or dismantling it! Nor did I ask for the power to make good on the choice that was demanded of me! But they gave me power, and I made a choice, and I have spent every day since living with the guilt of those actions, wondering if there had been another way! Wondering if I could've done things differently!"

Tynan remained seated, his body rigid as he fixed his fearful gaze on me, unable to look away.

"You see it now, don't you? You see the monster! This is how the world sees you, Tynan. And it terrifies you, doesn't it?"

"Yes," Tynan whispered. "Does it not scare you?"

"My whole life, I've never been afraid of monsters ... because there weren't any hiding in the closet or under my bed – all the monsters I knew lived inside my head! The only time I see a monster is when I look in the mirror, because all this time the monster has been me!

Only it isn't me, it's you. It's always been you! Your face, your actions, your mind. And all I ever got was the resentment, the burden, and the responsibility of dealing with your shit!"

I turned around and walked over to the observation window, then leant against the sill as strength gave way to weariness as my adrenaline faded. I watched the light cone flicker and dance as I tried to quell the rage inside me.

"From the moment of my inception, I think I instinctually tried to be everything you weren't, and for a time, I think that worked," I said quietly.

"What changed?"

"I was given an impossible choice. Alter the minds of billions of people against their will, without their knowledge. I could do it as me and make them good. I could do it as you and make them bad. I could do nothing and have it all happen anyway."

I closed my eyes and watched the light waltz over my eyelids as I focused on the past.

"I didn't like any of those options. Control over people's thoughts like that ... that is a power man should not have – only gods. So, I made a choice, but that wasn't enough; I also had to be the one pulling the trigger. Not just once but repeatedly. Afterwards, I asked myself, how do you destroy a monster without becoming one?"

"How do you?"

"I don't know."

The room filled with silence as we each quietly considered all that had been said. After a few moments of consideration, I realised I still had more to say, and I turned to look at Tynan again.

"The more time that has passed, the more I have come to realise that I will always carry you within me – the original you. I fight daily to control the dormant evil inside of me, and I am terrified that I will lose myself somewhere inside that darkness. You asked me how you get rid of guilt, and I said you can't." I paused as I planned my words. "It clings to you like never-ending honey – you can try to lick it off your fingers all you like, but your hands will always be sticky. It just becomes ... part of you, it's a burden you must carry. Life goes on, but it is never the same again."

Tynan seemed to deflate, his bubble of hope burst, popping any thoughts of escape from these feelings.

"And besides, even if you could get rid of the guilt and the pain ... I don't know that one should. Because without that feeling to remind you of the impact your actions have, you would just repeat them. Hurting, harming, and killing without a second thought, just like the old you. Maybe we feel guilty so that we think twice about an action before we make it."

"That's what makes you weak," Tynan said, a note of confidence in his voice again. "A powerful leader acts decisively, instinctively. While a weak one second guesses each step before they take it. I have always been strong. These feelings are *your* weakness! It shouldn't even be inside me. I will speak to the scientists and see about having it removed."

"You can't leave well enough alone, can you? After discovering you're more human, post-resurrection, your first instinct is to pull out the mind manipulation technology and start playing god again. Have you learnt nothing from everything I've been saying?"

"I've learned lots," Tynan said, getting to his feet and his tone turning condescending. "I'm Raith – poor me. I had to make some hard decisions, and now I feel bad every day. I'm ashamed of my noble face and the legacy associated with it, and I'm afraid my family will think I'm a monster."

"Leave my family out of this."

"See, more weakness. You are so bound to them and their fate. Tell me, how does it feel to be beholden to the welfare of another?"

I looked at Tynan's cruel smile and felt a surge of anger. Where he saw weakness, I saw strength. Yes, I was bound to my family, and their fate was my fate. This man, no, this *monster* was a constant threat to me and my loved ones. If he died, the danger would reduce significantly.

And we're all alone. There's no one here to stop me from taking him out.

A second surge of adrenalin coursed through my veins, and I rushed over to Tynan, grabbed him by his coat and hoisted him up into the air, surprising myself with my strength. I continued to walk forward until I'd slammed him into the wall.

"That's it, Tynan!" I snarled. "Keep pushing my buttons – keep winding me up – and let's see where things go, aye?"

The colour vanished from Tynan's face; his fear was almost palpable.

"Because as much as I fear the darkness asleep within me, it can do things I can't, things I sometimes wish I could. So, keep pushing!

Push me far enough, hurt those I love, and I will let that darkness out to play, and when you come face to face with the real you, then you will discover just how much of a pale imitation you are!"

Tynan reached out to the wall beside us, feeling around until he found the room's control panel. He slammed his fist onto it, simultaneously turning on all the lights and opening the doors. Blinded by the sudden illumination, I let go of Tynan.

"Guards!" he screamed.

Seconds later, I heard footsteps moving toward me before several hands grabbed me and wrestled me to the ground.

"Are you alright, Your Grace?" asked a concerned soldier.

"Yes, I'm fine. Just get this pathetic maggot out of my sight! Freeze him! Freeze him with the others!"

"Yes, Your Grace."

As the soldiers hoisted me back up, my eyes adjusted, and I turned to Tynan, watching him as they dragged me from the room.

"This isn't over!" I hissed.

"No ... no, it isn't," came the disgruntled reply.

Chapter 9
An Uneasy Alliance

2160, Common Era – Planet Gaia, Outer Rim, the Republic of Humanity

It turned out Tynan had mercy so long as there was some benefit for him, perceived or otherwise. He'd ordered I be put back in cryo for the rest of our journey to Gaia. As I vomited up cryofluid, I assumed we must be approaching our destination, but I noticed that they'd only woken me.

"Can you walk yet?"

I tilted my head back to find First Officer Faberson towering above me.

"Faberson. Hello, I –" I broke off to cough up more fluid. "Yeah, I think I can walk."

"Good. Ty … His Grace wants you on the bridge – immediately," Faberson said, offering a helping hand.

I grabbed his outstretched arm, and he pulled me to my feet, then helped me walk out of the room.

"Do you know what's going on?" I asked.

Faberson averted his eyes and stayed quiet. I assumed he'd been punished for his previous actions.

"Please, Faberson. Trust me now as you did on the bridge."

"I can't."

"If you don't help me now, I can't help you later."

Faberson grimaced. "What makes you think you'll be able to help me?"

"Let's just say I've got a solid hunch that things are going to change."

He looked at me wearily. He briefly closed his eyes and on a heavy breath and his shoulders slumped.

"Tynan has detected hundreds of ships outside Gaia. He thinks it's the entire Republic fleet."

"Why does he want me?"

Faberson shook his head. "I can't say any more."

Familiar metallic clicks and clacks suddenly echoed through the corridor. We looked up to see an Arachnobot visible behind a ventilation duct grate.

"Bitsy?" I exclaimed. My heart swelled with joy at the sight of my friend.

The robot jittered happily inside the duct.

"So that little critter is yours, aye?" Faberson inquired. "We'd given up on trying to catch it as it proved remarkably resistant to capture. Does it have aftermarket modifications?"

I nodded. "Oh yes, yes it does. I've missed you, buddy."

Bitsy jittered again.

"Stay out of sight and find me when it's safe!"

The Arachnobot jittered once more and then scurried out of sight. We listened to the waning sound of its footsteps and then Faberson turned to look at me.

"If you've had that running around the ship all this time ... you're owed more credit than I have given."

"I didn't tell it to do anything," I replied, meeting Faberson's gaze. "It's just loyal and capable."

Faberson furrowed his brow and pushed me forward, resuming our journey. I let the conversation lull, and we walked in silence the rest of the way. I contemplated where I'd left things before being frozen – the conversation with Tynan and his admission of experiencing guilt. Instead of the psychopath that the original Tynan had been, this clone was now human at best and sociopathic at worst. I was conscious of Zavis's plan to have the new Empire destroy itself from the inside out – and Tynan's guilt might just be the lever to pull to bring about that destruction.

As we entered the bridge, Faberson steered me straight to Tynan's side, sat as usual in his captain's chair.

I felt Faberson's firm grip as he tugged downwards, forcing me to my knees, and I found myself level with Tynan in his seated position. Tynan slowly rotated his head until he looked me in the eye.

"The traitor," he whispered.

"Your Grace," I replied.

A slight smile appeared on Tynan's face.

That's it – believe you are in control.

"The Republic didn't take too kindly to the destruction of their fleet, it seems," Tynan said sarcastically. "Now they've amassed all their forces and stationed them outside Gaia. Whilst this wouldn't be good for me all on my lonesome, we have a bigger common enemy to fight now, don't we?"

"Yes, Your Grace."

"Now, I could tell them as much, but we both know it would mean fuck all coming from me. Coming from you, on the other hand ..."

"I understand, Your Grace."

"Good," Tynan said with a nod. "Just to make sure we're on the same page, if we are to have any chance of beating that machine, it'll take our joint forces collectively hammering that Horror to take it down. We have the insight they need; they have firepower we need. But that union can't happen if they shoot us out of the sky when we arrive."

I had no desire to help Tynan avoid getting shot out of the sky, but it wasn't just him on this ship, was it?

The crew and my family, and myself, of course – we would all get shot down with him.

"Do we have an understanding?" Tynan asked.

"Yes," I replied, with a little more venom than intended. "Your Grace."

Tynan scowled. "Just because you add 'Your Grace' to the end of a sentence doesn't mean you can speak to me however you want," he said, slapping me up the back of the head.

"Of course, Your Grace," I replied more neutrally.

"Attaboy. Now get over to the comms station and get ready. As soon as we exit warp, I want you sweet-talking the Republic."

"Yes, Your Grace."

I stood up and moved to the instructed station, then sat down and familiarized myself with the console. Time to prep my speech.

What the hell do I even say though? Yeah, hi, don't mind my evil doppelgänger. Don't shoot us. Please.

I glanced behind me to my left and saw Faberson sitting there.

"What's our ETA until we exit warp?" I whispered.

Faberson looked away, pretending not to hear me.

"Come on, Faberson ..." I insisted quietly. "What's our ETA?"

"Two minutes. Now shut up."

Fair enough. Okay, time to focus.

I had two minutes. What did I need to do? I started building a mental checklist. Open a channel. State who I am and my credentials. State what I want.

That had to be a good start, right?

Everything after that would have to be reactionary, said in response to ... well, to what I say. Still, I could try to anticipate the things that might come up. Are we armed? Only rail gun and gauss cannon ammo, all other munitions expended. It's a military vessel? Yes, but there are civilians onboard.

The telltale light changes of warp exit appeared outside the bridge windows, the colours shifting through their transitions.

"Get ready traitor," Tynan drawled.

I looked out the window as the final light transitions occurred; violet turned to blue and then cleared to the star-studded universe, revealing Gaia in all her green glory. I felt my heart flutter as I gazed upon the world I considered home, a warmth spreading throughout my chest. But I had little time to appreciate the sight of her as I spotted the fleet positioned behind her, a chill replacing the warmth as my anxious heart skipped a beat.

"Fuck me," Tynan breathed. "There's got to be at least one hundred ships there – maybe even one hundred and fifty!"

I turned to the communications officer on my right. "Can you hail the fleet on all channels, please?"

The officer nodded and began tapping away at their console.

"We're hailing them. No response yet."

I watched their console while I waited for the indicator to show that they'd established a channel.

"They're firing their rail guns at us!" shouted Helmsman Nerys.

The ship lurched to the right and then to the left; the crew held onto anything they could as Nerys tried to avoid the worst of the incoming bullet streams.

"Open a goddamn channel!" Tynan yelled as he clenched the armrests of his seat, his knuckles turning white from the pressure.

"We're trying! We're hailing them on all frequencies, but they're not responding!" the communications officer shouted back.

"Prepare to return fire, then!"

"No!" I yelled. "If you do that, there's no way they'll communicate with us!"

A cascade of bullets bit into the Chupacabra's side. Warning lights flashed across consoles all around the bridge.

"We've got hull breaches on decks two, three, five and seven!" Faberson shouted.

I looked at Tynan. "Don't return fire!"

"What good will it do us if they tear us apart?" Tynan asked, his words tinged with an edge of panic.

"Just keep dodging – give them a moment to realise we aren't returning fire and that we're hailing them!"

"Fine!"

Another wave of bullets struck the ship, lighting up the consoles with another round of warning lights.

"More hull breaches! Decks one and six!"

The ship continued to lurch from side to side, and I kept a close eye on the console, but still our call went unanswered.

"They've stopped firing!" Nerys called out.

I watched the console indicators. Red. Red. Red. Green.

"Hello! Hello! This is Governor Raith of Gaia. We have civilians onboard; do not fire! I repeat: this is Governor Raith of Gaia. We have civilians onboard. Do not fire!"

There was silence on the other end of the line, and my heart pounded in my chest, hoping that there was someone receiving my message and they'd listened to what I'd said.

"Hello! Are you receiving me? This is Governor Raith of –"

"We are receiving you, Governor Raith. You are on an Empire ship, correct?" said a young male voice.

"Hi! Yes! Hi, um … yes, this is an Empire ship."

"What the hell is going on, Raith?" said a recognisable voice.

"President Knox?" I asked.

"Yes, it's me, Raith. Why on earth are you on an Empire ship?" the president demanded.

"That's a long story, Madam President."

"Well, you'd best tell it quickly, or I'm going to start shooting again."

I heaved a heavy sigh and felt a wave of frustration wash over me at the lack of trust. I knew it didn't look good, communicating from an Empire ship and all, but after all I'd done for the Republic, you'd think people would have a little more faith in me.

"The Empire intercepted the Stardove on its diplomatic mission to Akka. They cloned me and reconstructed Tynan Khidar's mind by interpreting scar tissue within my brain. Tynan then destroyed the Republic fleet going to Akka's aid."

"Shut up!" Tynan hissed. "Don't tell them that stuff!"

"No, you shut up!" I hissed back. "Least they shoot us down!"

I focused on my mic again – where had I been? Oh yes.

"I convinced Tynan to go to Akka's aid, and we fought the vessel mentioned in Akka's broadcasts but were unsuccessful in our offensive manoeuvres. We were able to rescue a few hundred civilians from Akka, though."

There was silence on the other end of the line. Did they believe what I had said? Were they preparing for another volley of rail gun fire while we waited for an answer?

"If you travelled to Akka via the coordinates where we lost contact with the support fleet, a round trip to Akka should've taken you nine months but you're three months late – how have you only just arrived here?"

I looked around the bridge, hoping someone would have an answer to that question.

Nery's supplied the information, "Our warp systems were damaged during our asteroid-pushing manoeuvre."

I gave an acknowledging nod and reopened the mic. "It has taken longer for us to reach you because our warp systems are damaged, Madam President."

A deafening silence filled the bridge, the tension almost palpable. What were they thinking?

"Honestly, Raith, this doesn't look good. Given your ... past, tell me why I shouldn't obliterate your ship where it stands?"

Sadness filled my voice as I replied, "Because you know me and we have civilians on board, Madam President."

How much convincing did this woman need?

"You know that I, Raith, am not the same person as Tynan. Yes, the Empire needs to be disbanded, and Tynan needs to face justice for his actions, but I'm asking you to trust me when I say that this isn't the time. There is a bigger threat out there, a threat that has destroyed Akka, and will probably head here next. We need to put aside our differences and unite to fight an enemy that threatens us all, regardless of our allegiances. Everything else can come later."

More silence. I really wished they'd stop doing that.

"Yes, yes." A heavy sigh sounded over the speakers. "I believe you, Raith. But only you, though – I don't trust Tynan or the Empire, so how do you propose we work through this?"

Knox's tone dripped with appeasement but not sincerity. Still, that was probably the most I was going to get out of her.

"Thank you, Madam President. We don't have the luxury of formalities, so can we all verbally agree to a truce, please?"

"Yes," Knox quickly replied.

Almost too quickly.

"Have Tynan go first," she added.

There it is.

I looked over at my doppelgänger, a scowl on his face, presumably at the lack of the formal address he so enjoyed.

"Please, Your Grace. As you said earlier if we are to have any chance of beating the Horror, it'll take our joint forces – we need to work together."

"Fine." Tynan snapped. "I, Tynan Khidar, do hereby agree to a truce."

"Thank you, Tynan," Knox replied, barely able to contain the smugness in her voice. "And I, Kylie Knox, President of the Republic of Humanity, also hereby agree to a truce."

"Excellent – thank you both!" I said and felt a measure of relief. "Now, there is much that needs to be discussed, so I suggest that we each gather a delegation and head down to Gaia – think of it as neutral territory. Once we're planet side, we can negotiate the terms of this relationship and decide how to combat the threat that hangs over us all. We'll also offload *all* the civilians onboard. How does that sound?"

Another moment of silence from the other side.

"I can agree to that plan," President Knox replied.

"As can I," said Tynan.

"Thank you both for your cooperation! I'll send through coordinates shortly, and we'll meet on the surface."

"Acknowledged. President Knox, over and out."

I turned towards Tynan, smiling. "I think that went well."

"It's not over yet," Tynan replied with a glare.

❦

To say that you could cut the air with a knife was an understatement. Two sets of chairs were arranged across from each other in one of Gaia's many fields, with a stunning panoramic backdrop of snow-topped mountains and greenery in all directions.

Tynan was in the centre of one set of chairs, Ichirō to his right, Phobus and Lorcan to his left, and a dozen soldiers surrounding them.

President Knox and several high-ranking Republic officials were seated on the other side, protected by their own group of soldiers — equal in number to Tynan's ensemble.

Despite my attempt to get all the civilians onto Gaia, Tynan had ensured that Amorina, Emma, and Zavis stayed on the Chupacabra to stop the Republic from destroying the only ship he had in the area.

"Thank you all for coming here today," I said, standing in no-mans-land between the two sides. "I appreciate that a meeting like this would be strange on any given day … but these are strange times we find ourselves in … and in that context, perhaps this meeting isn't so strange after all."

When I wasn't speaking, the atmosphere was heavy with tension as each side stared at the other in menacing silence. The pressure was on me to lead this negotiation calmly and constructively. With any luck, I'd be able to sweet-talk both sides into an alliance, regardless of how uneasy it may be.

"It is up to me to try and make peace between two sides that are so different because I, more than most, understand what it is like to have a past and a present that are so dissimilar to one another."

I glanced at both sides and could almost see the daggers soaring through the air.

"Cut to the chase, Raith," Knox snapped.

"Yes!" Tynan agreed. "An action we can finally agree upon."

Never mind that I'm trying to start things off calmly – no, they have to be all "hurry up Raith," and "get it over with Raith."

I inhaled deeply and reminded myself that I needed to be the guiding voice in this conversation.

"If either of you thinks this will be a quick and easy discussion, you are both sorely mistaken. If we are going to get through this discussion, it's going to take some time. I don't think I need to tell anyone how different each side is from the other."

Knox glanced away – was that a hint of embarrassment I saw on her face?

"You're right, and I apologise, Raith. The situation is obviously ... tense, but we shouldn't let that muddy the waters any further. Please continue," President Knox said solemnly.

I nodded an acknowledgement and continued, "Under normal circumstances, the Republic would be well within its rights, and justifiably so, to detain, persecute, and punish Tynan and his loyalists for the crimes they have recently committed."

Tynan snorted indignantly, but I ignored him and continued.

"Doing so here and now would weaken us more than can quickly be summarised, for there is a threat far greater than humanity's internal ideological conflicts. We must either face it united or fall before it, divided."

The president's face was solemn as she leant forward. "You've talked about this threat, but so far, all we have are unsubstantiated claims. Provide us with some physical evidence, any piece of data that proves, without a doubt, that there is an imminent danger that needs to be addressed. We need proof, Raith — actionable proof!"

I sighed. "Madam President, if you could please just be patient and allow me to —"

"I don't need to give you patience," Knox interrupted. "I just need proof! If you can't give me that, there's no need to continue this charade, and I will end Tynan and his forces."

"Earlier in space, I asked you if you trusted me. Please, trust me now. Trust me when I say that the threat out there is a threat to all of humanity."

"I trusted you enough not to obliterate the ship you were on. To trust you now, when you're asking me to work with a sworn enemy of the Republic, to fight a threat no one has given proof —"

"You want a description?" I snapped, tired of the mistrust. "I witnessed the Horror with my own eyes — a gargantuan machine that extended for half an astronomical unit! A machine that quickly and effortlessly shrugged off weapons of mass destruction like they were nothing more than BB pellets! A machine that caught an asteroid, split it in half and threw it back at us! Should I continue?"

Knox appeared a bit taken aback, and her stunned silence hung in the air as she raised her hands in a sheepish, apologetic gesture. I cleared my throat loudly and inhaled deeply, calming myself down.

"As I was saying before being interrupted again … Bitsy, please do the honours."

I'd reunited with my Arachnobot on the journey down to Gaia, my companion having snuck aboard the dropship. I watched the faces of Tynan, Ichirō, and the advisors as they recognised the Arachnobot, their expressions changing into looks of disdain and resentment. Bitsy scuttled over to a hologram projector and activated it with a few precise clicks. The projection burst into life, displaying a dot – Akka – overshadowed by the monstrous form of the Horror.

"This is Akka, and this tiny speck next to it is the Chupacabra." I pointed to the looming mass dominating the picture. "And this monstrosity is the Horror. You are about to see a mixture of footage captured by the Chupacabra's systems and a reconstruction of events as we understand them."

Bitsy tapped on the device a few more times and the holographic footage played, showing the gathered council the ineffectiveness of our offensive manoeuvres.

I watched both sides closely as they scrutinized the video: the subtle shame and embarrassment on Tynan's face, the simmering anger on the advisors' faces, the shock and awe on the faces of Ichirō and the Republic's representatives. But most of all, I noted the look of horror that appeared on everyone's faces, at one point or another, during the reel. As the footage ended, I spoke up again.

"This is the threat I have been talking about. This is the Horror," I said as I gestured at the hologram with both hands. "And as you have just seen, words could not do justice to the description needed to adequately detail this machine and its capabilities. Make no mistake, if we are to have any chance of defeating it, it is going to take our combined strength to take it on."

There was a moment of acknowledgement in Tynan's and Knox's expressions, an indication that they both understood what was required.

I turned towards the president. "I know you want to arrest Tynan, but you need to work together to fight the Horror first. And either Tynan will die during the coming conflict, or he'll survive, and you can see to it that he faces justice once we've all beaten this brutal machine."

"I understand," replied Knox.

I turned towards Tynan now.

"What?" he said. "What ultimatum can you give me to make me understand, Raith?"

"I've no ultimatum to give you, Tynan. All I have to say, really, is that karma loves the guilty."

Tynan squirmed at the word "guilty", much to my quiet enjoyment.

"Maybe you survive the fight, maybe you don't. Either way, you'll face your dues in one form or another."

Tynan's face became a shade paler, and I almost smiled. He hadn't seen that response coming.

"I understand," he said, his cockiness subdued.

"Okay, so we agree. We'll work together to fight the Horror. But we can't go up against it blindly – we need to know anything and everything we can about it," Knox said.

"Understandably, we know very little about the Horror. Fortunately, I anticipated the need for information and left behind some makeshift monitoring satellites that have collected data since our departure from Akka. Bitsy, if you please?"

A few more taps from the Arachnobot and the projection changed, showing an enlarged version of Akka, with a portion of the Horror looming over it. A vast cloud of the Horror's swarm surrounded Akka, with trails going back and forth between the planet and the machine.

"What's it doing?"

"As far as we can tell, it's using its swarm to systematically destroy any traces of organic life or technology and selectively mine mineral deposits from within the planet. These swarm tendrils are making their way to the planet, while these others are moving back to the Horror, bringing with them the collected elements. Now, we believe —"

"Raith — give us the laymen's version, yeah?" Knox interrupted.

I gritted my teeth and looked up, breathing deep breaths as I stared at the clouds above. I expected Tynan to play up, but, surprisingly, he was behaving rather well. Knox, on the other hand, was getting on my nerves.

"It's eating the planet," I said bluntly, looking back at Knox.

"Oh," Knox replied.

"We're monitoring it, obviously, but bear in mind that the latest data we have is already two months old when we receive it here on Gaia. Whilst the Horror hasn't left Akka yet, so far as we know, when we see it leave, it'll be imperative that we're ready for it, for its arrival would be imminent."

"Assuming it comes to Gaia."

"Exactly, but that is the next destination we have the most confidence in."

"Why?" Knox asked.

I felt my chest tighten — I'd been dreading this question and the reaction its answer would inevitably garner.

"The Horror emits a signal that, when our brains listen to it, induces theta waves."

"Oh, for fucks' sake! We — no, not we — *you* summoned it here with the mass conversion device, didn't you?" the president snapped.

A sickening wave of guilt washed over me, and my legs felt like jelly. Knox didn't know how much her words hurt, and my pain quickly turned into anger.

"First of all, you sanctioned those actions, so don't dump all the responsibility for this at my feet!" I retorted as I pointed at Knox aggressively. "And second, we had no way of knowing that this thing existed or that using the mass conversion device would inadvertently act as a dinner bell!"

Knox's eyes stood wide, her hands clenched and released. From the tension in her jaw, I could tell she had it clenched as well. But no statement was forth coming – really, what could she say?

"With this knowledge in mind, it's fair to presume that the Horror will travel from world to world, either by proximity or by which has the strongest theta waves being emitted. Currently, that would mean it comes to Gaia and then to Ares."

The president looked past me to Tynan. "And what about you? Where have you and your people been hiding?"

"Like I'm going to tell you that!" Tynan chuckled.

Knox turned to me now. "Either he reveals where his planet is, or this alliance is off!"

"Well then, we might as well go home now!" Tynan sneered.

"Well, that's a relief – these talks weren't going anywhere!"

"How could they? The Republic's bureaucracy is getting in the way, as always. This is why the Empire is superior – we get the job done!"

"Get the job done?" Knox asked incredulously. "What, like murdering innocent people? Hard-working men and women who had done nothing to harm or slight you, but you shot them out of the sky regardless?"

"Done nothing? Anyone who serves in the Republic has blood on their hands by association!"

Knox wiggled a finger in her ear. "I'm sorry – it sounded like you said Republic when you meant to say Empire, because our hands are clean!"

As the pair continued to shout at each other across the paddock, I looked down at Bitsy.

"It's like looking after children, isn't it?"

A message scrolled along Bitsy's back. *I cannot respond to that question.*

"Yeah ... I know, buddy. I know."

I checked out Knox, who had gotten to her feet, face flushed in anger as she yelled at Tynan, who seemed ready to tear across the field and knock her out.

"Both of you, please be quiet. This isn't constructive," I said firmly.

Obscenities continued to fly past, zipping back and forth, as they continued screaming.

"This isn't helping!" I said more loudly this time, though my plea fell on deaf ears.

"Silence!" I yelled; my words projected with authority that held an unwanted familiarity.

Much to my surprise, and probably that of all the onlookers, both Knox and Tynan fell silent. After a moment's hesitation, they both sat back down.

"Your actions should embarrass you both! You call yourselves leaders? More like children!"

Indeed, a look of embarrassment appeared on their faces moments later.

"To address the point you raised before, Knox, I know the planet that Tynan and his forces have been hiding on. They call it Erebus, and I can lead you right there."

"How do you know that?" Tynan asked.

"Because when you captured me, Bitsy escaped, and your loyalists couldn't capture him, so he recorded our entire journey to Erebus and back!" I smirked.

"Oh," said Tynan as he deflated like a sail losing the wind.

I smiled openly – it felt good to have one up on Tynan for once – I was no longer the one on the back foot.

I turned back towards Knox. "So, we're all good now, right? You'll know where Erebus is, and Tynan, you don't have to reveal where it is."

Tynan glared at me. He didn't like it, but he knew I had him on a technicality, which was always the best thing to pull someone up on.

"Okay, we agree to work together to fight this thing, but it has to be asked … with what? As you showed us before, rail guns, gauss cannons, Firecrackers, and nuclear warheads – even an asteroid – couldn't do any harm," Knox proclaimed.

"Well, I actually think all of those things might be capable of damaging it – one of the nukes Tynan fired struck the Horror and took a large bite out of its surface. It appeared to repair the damage promptly, but it proves that we can injure it. I think our earlier attacks were ineffective because there weren't enough of them, and the Horror could use its swarm to dismantle or redirect those attacks, rendering them useless. I believe if we can throw enough at it, simultaneously, that it will overwhelm the Horror's defences and we will break it."

Neither Knox nor Tynan spoke, both thinking through my theory. Did it have merit?

"I think, in principle, that's good enough of a plan, and at this point in time, it's the only plan that I think makes sense. I propose we begin evacuating Gaia immediately, just in case we can't defend it – we don't want a repeat of the lives lost on Akka," Knox said.

"I agree," I replied, then turned towards Tynan. "What do you think?"

Tynan nodded. "I ... I hate to say it, but I think I agree with Knox – in principle. It's the only good plan that makes sense right now."

"Okay. Do either of you have any additional weapons or ships that you can bring to bear?"

"We've got a few auxiliary ships we can bring here. We also have a planetary defence laser that we can install in Gaia's orbit."

"Please do both – we need all the firepower we have!"

I glanced over at Tynan again.

"We don't have much, for obvious reasons, but I have two other ships on their way here as we speak."

"Okay, thank you – that'll have to do. It has to be enough."

"So, it's settled then? We have a plan?" Knox asked.

"We do," Tynan confirmed.

"We do," I echoed. "So, let's make it so!"

"Let's make it so!" Knox and Tynan repeated together.

As the parties turned to leave, I spoke up.

"Um ... before you both leave, can we at least shake on it? Perhaps we can shake on the outcome instead of signing formalised treaties?"

Knox and Tynan glared at each other from across the field.

"Please. Don't do it for yourselves. Do it for all the people that follow you, that are loyal to you and your governance systems."

Both leaders thought about this momentarily, then Knox walked into the centre of the field and stood beside me. We both looked over at Tynan.

"Come on, Tynan!" I called.

This seemed to shake him loose from his steadfast position, and he finally walked over to the centre of the field. Knox made the first move, reaching out a hand, and after one last moment of hesitation, Tynan took her hand in his own for a brief shake.

"Thank you," I said to them both.

"It is probably us that should thank you, Raith. Without your mediation, we would've been fighting each other and missing the real threat," Knox replied.

"Don't thank me – just work together. Collectively, you're all that stands between humanity and the Horror. So, for the sake of all humankind, defend us."

Knox and Tynan nodded.

"Agreed. Perhaps to that end, we should discuss some strategy? Fleet formations and such?" Knox said to Tynan.

"Yes," Tynan replied slowly. "Let's talk."

❈

While Knox and Tynan discussed battle plans argumentatively, I walked over to where Ichirō sat. Phobus and Lorcan watched my approach closely, and the soldiers that surrounded them tightened the grasp on their weapons, ready to spring into action if needed.

"Easy, fellas," I said once I was within earshot. "I just came to talk to my son. That's all."

Some soldiers relaxed a little, but the advisors' gazes remained steady and unwavering.

"Go away," said Ichirō, glaring at me.

I knelt before my son and looked up at him.

"I just want to talk, Ichirō – that's all."

"Yeah, well, I don't want to fucking talk to you!"

"That's fair. Just listen then, okay?"

Ichirō didn't respond and averted his gaze.

"I'd ask if you were alright, but if you won't talk to me, I won't get a response. So instead, I'll say I hope you're alright. I hope you're healthy and safe and that being with Tynan is all you hoped it would be."

Ichirō continued to look away, but I watched his face shift and twitch subtly – at least he was hearing me out. I only hoped my words would sink in.

"And listen, if being with Tynan isn't what you thought – if you aren't healthy or safe – you can always return to me. The door is always open, okay?"

"That's enough," said Phobus. "He doesn't need your poisonous ideas in his head."

I turned my head slowly to look at Phobus. Our eyes met, and each refused to drop our gaze.

"Are you so sure that my ideas are the toxic ones?"

As we maintained our stare, a look of discomfort appeared on Phobus's face.

"Would you even recognise the symptoms of a venomous thought inside your head?"

Phobus appeared to squirm. What was he unsettled by? The gaze we were yet to break or my words, speaking a truth he didn't want to hear?

"Do you even know how and when to administer the cure before the damage becomes permanent?"

A look of recognition flashed across Phobus's face, and he looked away.

"Remove yourself ... or I'll have the guards assist you in leaving," he said half-heartedly.

I turned back towards Ichirō with one last thing to say. "Always remember, I love you, son."

With that, I stood, turned and walked away. I looked over at Knox and Tynan, both still deep in discussion. Hopefully, he'd been too busy to notice my interactions – and too distracted to realise I was sowing the seeds of dissent.

Chapter 10
Calm Before the Storm

2160, Common Era – Planet Gaia, Outer Rim, the Republic of Humanity

Once the negotiations had wound down, I was effectively told to stand down and stay out of the way – I had no military standing and no real authority above my governorship, after all. Part of me understood; the rest of me desperately wanted to help and hated that it couldn't. Part of me also knew I still had a role to play in the coming fight. I was certain I'd feel antsy about this at some point, but as the car sped down the road towards the farm, I knew more pressing events would distract me: reuniting with the rest of the family. My palms were slick with sweat as I nervously wrung my hands, a heavy feeling of dread in my stomach. It'd been three years – far longer than the one-year-round trip it was originally supposed to be. Thought after thought bombarded my mind, a ceaseless assault of worry and doubt.

Were they alright? Had anything terrible happened in my absence? How was Mother getting on with her illness? How was Father coping? Were Adanna and Winona okay? Had I let them all down?

The warmth of Amorina's hand resting on mine pulled me out of my spiralling thoughts, and I looked up to meet her gaze. Somewhat confident that he wouldn't immediately be destroyed, Tynan had released Amorina and Emma, although he had kept Zavis behind. I'd gotten Knox to raise Zavis's freedom with Tynan, but his ongoing imprisonment was "non-negotiable" apparently.

I hoped my old friend would be okay.

"They're going to be okay you know?" she whispered, her eyes filled with a comforting and understanding gaze that was all too familiar to me.

"I know that's probably true … I just worry about the possibility that it isn't."

"You worry too much."

"You said the same when I was worrying about the Empire's return — but I was right to worry about that, wasn't I?"

Amorina's face hardened as her expression shifted to one of betrayal. "I've already apologised for that — you can't keep welding that against me. I've admitted you were right about the Empire, okay? But here and now, I am right about our family. They'll be fine."

I nodded solemnly. "Sorry," I muttered. "I didn't mean to take a dig at you … it just came out."

We both swayed as the car turned and parked itself in front of the house. I leaned closer to the window, looking out at the house. I felt like it was only yesterday when I was here last; the house looked the same as it had three years ago. The front door opened, and a young woman stepped out.

"Is that … Adanna?" Amorina exclaimed.

The young woman gazed at the car with a confused glare. She stepped closer and raised her right hand to shield her eyes from the sun, and my brain finally recognised my daughter.

"Yes … yes, it is." My voice cracked, overwhelmed by the sight of my mature daughter.

She'd grown up so much in three years, and a feeling of lost time overwhelmed me — of memories I would never have a chance to create.

The car door opened, and I stepped out into the sun, allowing Adanna a moment to recognise me.

"Dad?"

I held my arms out, and Adanna let out a high-pitched squeal and sprinted across the yard, leaping into my embrace and wrapping her arms around my neck. I closed my eyes and enjoyed the moment, holding her close in a hug I'd not felt in a long time.

"You're back!" she whispered tearily, and I felt her chest heave as her sobs shook her body.

"I'm back," I whispered huskily.

Another squeal split the air, and I opened my eyes to see Winona running towards us. I staggered as she collided with us and wrapped her arms around Adanna and me.

"You're back!" she cried through her own sobs.

"Yes, yes! I'm back!" I replied as I choked on my words, tears streaming down my face.

"I'm back too!" came an insistent cry from Emma.

"Emma! Mum!" Winona exclaimed as she let go of Adanna and me and ran over to the awaiting ladies.

I put Adanna down, and she looked up at me. "We missed you."

"I could tell," I replied with a wink.

Adanna gave me a playful shove and we both laughed, and then she glanced past me at the other girls.

"I'll give you another hug later," she said as she squeezed my arm, then moved to join the others.

"Son?"

I turned towards the farmhouse where Father had appeared, and I was taken aback again. Unlike Adanna and Winona, who looked almost the same but had matured, Father looked older.

His wrinkles had deepened, and his hair had gone grey at the temples.

"Is it really you?"

"It's me," I replied as I shook off my shock, then jogged over and pulled him into an embrace.

"Oh, thank the heavens!" Father exclaimed. "I'd feared the worst and had begun to lose hope of your return."

"Ah, you know me. I was never one for conforming to the odds!"

Father chuckled and held me at arm's length. His eyes scanned over my face and body as his hands squeezed my biceps. His expression twisted from relief to concern as he took in my fresh scars and the gauntness of my body.

"Oh, my boy ... you've been through some kind of fresh hell, haven't you?"

"Yeah," I said with a solemn nod.

A pained expression crossed his face. "I'm so sorry, my son."

"I'm okay."

"Hmmm," Father hummed, knowing the truth was quite different.

I glanced back at the ladies, still catching up with each other, then turned back to Father.

"How have you been? How's Mother doing? How've the girls been? Did anything bad happen?"

"Whoa!" Father said as he held up his hands. "Slow down there, son. I'm okay, and the girls are fine. They've grown up frighteningly fast. I've chased off a bad boyfriend or two these last few years," he said with a chuckle.

I watched his eyes glance behind me and move four times.

He's counting.

"Speaking of boys, where's Ichirō?"

I averted my gaze as shame flushed my cheeks. "The Empire is still alive. They cloned Tynan, and ... Ichirō decided to join him."

"Ah," Father said, his simple word loaded with unspoken understanding. He gave the sentiment a moment to hang in the air, then continued. "As for your mother … your mother … her health is declining. Most days now, even the drugs don't pull her out of her zoned-out state."

I hung my head, feeling the weight of responsibility for my mother's condition. "I'm sorry. If only I'd made different choices … our 'quick' diplomatic mission may have been just that – quick."

"It isn't your fault … I sometimes think we all end up in hell, regardless of whether or not the path is paved with good intentions. The difference between an outcome that's intentionally bad versus accidentally bad is one's ability to sleep at night."

I gave my father a quizzical look.

Father sighed. "What I'm trying to say is you've got to stop beating yourself up. I know you. You're always trying to do the right thing – and that's the important bit. Negative outcomes probably would've happened irrespective of your actions, so stop punishing yourself for what has transpired and focus on what actions you'll take from here on out."

I nodded. "Ahh, *now* I understand."

Father chuckled. "I'm glad. Come on, let's go inside and get some food in you."

❧❧❧

The week passed quickly, with the family playing distraction from the war preparations happening around the planet and in orbit, but I still found myself pacing back and forth in the kitchen, desperate to do something other than domestic chores – which had certainly built up in my absence.

"You know, if you keep pacing like that, you're going to have to replace the floor," Amorina said as she walked into the room.

"Hmm," I grunted.

"Alternatively," she said with a smirk. "You could pace somewhere that's cheaper and easier to replace – like outside, for example."

"I know, I know," I replied and pulled out a dining room chair and sat down.

Almost immediately, my right leg began bouncing up and down, and my fingers tapped on the table, unable to keep still.

"You're driving me up the fucking wall with all your tipping and tapping as well!" Father said as he walked into the kitchen. "What's got you so increasingly wound up?"

"I feel so …" I throttled the air like I was choking some invisible individual as I tried to define my emotions. "Helpless – no, useless! I'm sitting here doing nothing while the Republic installs planetary defence lasers and coordinates the civilian evacuation and troop arrival. I want to help, but I'm told there's nothing for me to do, and I know there's nothing for me to do, but I feel like I should be doing something!" I ranted.

"I get that," Father replied. "Wanting to be of use and having to sit idle."

I nodded. "Yeah … it fucking sucks."

Amorina walked over and gently caressed my shoulders. "If only we could escape for a few days, just to unwind, you know? Have some us time."

"Maybe you can," Father said.

Amorina and I both looked at him.

"What do you mean?" Amorina asked.

"A mate of mine, he's got a cabin tucked away in one of Gaia's remote, mountainous regions … I forget which one – it's either the Limingnora or the Lantou Alps."

"And we could use it?" I asked.

"Oh, I'm sure of it. I'd just need to make a few calls, and then you could enjoy its serenity. I've taken your mother up there a few times – a truly spectacular and peaceful place."

I glanced up at Amorina. She didn't utter a word, but her eyes were full of a silent plea for me to accept the offer. I looked over towards Father again.

"We'd love to, but what about the kids? Your hands are full with Mother as it is," I said as I cast a glance at Mother staring vacantly into the distance.

"There's only one kid, and that's Emma. Winona and Adanna have been, and will continue to be, of great assistance in caring for your mother. Adding Emma into the mix will be trivial. Go! Take some time for the two of you."

A warmth spread through my chest as my heart swelled with pride and gratitude. Father was right, of course. Winona and Adanna weren't children anymore, and I'd seen that first hand this week, not only looking after Mother but keeping Emma busy as well. I knew they'd be alright for a few days while Amorina and I took the time we needed.

"Okay, thank you!" I said with a relieved smile.

"If you can arrange the cabin, I'll let the Republic know where we are, should we be needed."

"Of course! I'll call my mate now."

I looked up at Amorina again.

"Thank you," she whispered down to me.

"Of course, *mi amor*. We need this."

"Yes … yes, we do."

Father wasn't kidding when he'd said the cabin's location was spectacular and peaceful.

I lay on a king bed and looked out through a set of open French doors onto a splendid wilderness. In the background were the majestic snow-capped peaks of the Limingnora Alps. As far as the eye could see, the vast mountain range stretched from left to right, blanketed in thick, alpine forests, the trees looking like tall, grass-covered poles. A large glacial lake dominated the mid-ground, its pristine blue waters shimmering in the bright sunlight. The lawn was a lush, emerald expanse that occupied the foreground, stretching from the lake's edge to the patio of the holiday home.

The view quickly captivated you with its beauty, but Amorina, washing herself in the outdoor shower at the patio's edge, was the most beautiful part of it all. The sound of the water flowing over her body was calming; she was radiant in the sun's warm rays, its light glistening in the droplets that ran through her hair and down the soft curves of her body. She looked like a goddess, a personification of Gaia herself, surrounded by life-giving water and light. Watching her, set against this stunning wild backdrop,
it was almost easy to forget the frightening reality we'd briefly escaped from.

High above, in orbit and all around the planet, the Republic war machine was busy at work, preparing for a horror the likes of which few had encountered, and fewer had survived. Even here, as far away from civilisation as one could get, you couldn't escape the in-progress preparations. Any time of day, you could look up into the sky and see Republic or Empire ships passing overhead, and sometimes I could even spot the orbital laser making a flyby.

Tynan was out there too, of course; his existence allowed to perpetuate due to the unprecedented circumstances. Our recent interactions looped through my mind like a background process I couldn't terminate, and the more I thought about it, the more I concluded he was an imperfect copy, still dangerous but not on the same level as the original man. This version of Tynan had too much of Raith in him to truly be as bad as he had once been. But the inverse thought sent shivers down my spine – that too much of Tynan was in me. Part of me had known that for a long time, but it wasn't until my outburst with Tynan that I'd acknowledged that fear that Tynan, the real Tynan, was still inside me. If I was pushed hard enough, if I went past the breaking point … would it be possible for him to resurface?

"You have your thinking face on."

I snapped out of my concentration and realized that Amorina was lying beside me on the bed.

"I have a thinking face?"

"You sure do," she said softly, and then her expression darkened.

"Sometimes I look at you and it's like your body is sitting there, but your mind," she paused, glancing around as if seeking the right words to say, then shook her head and continued, "Your mind is who knows where, and you have this thousand-yard stare that just seems to cut through everything in its way. Your body will look so … heavy, like it's bearing the weight of the universe upon its shoulders."

"Huh." I replied, taken aback by this sudden confession. "I didn't realize I did that."

Amorina's face was a portrait of concern, her brows furrowed with worry, and her shoulders slumped in sadness.

"Does it worry you?" I asked.

"Yes," she replied with a sombre nod. "I want to help you, I want to support you, but when I see you so deep in thought, it often feels like I can't help. I feel powerless, like if I were to take the weight off your shoulders and put it onto my own, it would crush me."

Amorina looked away, and I watched a tear streak down her face.

"I wish … I wish we could bring the kids to a place like this and never leave. To never have to deal with the universe and all its bullshit ever again. To just live a good, simple life, but it feels like that's an impossible dream, like we're not destined for peace or something."

I felt a palpable ache in my chest as my heart sank like an anchor. She wanted what I wanted, yet, because of who I was – who I am – the simple happiness we sought was unobtainable.

"Do you regret getting to know me? Do you – ow!" I cried out and clutched my arm where Amorina had punched me.

"What was that for?" I exclaimed as I rubbed my tender flesh.

"Don't you ever think that I regret being with you!" Amorina snapped. "Who else would've travelled across the stars to rescue me? Hell, if it hadn't been for you, I'd probably have died a sex slave on Earth many years ago!"

"I'm sure you would've gotten out."

"Maybe, but I wouldn't have a beautiful daughter … daughters, or a son, misguided as he is. I wouldn't have had so many passion-filled nights and quickies among the hay bales."

I snorted with laughter. "The barnyard quickies are a highlight of your life, are they?"

"Oh, shut up – you know what I meant!"

"No, I don't think I do," I chuckled. "Please explain it to me."

That earned me a glare.

"My point is," Amorina said as she moved right on past my question, "the time I've shared with you has been amazing. And sure, I wish life was simpler or that we didn't have to face the uphill battles that we do, but you know what?"

I shook my head. "What?"

"There isn't anyone else I would want to face them with," she said as she leaned in and kissed me on the cheek.

I couldn't help but smile as I pulled Amorina close. I leaned in and kissed her lower neck, then rapidly peppered her neck with kisses and ended with a few pecks along her jaw, causing a fit of laughter that was music to my ears. She gently pushed me away and looked into my eyes.

"As I said on Tynan's ship: I'm sorry I didn't believe you earlier. It's … recontextualized times when you've seemed absent or been in a particularly long thinking session. I have a better idea now of some of the things you might've been turning over in that head of yours."

"Thank you, *mi amor*. You and your support and companionship … they mean the world to me. I will never stop fighting for us, to make sure we have the simple life we envision."

Amorina smiled, and suddenly the world seemed brighter.

"Well, you know what I've been dreaming about today?" she asked, her smile becoming coy.

"I don't, but you should absolutely tell me about it. I might be able to make a few dreams come true."

"I dare say you can," Amorina said as she reached out, running her hand down my chest and onto my already hardening cock.

"I've been dreaming about … stroking things," her words matched her actions, and I felt myself becoming fully erect, a small groan escaping my lips.

"What else have you been thinking about?" I gasped, rolling onto my side and running a hand down the side of her body.

"Many things. Rubbing. Grasping. Grabbing. Licking. Kissing. Sucking," she replied, biting her lip suggestively.

"Is that all you've been dreaming about?"

"That was just the foreplay … I was also thinking about penetration. Thrusting. Pounding …"

As the sun set and the stars glittered in the night sky, I left Amorina sleeping peacefully and made my way to the lakeside. I settled on a conveniently placed bench and watched the water's steady ebb and flow, bringing my reflection in and out of focus. As I caught glimpses of myself, it was hard for me to see the farmer, the father, the husband – these identities seemed … absent, somehow.

In its place was a different someone, a person moulded by torture and stress, in a thin body that bore many fresh scars and bruises. But the battle-hardened leader that looked back at me was wrong – this wasn't who I was supposed to be – it wasn't who I wanted to be. It was as if I'd become a caricature of myself, twisted and exaggerated into some grotesque monster.

You see it now, don't you? You see the monster!

As my words echoed through my mind, I felt my skin grow hot and prickly with … shame? Guilt? I couldn't even tell what I was feeling.

"Yes," I whispered in response to my thoughts. "I see the monster."

My mind recalled further moments from that earlier conversation with Tynan. How *do* you destroy a monster without becoming one? The monster looking up at me in the lake water didn't know. How could it? This twisted man with a scrambled brain, definitely not Tynan but not quite Raith either – some sort of hybrid – a personality with elements of both.

When all of this was over – *if* all of this was over – would my family recognise who I was becoming … what I was becoming? This place was stunning, but it was a temporary distraction.

A beautiful wilderness that masks the frightening reality out there.

I looked at the night sky and saw the orbital laser passing by. I looked past it at the distant stars that shimmered and shone. Somewhere out there, maybe still devouring Akka or maybe on its way to Gaia, was the Horror – that mechanical monstrosity that threatened humanity's very survival. The personal threat, of course, was that it would take a monster to defeat a monster.

I stood up and spread my arms, offering myself to the universe. "Here I am – here's a monster I prepared earlier," I shouted as if I were some dish on a cooking show. "A few years in a pressure cooker of torment and pain, and you too can have your very own monster, ready to fight the battles you cannot, a man who can make the impossible choices no one else wants to!"

The night sky looked down silently, as unaware of me as I was of microbes beneath my feet. I slumped back down onto the bench, weighed down by a feeling of isolation and hopelessness. If I had a choice, I'd just stay here with Amorina … forever. I'd bring the rest of the family out, and we'd live out our days in peace.

The fleet would defeat the Horror, and Tynan would be imprisoned – and I wouldn't have to deal with any of it. But every fibre of my being knew that couldn't come to pass; my fate was interwoven with Tynan's. There was no escaping any of this while he was alive and well.

"Why does it have to be me?" I whispered. "Why is the champion required to fight the approaching menace *me*?"

I was tired of the politics, the existential threats, and the power struggles between the wolves within. Couldn't one of them surely win by now? Let me retire to the fields of Gaia and farm them with my family for the rest of my life, seeing out my days in a peaceful and harmonious existence.

Is that too much to ask, Universe?

Chapter 11
The Battle for Gaia – Part 1

2160, Common Era – Planet Gaia, Outer Rim, the Republic of Humanity

With each passing day, I felt my anxiety ease, and the more I relaxed, the more my body healed. Freed from the weight of responsibility and duty, and released from the grasp of fear and uncertainty, I could finally experience a period of unbroken serenity.

We immersed ourselves in the beauty of nature, living au naturel, swimming in the lake, sunbathing on the deck, and rolling about on the lawn – equally engrossed by the feeling of the grass and each other's bare skin.

The cabin was well stocked with healthy, nutritious food, and in combination with the fresh air and the clean water, I was gaining weight and putting on muscle – reclaiming the strength that had been stolen from me.

Our sense of time distorted as well; with no demands on our time, we were free to do as we pleased. The days felt like they were never-ending, yet as each one drew to a close, they felt like they had gone by too quickly.

"Hey, Bitsy – what's the date today?" I asked, glancing at the Arachnobot on the bedside table.

Bitsy tilted its abdomen towards me as the answer displayed, *Today is Monday, the 27th of October, 2160.*

It's the 27th already?

I shook my head, wondering where the last three weeks had gone. I glanced to my right and gazed at Amorina's naked form, my brain still happily flooded with oxytocin, endorphins, and dopamine.

We had unknowingly formed a habit of doing similar things every day, and today would be no exception; we'd made love just as the sun was rising, and soon we'd leisurely enjoy breakfast before taking a dip in the lake. We'd have a few hours to ourselves to read or sunbathe or nap, then indulge in another passionate duet, closely followed by lunch. A walk through the bush and another nap would round out the afternoon; then it'd be time for dinner, and the day would end with a last dance for dessert.

Now, as I lay in post-coital euphoria, all I wanted to do was hit the universe's pause button. If I could stay here in this moment with Amorina forever … I'd be good with that. Soaring on a natural high, surrounded by beautiful wilderness, with a gorgeous naked woman beside me. There was no danger and no stress, no worry or doubt – only peace and bliss, elation and harmony.

Could I ever hope for a better moment than this?

I rolled onto my side and carefully shuffled over until I was spooning Amorina. I wrapped my arm around her, enjoying the warmth radiating from her skin and the rhythmic rise and fall of her chest. I propped my head up on my right arm and looked down at her face, admiring how relaxed she looked. There was movement behind her closed eyes – perhaps she was dreaming.

"Question is, what is it you are dreaming about?" I whispered as I watched her eyes move. "Is it me you're seeing?"

A smile flashed across Amorina's face, and I wondered where she was in her imagination. Was it here? Or was it somewhere else? Not that it mattered either way – her joy was my joy. I closed my eyes and lay back down, listening to the sound of her breathing and feeling her heart beating.

"Truly, this is a sweet surrender," I mumbled to myself.

I suddenly winced as I felt the metallic points of Bitsy's feet digging into my skin as the Arachnobot climbed onto my side.

"Bitsy – what are you do –" I stopped when I saw the message scrolling across Bitsy's screen.

Something is coming.

I let go of Amorina and offered my hand to Bitsy, who promptly climbed onto it, and then I sat up.

"What's coming?"

A ship.

Suddenly, there it was – a faint hum in the distance. A familiar sound if you knew what you were hearing – ship engines. The noise was rapidly growing louder.

It's moving with urgency.

I knew there was probably only one reason a ship would be approaching quickly.

The Horror ... it's on the move again.

I looked down at Amorina.

"I'm sorry, my dear," I said as I gently shook her shoulder.

She stirred and looked up at me. "Uh?"

"I think our time here is at its end. We need to get ready to leave."

She didn't say anything, but her expression said it all: sadness that our retreat was over and fear of what was coming. She nodded, swung her legs over the side of the bed and began finding her clothes. I did the same, and as I pulled on a pair of pants, the ship roared overhead, setting itself down on the lawn. As Republic soldiers climbed out of the ship and headed towards the cabin, I knew my suspicions were true.

"Let's do this."

The soldiers were extremely tight-lipped, refusing to explain the circumstances behind our pickup. The pilot was pushing the ship, working it hard to get us to our next destination as quickly as possible, which, as it turned out, was the farm. As the ship touched down, Emma, Adanna, Winona, and Father stepped out of the house, staring at the ship in confusion.

No doubt rudely awoken from a deep sleep.

Amorina and I stepped out of the ship when a soldier placed a hand on my chest.

"Not you, sir, only your missus."

I looked past the soldier at Amorina.

"It's all right," she said with a reassuring nod. "Do what you need to do."

I sighed. "Okay. Give my love to the girls and Father."

"I will."

I watched Amorina climb out and run over to the rest of the family. The ship lifted off as soon as she was clear, and I watched their sleepy, confused faces grow distant as we raced away.

"Okay – now, can you tell me what the hell is going on?"

"Yes, sir. Apologies for the silence; we were under strict orders that this information was for your ears only."

With a circular wave of my hand, I gestured for them to cut to the chase and give me the details.

"Sir," the soldier said, acknowledging the motion. "About five hours ago, the surveillance satellites captured the Horror moving away from Akka.

The transmission feed from the first satellite ends shortly after that, and the second satellite captures the first's destruction before going dark itself."

I nodded solemnly.

The clock is ticking now. Time is running out.

"The Horror is on its way," I muttered quietly.

"Yes, sir."

"Don't call me sir."

"Yes, si – ah ... Governor?"

I shook my head. "Just call me Raith."

"Of course, Raith."

I glanced out of the ship, watching the scenery flash by below us.

"Where are we going now, then?"

"The GBDOC," the soldier replied.

I raised an eyebrow. "The what now?"

"The GBD – oh, right. The Ground Based Defensive Operations Centre."

I acknowledged the soldier's explanation with a nod, then looked away and rolled my eyes.

I think the Republic loves their acronyms a little too much.

In the distance, I could now see a collection of tents, satellite dishes, and radio antennae. As we got closer, I could see people running about everywhere – from this tent to that tent, from this dish to that antenna. Ships were coming and going, dropping people off and picking people up.

"We're going to need to make this drop off quick, Raith," the soldier said as the ship descended towards a landing zone.

"Got it."

The ship jolted as it landed, and I leapt out, dashing away to give the ship enough space to take off again, which it promptly did. I turned and watched the ship soar away.

"Welcome to GBDOC, Governor Raith."

I jumped and spun around to see a Republic officer standing behind me.

"President Knox is waiting for you," they said, giving me no time to respond. "Follow me, please."

"Yep, okay."

The officer led me this way and that through the maze of tents, and I marvelled at what they had put together. With only the supplies available onboard the Republic fleet ships, the crew constructed an impromptu setup on short notice – they'd utilised the last four weeks well, doing their best to anticipate what this operations centre would need to manage.

I wondered whether the Empire's version of this would look anything like this if the same kind of response was expected from them. Try as I might, I just couldn't see it.

"Just in here, sir," the officer said, pulling back the flap of a tent.

"Thank you," I replied, stepping inside.

Within the tent, a large war table occupied the centre of the room, with numerous Republic officers gathered around it.

"Ah, Raith – you've finally joined us. Enjoy your little jaunt in the hills, did you?" Knox asked sourly, barely looking up from the war table as I entered.

"Yes, I did, Madam President. You should try it sometime – it might make you a bit more relaxed."

I pretended to be oblivious to the intense, burning stare that Knox directed my way.

"Anyway," she said, clearing her throat. "This is a real-time view of Gaia, the orbital defence laser, and all the Republic and Empire ships, respectively," she said, pointing to the different parts of a hologram in the middle of the war table.

"Where is Tynan?" I asked, noticing the lack of any Empire presence within the room.

"I invited the Empire to have a presence here, but they didn't even have the curtsy to refuse the request," Knox replied dismissively.

"I see," I said, as I felt a shiver run down my spine.

If Tynan isn't here, preparing for the Horror's arrival, then where is he and what is he doing?

"Now, as I was saying, these are the positions of our defensive forces. We've evacuated roughly sixty percent of the civilians and tasked all our smaller vessels and commandeered any nearby private and commercial vessels to help evacuate the remaining citizens. They're all being taken to Machina Station. Other vessels are taking them onward from there to Earth."

"How long do you think we need to evac the last forty percent?"

"Ideally, as much time as possible ... realistically, as much time as we can get."

I nodded. It was better than Akka, but it still wasn't great. If the Horror turned up now, were we even capable of holding it off for long enough to enable those other citizens' safe passage away from the coming destruction?

"Okay, it seems like we're pretty ready here – what communication has there been with Tynan regarding the readiness of their shi –"

Suddenly, the earth lurched beneath us, and we were all thrown to the ground – objects falling all around and on us. Before we could get our heads around what had happened and gain our footing, the earth began to shake so violently that it was impossible to stand back up. People began screaming, both outside and inside the tent, and we scrambled for cover under the war table, holding on tightly to anything we could reach. My hands were shaking as I held onto the table leg, my heart pounding with fear and bewilderment at the situation.

Everyone stared, terrified, at Knox, waiting for her direction.

"What is happening?" I shouted over the rumble of the earth.

"I don't fucking know!" Knox shouted back at me.

I looked over the edge of the table at the hologram, which was in the process of updating. As the latest information was rendered in the air, my stomach dropped: the Horror was here, displayed in all its terrifying might, looming over everything – its girth so huge that it stretched beyond the hologram's projection limit. As the quaking finally subsided, reducing to a constant background tremor, everyone slowly rose to their feet and gathered around the table. A quick glance around the room showed that no one in here was severely injured – but others had been less fortunate from the continued screams coming from outside. The projection of Gaia updated again and now showed volcanic plumes rising into the air from multiple locations around the planet.

"What the fuck just happened?"

Knox shook her head. "I can't say for sure, but the only thing that comes to mind is the theoretical effects of a gravitational quake – that thing must have quite the gravity, and for it to just drop out of warp beside the planet ... well, we all just felt what that feels like."

A stronger quake rolled through the ground beneath us, and the hologram showed a new volcanic eruption bursting forth from Gaia's surface.

"And so it begins," I mumbled as I took in the unfolding events.

This was different to Akka; the Horror's approach there had been slow and cautious, now it was coming at Gaia with speed and confidence.

That was a problem because all the Republic's strategy would've been built off the intel I provided based on how the Horror had attacked Akka.

I glanced at Knox, and she nodded. I watched as she took a second to compose herself, and then she was in her presidential mindset. "Everyone, you know the plan, you know your duty. The Horror is coming at us differently, but the plan remains unchanged. Let's get out there and show that thing what we're capable of – move out!"

The officers responded immediately, running out of the tent with predetermined plans to enact. I ran out of the tent with them, turning to the right as I exited.

"Raith, you're with me!" Knox yelled behind me.

"But I need to get my family!" I said, turning around to face her.

"Don't worry about them – I've already instructed a dropship to evacuate them."

I stopped, trying to decide what I should do – did I trust what Knox was saying?

"Look, I get it," Knox said. "We've a rocky history, relationships aren't exactly on the best terms right now, etc. But when the Republic says it will do something, that thing will be done! Trust me, someone is on the way to them as we speak – and I will personally check that they've safely been evacuated."

I hesitated. I wanted to trust Knox, but I also wanted to see that my family was safe with my own eyes.

"Come on! We need to go now!"

"Okay, fine!" I snapped, running over towards her. "But I want that confirmation that my family is safe!"

"You'll have it!"

I followed Knox as she led me out of the GBDOC and into an awaiting dropship.

As soon as the vessel's exterior doors were closed, it took off, rocketing towards space before I'd even had a chance to sit down. I watched a Republic officer speak to Knox, showing her things on a tablet.

"What's happening?" I asked.

"Because the Horror dropped out of warp so much closer to Gaia than it did to Akka – it's already pulling Gaia away from its normal orbit."

"What can we do about that?"

"Right now? Fuck all! The best thing we can do for Gaia now is to get rid of the Horror as soon as possible and try to minimize the damage caused by its presence in the system."

"And what about my family?"

"Let me check."

I watched as Knox summoned the previous officer and spoke to him again. He quickly began tapping away at his tablet.

"It's even better than I told you before," she stated after he had re-laid his findings. "Two dropships ended up going to your farm and picked all of your family up. They're safely flying away from the planet as we speak!"

I sighed in relief, feeling my shoulders drop and some of the tension leave my body. They were safe. They were heading for safety. Regardless of how today turned out, I knew they would be okay.

"Thank you, Knox. This means the world to me!"

"No worries, Raith," Knox said, looking out the dropship window. "We're almost at my capital ship, so I need you to focus now, okay? It's going to take all our attention to win this fight!"

"Understood!"

It was my turn to glance out the window now, watching as Knox's ship grew closer and closer, its name proudly emblazoned on its side – the ROHS Celestial.

I inhaled and tried to focus – Knox was right. This was going to take all our concentration!

❦

Minutes later, the dropship had docked, and we'd been rushed to the bridge and debriefed, bringing us up to speed on the latest intel; the Republic and Empire ships had moved forward, placing themselves between the Horror and Gaia, and the monstrosity itself had ceased its movement, much to the concern of the fleet. One question seemed to permeate everyone's minds: What will this thing do next?

"What's your plan, Knox?" I asked when the officers finished passing on their information.

"First and foremost, we're going to be reactionary – if that thing does something, we must be ready to respond swiftly and flexibly. If it doesn't give us anything to react to, we're going to synchronize all our ships and fire a simultaneous, multi-weapon volley. If we can punch a hole in its exterior, we'll fire a blast of the orbital defence laser into its internals!"

I nodded – that seemed to be a solid plan – now I just hoped it worked.

"Raith? What's going on?"

I spun around to find Amorina and Emma standing in the entranceway to the bridge.

"What are you doing here?" I exclaimed, rushing to them. I ran my eyes over them both, checking they were okay. A feeling of dread flooded my body with a shudder, and my stomach dropped.

"I don't know!" Amorina angrily retorted, her gaze fixed on me as if I had just said something foolish. "Two dropships arrived to evacuate us, and they split us between them. I watched the other one take your parents, Adanna, and Winona towards one of the evac ships, but our one dropped us off here?"

I turned towards Knox. "Did you know about this?"

"No, I didn't – they should've gone to the evac ship with all the other civilians!"

"Well, we have to get them to an evac ship!"

Knox shook her head. "There's no time. They're here now. They'll have to stay here."

"We're about to fly into combat! This is the opposite of keeping my family safe!"

Knox held up her hand and waved a crew member over. "Private Ivan, please escort these ladies to the engineering core. See that they are comfortable and secure, please."

"Yes, Madam President!" Private Ivan replied, then turned towards the girls.

"How is that going to help?" I demanded. "Why the engineering core?"

"It's centred in the ship's superstructure – it's one of the ship's strongest and safest areas."

I glanced at Amorina, whose single nod said so much. *That will have to do for now.*

I turned to Knox again and nodded. "Thank you."

"Yeah, don't sweat it," Knox said as she pointed at a console.

"Can I get you over here on comms please? We need to synchronize the fleet."

I nodded, watching as Amorina and Emma followed the private out first, then turned towards the desired console.

"Of course," I replied, heading over to the station.

I sat down and quickly got acquainted with the controls, and then I glanced over my shoulder. "Who should I contact first?"

"Why don't you liaise with the Empire vessels? You seem to be quite good at the role of mediator."

Figures.

"On it!"

I put on the wireless headset and swiftly configured a communications channel. I began hailing the Chupacabra, and after a few moments, Tynan accepted the channel, his voice coming through the headset.

"What?" he barked curtly.

"This is Raith calling from the ROHS Celestial."

There was a pause on Tynan's end – a hesitation, or a contemplation perhaps, on how to respond.

"As I said ... what?" came his reply, more calculated this time.

"We're establishing communications with all ships in the fleet so that we can synchronise against the Horror. The Republic ships do this automatically, but since your fleet is not part of the Republic, it needs to be done manually."

There was another pause.

"Whatever. I make no apologies for not being fully compatible with inferior technology."

"If you say so. The important thing is that the Empire vessels are ready to receive orders."

"Yeah, got it. Give me an order when there is one, but otherwise, shut up."

"Gotcha," I said, putting the call on mute.

I turned towards Knox and gave her a thumbs up. She nodded in acknowledgement and continued with her work – what appeared to be monitoring the statuses of all the ships.

The fleet was already positioned between the Horror and Gaia, so it was just a matter of powering up weapons stations, allowing the crew to ready battle stations. As the ship icons on Knox's screen slowly turned from red to green, I assumed she would issue the first order once each ship had reported in as ready.

I turned back to my console and unmuted the call.

"Is the Chupacabra, the …"

"The Chupacabra, the Piranha, and the Moray."

"Ah, thanks. Are they battle-ready?"

There was a pause.

Not a hard question, Tynan. Are they battle-ready or not?

"Yes, yes, they are," finally came his reply.

"Great. Thanks."

I turned to face Knox again and noticed that most of the ship's icons were now green. Knox caught my gaze and looked over at me.

"Are the Empire ships ready?" she asked.

"Yes, they are."

"Thanks."

I watched Knox interact with her console, and then three more ship icons turned green. As the last few icons changed over, Knox signalled her comms officer, who was sitting at the console in front of me. The officer promptly turned around to face me.

"I'm going to open a channel to the Republic fleet and isolate Knox's audio for the broadcast – can you copy what I do to the Empire fleet?"

"Sure thing,"

"Thanks!"

The comms officer began tapping away at their console, and I tried to keep pace – as far as I could tell, I more or less replicated the process.

With a quick check from the comms officer, I gave Knox a thumbs up. She stood, straightened her uniform, and began her speech.

"This is Kylie Knox, President of the Republic of Humanity. The situation is clear, the enemy obvious, and the stakes have never been higher – either we end the Horror now, or there will be no humanity left to make a second attempt."

She paused, allowing time for her message to be transmitted and received.

"Therefore, we must act swiftly and in unison, focusing our firepower on the same portion of the Horror's exterior – you should receive the coordinates now."

A pop-up appeared on my console, displaying a set of coordinates, and I noticed the same thing had appeared on the comms officer's screen. As he sent the coordinates to the Republic fleet, I mimicked his actions as I had before.

"On my mark, all vessels are to move forward into a clustered attack formation, then on my second mark, commence fire. When we punch a hole in the Horror's exterior, we'll fire the orbital defence laser into the newly created opening. We're assuming that the Horror will repair the exterior hole, so the fleet will rinse and repeat the manoeuvre until we have destroyed it."

Knox paused again, allowing her plan to be heard and understood.

"Now, it's important that we maintain a tight formation so that our point defence systems are most effective, as based on our understanding of –"

"Madam President – there's movement on the Horror's right flank!" interrupted the first officer.

A few people immediately moved closer to the bridge's windows, whilst others focused on the various screens around the bridge as a video feed of the Horror was brought up. The footage showed the swarm dispersing from the right side of the Horror, surging away from it like a great tentacle, arced through space, heading towards the fleet's left flank where the Empire's ships were.

"Tynan, the swarm is heading right towards you and your ships!" I yelled into the Empire communications channel.

"Ya think?" Tynan fired back. "We're seeing what you're seeing!"

I looked up at the nearest screen and watched helplessly as the swarm engulfed the Empire's ships. Explosions and screams rang out in my headset, and the line went dead. On-screen, the swarm punched holes through the vessels, which quickly lost power and then listed, seemingly easily pushed around by the enemy cloud that enveloped them. My heart fluttered at the thought that Tynan had gone down with his ships, but then my stomach dropped as I remembered that Zavis and Ichirō were onboard those ships, too.

"All vessels, move forward into formation now!" Knox ordered.

The Republic fleet responded immediately, moving forward and closer together.

"What about the crew on the Empire ships?" I shouted, standing up and facing Knox.

"If we stop to help them now, we risk the entire fleet! Now is our chance to strike!" The president retorted.

"Hundreds of people are on those ships, including my friend and son!"

Knox smirked and quietly said, "Well, maybe it's good riddance. They got what they had coming to them."

I clenched my fists. "You're just as bad as the Empire! The people onboard those ships are just as deserving of your support and aid as any crew member aboard a Republic ship!"

Knox turned towards me; her face twisted in rage. "Don't you dare demean me on the bridge of my ship, Raith! I will not apologise for taking joy in seeing the Republic's enemies destroyed by circumstance, nor will I apologise for giving orders that best serve the Republic and its people. And before you argue further, remember that nobody here has forgotten who you are ... traitor!" Her last word was said in a low growl.

I felt my chest tighten painfully; her comment felt like she had stabbed me with a knife. But she wasn't done yet.

"Even though you may technically be a different person, you will always be Tynan, your hands will always be bloody, and your past actions will always stain your soul. Now get off my fucking bridge!"

My face felt hot and prickly, my shame burning brightly in my cheeks. Tears burned in my eyes then tears streaked down my face. Knox's words weren't only a low blow; they were cruel, targeted, malicious words intended to do one thing – hurt me – and it had worked. She'd awakened a bubbling anger within me – an anger quickly building up pressure, turning into a fiery rage.

"You're right," I hissed. "I *was* Tynan. And now, I *am* Raith. Believe me when I say that I am painfully aware of my stained soul each and every day!" I paused, trying to steady my shaking hands as I pointed at Knox. "But at least I have a better moral standing than you! Because there was at least one thing the Empire had right: a united humanity is stronger than a divided humanity ... and all you have just done is split us apart!"

As I turned and walked out of the bridge, my departure was accompanied by a sense of loss. Zavis and Ichirō, even if they had survived the initial attack, they would be dead by now, at the mercy of the vacuum that permeated those crippled ships.

Damn you Knox!

❈ ❈ ❈

A few minutes later, I was stalking through the halls, feeling the Celestial shake beneath my feet as it participated in the first volley against the Horror.

I was taking deep, long breaths, slowly calming the simmering rage within, and as the anger subsided, I noticed another feeling within me: unease.

Why was I feeling uneasy? Was it the loss of the Empire's ships and crew? I mean, sure, that had been … unexpected. It had been shocking, but did I feel uneasy because of it? Not really. The Republic portion of the fleet was much bigger, had more firepower, and was arranged in a tighter formation that could better defend itself. Was I uneasy because of Knox's personal attack? Again, no, not really. Sure, her words hurt, but they'd prompted a response of anger, not unease. I also noticed that the more I walked, the greater this feeling became. I noticed an auxiliary command room up ahead and quickly made my way over to it. As I stepped inside, I startled the crew within.

"Governor Raith. We weren't expecting you," one of the crew said, quickly standing and facing me.

I scanned the woman's uniform, paying attention to her chest badge that indicated her rank and name. "Don't worry, Lieutenant Nye – I wasn't expecting me either."

Lieutenant Nye smiled briefly but quickly restored her professional neutral face. "Was there something I could help you with, sir?"

"Just to ask for your permission to sit in here and observe?"

"Granted, sir, absolutely."

"Thank you, Lieutenant. And please, just call me Raith."

"Of course, si – Raith."

The lieutenant returned to her seat, and I made my way over to a vacant console, sitting before it and pulling up an external view.

The last traces of the first attack were fading away, revealing a deep gash in the Horror's surface – although still not deep enough to break through to whatever was underneath, it was certainly a solid strike.

I watched as the Horror now retaliated, several portions of its surface dissolving into swarms, and noticed that feeling of unease again.

What am I missing?

I leaned closer to the monitor, watching the unfolding action more closely. The metallic clouds had quickly crossed the distance between the Horror and the fleet and were now plunging into several Republic ships, easily tearing them apart and ripping them into multiple pieces.

The sense of unease slammed into me now, and I had a feeling as to why. I stopped the live feed and pulled up the footage from the Horror's first strike against the Empire ships. I watched the formation of the swarm, which looked exactly like what I'd just witnessed, but one key element was missing: the surface of the Horror wasn't changing. The swarm had just materialised from nowhere.

I fast-forwarded the footage – the swarm appeared to punch a few holes in the Empire ships, causing complete loss of power – but I had literally just seen the actual swarm attack Republic ships, shredding them from end to end.

I switched back to a live camera feed and pointed it at the Empire ships. They were still sitting there, surrounded by the "swarm", unpowered and floating randomly. Suddenly, I had a terrible hunch. I leapt out of my seat and ran for the exit.

Leaving the auxiliary command room, I sprinted down the hallways, heading for the ship's rear, skimming the signage as I ran past until I found the room I was looking for – a rear-facing observation deck.

I charged into the room, racing to the far end of it, and placed my hands on the windows as I started scanning the space behind the fleet.

I could see where the Empire ships were supposed to be, their floating carcasses an eerie sight, still surrounded by a swarm. Now I searched the darkness for where the ships actually were. At first, I couldn't see anything, and I briefly entertained the idea that I was wrong. Then I saw it – a dark outline, barely visible against the black void of space. And once I saw one, I could spot the other two: one ship to the left of the Republic fleet, one to the right, and one centred. On one hand, Zavis and Ichirō were alive, but on the other hand, so was Tynan.

"Damn you, Tynan," I muttered.

The truth was slowly sinking in; a painful, embarrassing truth that we … that I had been played. I could've guessed what would happen next, but I didn't need to as a light appeared beneath each of the Empire vessels. Moments later, Firecracker warheads moved away from the ships.

I could just imagine Tynan standing opposite me on the bridge of the Chupacabra, watching the unfolding scene as I was. I could picture his face ... my face, looking on coldly; his dark, unfeeling eyes watching the warheads streak towards the Republic fleet, waiting for them to detonate – for the chaos to erupt. His pursed lips would soften and twist into a smirk. He enjoyed the death and destruction he was unleashing; he liked the pain and the cessation of life he was about to create – this was a source of pleasure.

This was humiliation and pain for me: embarrassment that I hadn't anticipated Tynan's plans and anguish that I couldn't stop it.

I was powerless – there was no time to warn anyone, and even if there was, even if I could run all the way back to the bridge and notify the entire fleet of the threat coming up behind them, there wouldn't be any time to manoeuvre out of harm's way. I knew how destructive Firecrackers could be, although the fleets rear profile was being attacked, not its side profile, and whilst I didn't know what difference that would make, at best the fleet was still going to be crippled, and at worst destroyed. A wave of fear gripped me as I thought of Amorina and Emma huddled in the engineering core. Would they be safe there? I didn't know, but I hoped that the ship's superstructure was as strong and as safe as Knox had claimed it was.

This wasn't just an attack on the Republic fleet, though. It was a personal attack on me, on my family, and Tynan knew it. Just the thought of Tynan looking down on the chaos that was about to unfold was infuriating, and I yelled at the window as if that would help.

"Damn you, Tynan! You goddamn son of a bitch!"

I knew yelling like this was pointless, but it provided some comfort to think that Tynan could somehow hear my screams and know of my sheer displeasure.

"You fucking coward! You backstabbing arsehole!"

I felt the Celestial shake beneath me and realised that the Republic fleet had fired another volley of ammunition at the Horror, and I could see the orbital defence laser charging up in the skies above Gaia. But I knew they'd never get to see the fruit of their labours, for they'd be destroyed from behind before then. Another realisation jolted through my mind – I was standing at the back of the ship!

Chapter 12
The Battle for Gaia – Part 2

2160, Common Era – Planet Gaia, Outer Rim, the Republic of Humanity

The initial detonation of the three warheads resulted in a burst of light, spreading their payload out.

"Motherfucker!" I screamed out a final obscenity as the intense light overwhelmed me.

I whirled around, my heart thumping, and careened forward. My vision was still white and overexposed, leaving me to guess how much ground I'd covered as I stumbled towards the back of the observation deck. I imagined the confusion spreading across the fleet as the crews examined their sensors in bewilderment as light radiated from behind them.

I hit the wall at the end of the observation deck and was sent tumbling to the floor. I felt a dull ache in my head, but between the rush of adrenaline and my hazy vision, I couldn't tell what was causing my pain. I rolled over onto my knees, fighting the panic rising in me, frantically running my hands along the wall, searching for the door controls. My heart thumped faster, and my breath came in quick gasps – I knew time was running out. Every second counted if I was going to survive the coming destruction.

I blinked hard until I could make out the blurry square panel with lights.

That must be the door control!

I hit what I thought was the right button, but nothing happened. I pressed another button, but again, no response.

"Come on!" I hissed as I glanced behind me, now punching the buttons.

I could see the cloud of projectiles tumbling towards the fleet. There was a flash above Gaia, and then a beam of blue light streaked across space, passing underneath the fleet, presumably targeting a hole successfully blown in the Horror's exterior.

The door hissed open, and I tumbled into the hallway. I scurried forward on my hands and knees and then pushed myself off the ground and rushed over to the nearest in-wall emergency unit. As I pulled open the hatch to the unit, there was a flash of light to my left – the Firecracker's secondary detonations had begun. I rummaged through the emergency unit until I found what I was looking for – a Rapid Autonomously Deploying Life Support Suit, or RADLSS for short. I grabbed the RADLSS and unfolded it into two interlinked pieces: a full-face respirator and a chest unit. I placed the mask on my face and the unit on my chest, then pressed the activation button. Immediately, I felt cool fresh air inside the respirator, and a gel spread rapidly from the chest unit.

I turned away from the observation deck and sprinted down the hallway, the gel from the RADLSS almost having covered my entire body now. As I ran, I desperately tried to remember the decompression survival training I'd received a long time ago. I was already working towards step 1 – get as far away as possible from the environment breech.

What was step two again?

I heard the shattering of glass and the sheering of metal behind me and suddenly remembered step two.

Stick as close to the internal walls as possible.

I dived to the side and grabbed hold of a railing. For a few moments, I felt the air as it rushed past me, evacuating into space through the newly ruptured exterior.

Make your body as small as possible and cover your eyes and ears.

Doing my best to get as close to the wall as I could, I was thankful the RADLSS was managing one of the most essential components of step three for me – covering my eyes and ears. The flow of atmosphere halted abruptly, causing a strange, eerie stillness.

That wasn't so bad …

Shrapnel suddenly filled the air, tearing the ship into pieces around me. There were flashes of light as the ongoing explosions continued, the Firecrackers grenade-like projectiles now exploding within the confines of the ship. The projectiles released from each explosion ripped apart anything they encountered, creating a cascade of debris that collided with everything in their path.

I clung to the railing, my breath coming in shallow gasps as I tried to quell the panic flooding through my body, hoping that I could somehow avoid being hit. The wall beside me shredded apart, obliterating the foundation into which the railing was embedded, sending both me and the railing tumbling through a sea of particulates.

I felt completely disoriented as I whirled around; my stomach lurched as a wave of dizziness and nausea joined my growing sense of panic. The dizzying whirl made my head spin, and all sense of direction was lost. Everywhere I looked, debris was flipping around. The shrapnel had enough velocity to cause harm, but the RADLSS gel absorbed the impacts. Even so, I could feel little pricks of pain all over my body as larger or faster objects penetrated the protective layer.

"Argh!"

Pain radiated throughout my shoulder as something slammed into it. The force of the hit smashed me into a wall and sent shock waves reverberating through me. When my senses finally began to clear, I found myself fastened to the wall.

The impact must've created suction between the gel and the wall.

Now that I was no longer tumbling about, I could look around and try to gain some perspective. I noted my physical condition first; there were points of pain all over my body. It radiated in my arms and legs, all over my torso, and even on my neck and head – no doubt these were all shrapnel impact sites – but everything else seemed to be intact. The worst pain was coming from the back of my right shoulder, but even that was lessening as the RADLSS gel numbed the wound.

I peered to the right and saw a vast expanse of debris, filled with secondary collisions and the occasional explosion, silently erupting into the void. The three Empire ships were still visible in the distance, watching over the carnage they'd created. I peered to my left and saw a semi-intact hallway filled with holes and out of power. I stared into the darkness and saw something was moving towards me.

No, someone!

"Hey!" I shouted, waving my arms. "Over here!"

The figure floated out of the darkness, twisting and turning. I recoiled as its torso spun into view; there was a gaping hole where its chest should be, blown clean through. The body was hit by another piece of shrapnel and its rotation ceased, leaving the wide eyed, blank stare of the dead gazing back at me. I fought a wave of nausea as the body passed by, turning away as they continued their journey on their endless float through space, and then noticed a sign on the wall opposite me; according to it, this was Section R, Deck 9.

Bloody hell!

That meant that the back third of the ship was completely gone, and I'd somehow gone up three decks.

Some movement in my peripheral caught my attention, and I focused on the small, dark, malicious object tumbling into view. A chill ran down my spine – it was a Firecracker projectile.

Maybe this one is a dud? Perhaps it won't detonate?

A wave of dread washed over me as a red glow suddenly appeared in the depressions of the ordinances surface, and I knew right away that it was about to detonate. I raised my arms up in front of me, a defensive action that felt like I was doing something and at the same time was probably entirely pointless.

There was a flash – the detonation – then a wave of light washed over me, the light passing right through my arms, making them almost translucent, illuminating the bones and veins in my arms like some sort of x-ray. Then my left forearm exploded; a projectile ripped straight through the RADLSS and into my flesh and bone.

Time seemed to stand still as I watched, horrified, as chunks of my arm, destroyed flesh, bone, and blood shot in all directions. My arm was destroyed, but the projectile didn't cease there as I watched it continue forward, crossing the short distance between where my forearm had been and where my upper arm still was. Again, the protection of the RADLSS gel was no match for the energy being imparted by the shredded piece of shrapnel, which after the massacre of my lower arm, had now embedded itself in my bicep.

I was aware of the speed of everything, yet it felt so slow in my mind, my brain attempting to give me a chance to react and lessen the destruction – there was no way to avoid this devastation. I stared as the metal bore through the muscle and into the bone, sawing through the triceps and out the other side.

The RADLSS had sealed over the end of my destroyed arm and now the gel was expanding as the remnants of my arm swelled. For an instant, I thought it might hold, that maybe the metals destruction had stopped. But then, like a macabre balloon, the gel burst and more of my arm was flung into the dark vacuum of space.

The projectile slammed into the wall behind me, and suddenly I was dislodged and tumbled around once more thanks to the force of the exploding wall. My body rag-dolled left and right as the cascade of destruction continued to unfold around me. I slammed into the body that had drifted by earlier; the collision bounced me downwards, somewhat stabilising my own trajectory.

Suddenly, my nerves registered the absence of my left limb, and a searing pain erupted throughout my body.

"Aaarrrggghhh!"

It felt like my arm was still there, and this phantom limb was on fire – the burning agony was shooting through my stump into my body. I wanted to do something, *anything*, to stop the pain, but what could I do?

I screamed again, pain and frustration blending together. Then the pain started to subside, and I stared at the stump of my arm; the RADLSS gel had expanded over the wound, sealing it in and restoring suit integrity, as well as applying its numbing agents. I took in a deep breath and focused, releasing the pain as I exhaled. What to do now?

Step 4 of decompression survival training: after the decompression, make your way to a pressurised area a quickly as you can.

I was still drifting through space and now looked around – was there a pressurised area I could make my way to? Up ahead, I saw what I was looking for: the open entrance to a hallway that still had power.

My current flight path was too wide, though – I was going to miss the passageway – but then I noticed a large piece of structural steel floating up ahead.

That's what I need.

As I passed by the beam, I pushed off it with my right arm, altering my course.

Not perfect … but close enough.

I looked ahead and saw I was still slightly off to the side, but at least I was heading in the right general direction. As I drew nearer, I noticed the jagged edges of the entrance – which made sense, considering it had been ripped apart. This was going to hurt. I worked out that my upper half lined up with the hallway, but my legs were going to hit the wall around the opening.

Moments later, my left leg hit a relatively flat area, whilst my right leg hit part of the jagged, ripped edge, the metal spikes driving themselves through the gel and into my thigh.

"Unngghh!" I groaned as a fresh source of pain spread through my body.

The collision bounced my legs back outward, yanking them off the spikes with another burning surge of pain, whilst my upper half continued moving forward, rotating me, and sending me headfirst into the hallway.

At least I'm inside the ship again.

I floated down the hallway, scanning left and right, looking for any nook or cranny that might serve as a safe harbour.

There – a supply closet!

As the closet came into reach, I slammed my fist into the control panel, triggering the door to open. The force of my strike sent me sideways, where I bounced off the opposite wall and tumbled into the closet, hitting the control panel within to close the door behind me.

With my adrenaline wearing off, the shock of the situation was setting in. My entire body ached with a dull, pulsing pain that seemed to grow with each passing second. I felt my head spinning and my eyelids drooping – I assumed my blood pressure was dropping, and my body was urging me to faint, to collapse onto the ground and let my blood flow more easily to my head.

Who am I to resist such urges?

I felt my eyes close, and my body slumped forward as the world faded away.

※ (∨) ⁂

I lost track of time, vaguely aware of the growling of my stomach and the dry ache in my throat as I faded in and out of consciousness. The strength I'd gained back during the weeks in the cabin was seeping away, and I grew weaker by the day. My injuries prevented me from getting up and going to an escape pod or a docked vessel; I knew my situation was dire. I was starving, dehydrated, and cold. Life support still seemed to be on, which was probably the only reason I hadn't been frozen or choked to death already, but if help didn't arrive soon, I would be a dead man. I didn't care about my life, though.

Hell, this world would probably be better off without me in it.

What I did care about was Amorina and Emma. I hoped that they'd survived the Empire's attack, that they'd been escorted to an escape pod and gotten off the ship, or if they were still here, that they were safely contained within the engineering core and would soon be found by rescuers.

There would be rescuers, right?

There had to be. Surely somebody would come and find them.

Suddenly, sparks lit up the darkness at the far end of the supply closet. Something, or someone, was cutting through the metal safety shutters. The sparks continued, and a red glowing circle slowly appeared as the glowing metal shards continued to shoot out and rain down. When the circle was complete, the circular cut-out fell to the floor, the vibrations of its collision with the floor reverberating around the room. An Arachnobot scuttled into the room, followed by beams of light.

Head torches?

Several lights entered the room and walked through the darkness towards me. How long had I been here? Who were these people? Were they people? Did they belong to the Republic or the Empire? I raised my remaining fist, unsure of whether I had to fight these approaching figures.

"Easy there, mate. It'll do you no good startin' a fight. You're with friends, you are. Let us do the rescuing, aye?" said an oddly familiar voice.

"Yo re fry ends?" I asked, my speech barely intelligible. "Re bub like?"

"Of a sorts, mate, of a sorts. Don't you worry; we've got you. You just lie back now, and we'll hav' you back on your feet in no time at all!"

The Arachnobot had now scuttled up onto my lap and jittered about. *Are you okay, Raith?* the text scrawling along its back read.

"Bitsy?"

Yes, it's me.

Huh – maybe I am among friends after all.

\\ \ v / //

I awoke to a bright fluorescent light that filled the room.

I attempted to sit up but was met with a sharp, stinging sensation as my head struck the low ceiling above me, producing a loud, echoing thump.

"Ow!" I cried as I fell back onto the bed.

"Easy there, mate."

I looked to my right and saw a grizzly, older man sitting beside me. It took me a moment, but suddenly his face registered.

"Arty?" I exclaimed.

"In the flesh, mate."

"What are you doing here?"

"Long story short, our mutual acquaintance had the good sense not to disband the Insurgency after the fall of the Empire. Should our enemy ever arise again, we'd 'ave to be ready to rise too."

Our mutual acquaintance? That had to be Zavis, surely.

"Where are we?"

"In the medical bay of the ship we're on. Nothin' special, but good enough to do what we need it to."

"How did you find me?"

"Via your little friend o' course. The jailbreaking your bot got all those years ago saved your life. An Insurgency installed 'n' accessible tracking system – led us right to you, it did."

I chuckled. Wasn't it funny how the choices of the past affected the actions of the present?

The feeling of joy that had filled me was suddenly replaced by unease. "Did you find anyone else on the ship? In any of the ships?"

"I'm sorry mate, we didn't. Yours was the only life sign amongst a whole lotta bodies."

I felt a shiver course through me, and my skin prickled with goosebumps.

"There was ... there was no one else?" I whispered.

Arty slowly shook his head.

My heart dropped as the implication of Arty's confirmation sank in: Amorina and Emma were out there, dead and adrift in space.

They couldn't be dead.

"Where are we? In space, I mean – I know we're on a ship."

"We're still in the Gliese 570 system."

"Show me –" I cut my sentence short as I reached out with my arm, only to realise there was no arm there.

As I stared down at the empty air where an arm should be, the events that took my arm came rushing into my mind. I slowly lifted my head and looked at Arty; his expression softened into a knowing, sympathetic look.

"Yeah ... you're a ... well, you're short an arm. No easy way to say it, mate. On the bright side, though, you've met your weight loss goals for the year."

I would've smiled on any other occasion, but right now, I only wanted to cry, shout, and scream.

"This ship doesn't have the equipment or the parts to set you up with a replacement, but we cleaned it up the best we could. Shaved off the rough edges and applied a trauma kit to seal it up."

I looked down at the metal cap that now enclosed the end of my stump. It wasn't pretty, but it was functional.

"Thanks." With the shock wearing off, my mind returned to its previous priority. "Can you help me up, please? Show me the wreckages."

I needed to see it for myself, to prove that it was real. I couldn't believe it was real. I didn't want to believe it was real.

It can't be real ... it can't be!

Arty reached an arm behind me as I swung my legs out of the recess in the wall where the bed sat.

Every movement hurt, and I winced as my body tried to support its weight.

"Yeah … you're gonna hurt for a while, mate. We fished sixty-one pieces of shrapnel out of your body, plus you got some deep cuts in your leg, and your shoulder was pretty banged up too," Arty explained, listing my injuries. "An' your arm, of course."

"I don't care about my injuries – just take me to a window!"

"Alright, mate."

Arty walked me through the ship, and the further we went, the more it felt like this was all real.

It can't be real.

I had to be hallucinating. This was just some fever dream as I lay dying in the supply closet, my hunger and thirst finally catching up with me.

It can't be real.

Yet with each step, with each painful contraction and expansion of my muscles, it felt real. Arty's arm, wrapped around me, supporting my weight and helping me stand, felt so real.

It can't be real.

It couldn't be real … because the truth would be too much if it were.

We rounded a corner and stepped into a small observation lounge, a large window dead ahead. Gaia was immediately visible in the distance, that beautiful green orb I called home.

But the view wasn't beautiful – it was hell. As I took in the destruction, a numbness spread through my body, and a piercing white noise filled my ears.

"It's real," I whispered as my eyes moistened.

The Horror had moved in on its target, ploughing into the ruined fleet as it had moved closer to Gaia, sending the carcases tumbling off into space, where they were now being dispersed into the orbit of Gaia's trinary star system, forming a great cloud of death and debris.

"Oh god … it's real, all of it is real," I whispered, as the first tear rolled down my cheek.

The Horror had destroyed my home, stripping Gaia of its greenery and now seemed to be sucking up its ocean.

It's real.

My wife was dead. My daughter was dead. Tynan had killed them.

All of this is real.

Their bodies were in a cold orbit, alongside thousands of other murdered people, in a floating grave of shrapnel and debris.

"Nooo!" I screamed, my entire body trembling as tears poured down my face.

My legs buckled beneath me, and my bodyweight, light as it was, was too much for Arty to handle on his own. I dropped to the ground, feeling the impact of the hard floor, but the physical pain didn't register. How could it in comparison to the overwhelming emotion surging through me? My body quaked uncontrollably, and my soul ached as a deluge of grief cascaded through me, wave after wave piercing the core of my being, tearing it apart and leaving me shattered.

"No, no, no, no!" I cried as if my shouts could somehow erase what I was seeing … and somehow bring them back.

My sobs reverberated around the room, and my anguish was the only sound to be heard.

I could see a blurry reflection of Arty in the window, his face set in an expression of helplessness, unable to offer any words of comfort. I looked out the window, past Arty's reflection, at the Horror, its great swarming tendrils tearing apart my home, the only home I've ever known. It was taking away my dream, my farm – the farm I was supposed to grow old on with my family and their families – the farm that would've held my grave. Now, it was all being consumed, gobbled up into the belly of the beast. But for all the Horror had done, it hadn't killed my family.

Tynan did that.

My doppelgänger, my evil twin, my dark self.

He had done this. All of this.

Some part of me knew – he was behind everything. He had taken *everything* from me.

"Where is Tynan?" I asked as the tears stopped falling and my body stopped shaking.

"What?" Arty asked.

"Where … is … Tynan?" I growled.

"I dunno, mate. The Empire wasn't 'ere when we arrived."

I grabbed the windowsill and felt the cool metal against my skin as I pulled myself upwards.

"I will find him … I will make him suffer!"

I was standing upright once more, filled with anger as I looked out at the Horror.

"I mean, sure, but shouldn't we tackle that thing first?"

"That thing is here because of Tynan!" I yelled, turning on Arty. "That thing can go to hell! It's Tynan I want!"

"Yeah, I get that, mate, I do. But Tynan will be there after we get rid of that monster."

"You're not listening," I hissed.

Arty took a step back, his face twisted with concern.

"I don't give a shit about the Horror! Bring me … Tynan!"

Spit flew from my mouth as I issued my command.

"I can't do that. You'd know that if you were yourself. But you aren't right now, mate."

"I am me! This is who I am!"

Arty continued to step backwards, creating a space between him and I.

"I don't think so, Raith. This isn't the you I know."

"Maybe I've changed! Maybe your memory is failing you, old man!"

Arty had now worked his way back to the doorway, standing inside the frame.

"I may be old, but my mind is still sharp – I promise you that, mate."

"I don't care!" I growled. "Obey me! Do as I command! Bring me Tynan!"

"Or what?"

"Or I will find someone who will …"

"Then maybe … maybe you'd best do that then, yeah?"

"Aarrgghh!" I yelled, rushing forward.

Arty stepped aside, and another familiar, towering figure appeared in his place – Doug. "Hello there, laddie," he said, swinging his fist towards me.

I had too much momentum to stop, and there was no avoiding the collision that followed.

I awoke to a pounding headache and opened my eyes to find myself in a dimly lit room.

What happened?

The previous events suddenly flashed through my mind: the disbelief, the grief, the sorrow, and then the pain.

The hot white rage burning through my veins, and the anger I had turned upon Arty, and then Doug's fist swinging towards me. I sat up and slowly looked around the room. It was a tiny room, devoid of any furniture or decoration, and I was the only one in it. It was cold, it was dark, and I was alone.

All alone.

I stood up and stepped over to the door, banging on it as I called out, "Hello?"

Only silence responded to my call.

"Hello? Is anyone out there?"

I felt a growing sense of unease, and I glanced behind me. The room walls felt as if they were closing in around me, restricting my space, trapping me.

"Hello? Please! Don't leave me in here!" My voice cracked as I let out a sob. "Please!"

The air seemed to thicken around me as I gasped, overwhelmed by my loneliness and the constricting space. I felt as though I was trapped in a prison of grief, with no way to run or hide.

"Please!" I cried feebly, tears streaming down my face.

My legs trembled, on the verge of collapse, unable to hold up the weight of my sins. With one last violent shake, they folded beneath me, and I collapsed to the floor.

"Please don't leave me in here!" I pleaded desperately one last time. "Don't leave me on my own!"

The world outside the room remained silent. I turned around, pulled my knees up to my chest, and rested my head on them.

Alone.

I was truly alone. My family was gone; my wife and daughter were dead, my son was standing by the enemy's side, my parents and daughters fleeing from the world-eating monster.

My friends … well, my family were my friends, and the few other people I considered that close, like Zavis, were … well, I did not know where he was. As for the acquaintances who'd come to my aid … I'd turned on them, I'd pushed them away, and now … they were also gone.

Family gone.

I clenched my fist, trying to control the trembling of my limbs.

Friends gone.

The darkness surrounding me seeped into me, snuffing out every ounce of joy and happiness I'd ever felt or would ever feel again.

Home gone.

My sorrow was drowning me, and my anguish was burying me alive.

And the worst part is … it's your fault.

"Stop it," I hissed at my thoughts as if that would stop them.

Your choices summoned the Horror.

"Stop it!" I said more insistently.

Your mercy let the Empire survive.

"Stop it!" I cried, desperate for the train of thought to end.

Your actions killed your family.

"Aaarrrggghhh!"

Chapter 13
A Hail Mary

2160, Common Era – Planet Gaia, Outer Rim, the Republic of Humanity

"Hello there," said a familiar voice.

I looked up to see a hologram flickering to life, and I wiped the tears from my cheeks.

"Zavis?"

The hologram focused and stabilised, and Zavis's kind eyes looked down at me.

"Who else would it be?" the old man replied with a wry smile.

I sniffed to clear my blocked nose. "I … where are you?"

"I'm onboard the Chupacabra, hiding. The search for me has been going on for some time, and I'm not sure how much longer I can remain hidden; I need you to listen to what I have to say, Raith. Can you do that?"

I nodded. "Yes. Yes, I can."

"Good man. Let me start by saying I am so sorry for your loss, my friend."

I furrowed my brow. "How did you know?"

"The others … they told me what happened."

I nodded. Silence filled the room, and I just sat there with Zavis looking over me.

What is he waiting for?

Did he want me to say something? Was he expecting an outpouring of emotion? Was I supposed to confess my sins? Or own up to my actions and apologise for the misdeeds that had led –

"I didn't … I didn't even get to say goodbye," I whispered as fresh tears ran down my face.

"Oh, my friend," Zavis said, with pain in his voice. "I know what that's like … how hard it is to lose someone so suddenly, so … unexpectedly."

I bowed my head, resting it in my right palm. I just wanted to implode – to fold in on myself and blink out of existence because at least the pain would stop.

"They say that the worst day of loving someone … is the day you lose them," Zavis continued. "I can see your despair. It emanates from you, seeping out of you and surrounding you like a depressed aura."

I looked up into Zavis's holographic eyes and saw that an experienced sadness filled them.

"I, too, know what it's like to be wearing those shoes." Zavis's pained expression showed that he remembered it all too well. "The grief and the pain. The desire to blame someone for your losses. And the hopelessness when you realise nothing will ever truly take that pain away."

I hung my head again, remembering my denial – that surely this wasn't true, it wasn't happening. The anger that had followed as I lashed out at the people who were helping me, desperate to blame someone, eager to unleash my rage upon them.

"I lashed out at Arty – I turned on him. I was cruel and demanding … and demeaning," I said as I looked up at Zavis again.

The old man nodded. "You weren't quite yourself for a time – something of a darkness overcame you, as I understand it."

"Yeah," I replied, bowing my head as my cheeks grew hot.

"They understand, you know?"

"How could they?"

"Because almost all of them joined the Insurgency after losing something at the Empire's hands. Mothers and sisters, fathers and brothers, sons and daughters, friends, and lovers – all of them have suffered – that is what united them under the banner of rebellion."

I considered all the raw emotions that were coursing through me, and imagined those feelings running through Arty, Doug, or any of the other Insurgency members.

"I ... I didn't know," I said as I shook my head. "Although ... it makes sense."

"So, believe me when I say an apology will go a long way with them. They've all had to atone for an outburst or two."

I nodded. "I will apologise."

"I know you will."

I looked up into Zavis's face again, his kind eyes gazing upon me knowingly.

"Now, I know there's no right or wrong way to grieve, and I, of all people, want to be the last person to tell you how to mourn, but I must ask you to postpone your grief."

"I've done enough," I muttered. "There's nothing left to fight for."

"I'd say your parents, Adanna, and Winona would disagree with that statement – they are all on their way to Machina Station."

"How do you know that?" I asked with a slightly accusatory tone in my voice.

"Tynan may have kept me captive but that didn't stop me keeping a watchful eye over you and your family. I was watching your farm from the Chupacabra earlier and saw the two dropships land. I watched them split your family between the vessels. One flew to the evacuation ships, the other flew to the Celestial. Why that happened, I do not know. But I know who was on which shuttle."

I nodded. That made sense, and it touched me that Zavis had been keeping an eye on my family, even from the relative captivity onboard the Empire ship.

"They aren't out of danger yet. Do they not deserve to be fought for? And what of Ichirō? He's fallen, but he is not yet irredeemable. They still need their father and their son. So don't give up, my old friend, for their sakes, if not for your own!"

I felt a flicker of hope rekindle inside me, and I nodded. "I'll try,"

"Good man."

"What do you need me to do? What can I possibly do? The Republic is defenceless! The Empire and the Horror outgun us. We threw everything we had at it and achieved what – we opened a hole in it for thirty seconds?"

"I know you think we did all that and only got a drop of metaphorical blood out of it, but I'll tell you what I think," Zavis replied with an optimistic smile. "We made it bleed. That might not be much, but it shows us it is not invulnerable. We can harm it. We can break it. We can kill it."

"That's all good and well, but as I said, we've nothing left to throw at it." I waved my arm in frustration.

"Maybe it's not a case of throwing something at it now ..."

I looked up at Zavis's hologram and swore I could see a twinkle in the old man's eye.

What are you planning?

"Maybe it's a matter of distracting it for long enough that we can build bigger, stronger rocks to throw," he finished, a knowing grin spreading across his face.

"Where does Tynan fit into this?"

"I have a plan for Tynan, too. In fact, maybe the plans for the Horror and Tynan are one and the same."

I raised an eyebrow. "You have a plan that can take them both out?"

"I hope so … but I won't lie. It's a long shot. But I have faith – in you, in the Insurgency, in the fact that evil cannot win – it cannot be allowed to win. And for it not to succeed, that must mean that *we* succeed."

I felt my tiny spark of hope grow, and my heart beat a little stronger. Maybe this old man was on to something after all.

"Okay … you've bought me some hope. Now, how about you tell me this plan of yours?"

Zavis smiled.

"Thank you, my friend. Thank you for believing in me. Why don't you rejoin the others in the dining room, and we'll get some plans in motion, aye?"

The door slid open behind me, and I got to my feet.

"That sounds like a plan."

Zavis smiled again. "See you shortly, then!"

❊❊❊

The doors to the dining hall opened, and I entered the room where two dozen Insurgency members were waiting. Many an eye lingered on my stump as I walked into the centre of the hall, and they formed a circle around me. Zavis's hologram flickered into life in the middle of the room.

"Hello, everybody!" Zavis said.

As the gathered crowd said hello to Zavis, Arty stepped forward and offered me a worn and weathered hand. When I looked at him, I saw his expression was benign with no trace of ill will. I searched his face for any sign of a grudge, and all I found was understanding and compassion.

"I'm sorry," I said, as tears filled my eyes.

"I know you are, mate. It's a sad truth, but the fact of the matter is that you are not alone in your pain. None of us are … really very good at talkin' about it, but it's there, inside us."

I nodded and took a hold of Arty's hand, and with a solid tug, he pulled me close and embraced me. Then he let go and stepped back into the crowd, and I joined him, standing shoulder to shoulder with my brothers and sisters of the Insurgency.

"The floor is yours, Zavis," I said.

"Thank you, Raith. And thank you, ladies and gentlemen, for answering my call. I'm sure you're all aware by now that the Empire has been resurrected and its emperor reborn. But the bad news doesn't end there, I'm afraid. A great, technological monster that we've taken to calling 'the Horror' has attacked and destroyed the colonies of Akka and Gaia. Both forces are working against us, although thankfully not working together."

I glanced around the room. These people were afraid. They weren't fools; they knew the odds were stacked against them, but they still had hope shining in their eyes. They had good cause to believe Zavis – he was the architect of the downfall of the first Empire. And they were all listening, waiting for him to tell them how they would bring about the downfall of the second.

"So, we have two problems, two dilemmas in need of solving. Double the trouble, you might say. But the only thing two enemies means is that twice as many opponents will fall before us."

The crowd murmured in agreement.

"Let's start with the Horror. Our technology is potentially strong enough to destroy it, if only we had enough weapons to utilise against it.

But we don't have enough, nor do we have the fleets to deliver those munitions against our foe."

A concerned whisper moved through the crowd.

"Our advantage is that we have knowledge. I believe this machine works in a very particular way – it detects the theta waves emitted by living things. This is how it finds worlds to destroy. Now I know this will sound familiar to you all because, of course, the mass conversion device also emitted theta waves."

"An de ye happen to know where that device is?" Doug asked.

"I know that the device you're thinking of is buried on Gaia. I don't know where, and even if I did, it's inaccessible to us right now for obvious reasons, and even if we could get to it, assuming the Horror didn't eat it, there's no knowing what state it would be in."

"Fat lot a good that does us then, laddie. I hope yer've got more than that up yer sleeve!"

"There is a second device, a prototype actually – I don't know exactly where it is, but I know where we can look for it."

"It's on Erebus," I said, beginning to catch up with Zavis's train of thought.

"Oh, it is, aye?" said Doug, glancing at me, then turning back to Zavis. "An' ye dinna think that might be an issue?"

"It's definitely an issue. Yes, Raith is correct – the prototype is on Erebus. My plan would be for you to assemble a strike force amongst yourselves, go to Erebus, find and extract the prototype, and then find the Horror. I believe that if we programmed the device to activate on a cycle, emitting small, localised bursts of theta waves, that it would overpower any organic sources of theta waves and sufficiently fool the Horror into thinking that the device is the closest, most populous source of life."

"What bloody good does that do us?" a woman called out.

"Well, for a start, it would allow us to lead it away from our remaining worlds, saving countless lives and enabling the ongoing survival of our species. I also believe it would allow us to lead the Horror to Erebus. We already know the Empire would be unable to defend itself against its attacks. Once it has vanquished the Empire once and for all, we lead it away again, deep into space, where it can't harm us again."

A shiver ran down my spine; this plan, it was mass murder – the same mass murder I'd sought to prevent when I thought the Empire vessels were adrift and floundering. But as I pictured Amorina and Emma's bodies floating in the cold emptiness of space, I pushed my compassion aside – the situation had changed, and the Empire could go fuck itself.

"That's something, mate. But what if it finds us again? Or finds some other people out in space?" Arty asked.

"A valid concern. I'm not saying we lead it away and forget about it forever more. On the contrary, I think we lead it out of harm's way and improve either the quality of our weapons, or the quantity – or both. Once we have sufficient strength, we go back and finish that monstrosity off for good."

An approving murmur moved through the crowd. This plan actually sounded okay.

"Now I know this all relies on a lot of things working out. That we can actually get in and out of the Empire's facilities on Erebus with the prototype. That once we have the device, that it actually has the desired effect on the Horror.

Without doubt, there will be complications, but you don't need me to be there holding your hands. Doug is a great strategist; Raith is good, too. I have faith in all of you and your abilities. I know you can execute this plan and adapt to the complications you encounter along the way."

Louder, more positive affirmations spread throughout the crowd now, inspired by Zavis's confidence in them.

"It is a Hail Mary plan, but it's the only plan we've got right now. And as I always told you in the days of the Empire, I can't guarantee anyone's safety, but live or die, I promise your actions will have a positive outcome and your deeds will be remembered."

"Mate, if Tynan and his Empire are back, then the Insurgency is back too. And if we're back, then we do what we do best, which is fucking up the Empire and their schemes!" said Arty.

"Aye!" Doug said. "Here's ta fuckin' up da Empire!"

The crowd cheered, and Zavis smiled.

"That's the spirit. I must go now; I fear my hiding place may be secure no longer. Good luck to all of you!"

The transmission ended, and the hologram faded away.

"Alright, ye Insurgents – ye heard da man, let's get organised!"

❦

As Doug, Arty, and the other insurgents discussed who would be part of the strike teams, I made my way back to the observation lounge. There was still chaos in my mind and pain in my soul. Being in the presence of so many people was overwhelming; too much noise, and too many eyes looking at my wounds and scars. As I entered the room, I couldn't help but be captivated by the looming darkness of the Horror above Gaia.

Quickly, I turned away, not wanting to let its oppressive sight bring me down further. I sat down and leaned against the wall, staring at the back of the observation lounge. An eerie light show danced across the surface, the shadows cast by the Horrors' planetary consumption. I closed my eyes and exhaled, letting my head rest against the wall as I soaked up the silence. In my mind, I pictured Amorina and Emma, smiling and laughing, playing in the sunlight on the farm.

Alone.

The image glitched, and a chill ran down my spine as darkness replaced the bright scene. Amorina and Emma's frozen, contorted bodies were floating in the void, their faces twisted into expressions of terror.

"No!" I snapped, opening my eyes, replacing imagination with reality.

Family gone. Friends gone.

Tears welled up in my eyes and ran down my face. The insidious thoughts seemed to multiply with each passing moment, and with every additional thought, the dark sentiments became harder to ignore. My reservoir of guilt grew and grew — how much could I take before the dam broke?

Arm gone. Alone. Home gone. Your fault.

My body trembled, and I clenched my fist, willing the darkness away as the noise inside my head increased.

Wife dead. Family gone. Alone. Daughter dead. Son lost. Alone. Your fault. It's all gone.

"Stop it!" I cried as I started hitting myself in the head. "Stop it!"

You let the Empire live. Your mercy killed her. Alone. Your choices conjured horrors. You lost your home. Alone. You destroyed your family. It's all your fault.

"Stop it!" I yelled as I leapt to my feet. "Stop it! Stop it! Stop it!"

I stood there, huffing and shaking with rage, as I slowly realised that my mind was silent now.

"Argh!"

I wiped the tears off my face and turned towards the window. I needed to distract myself, to focus on something else to keep my thoughts quiet and drowned out. I'd intentionally avoided looking at the Horror when I'd entered the lounge, but now it was perfect for drawing my attention.

"Are you having a good feed?" I muttered as I stared out the window at it.

The monstrous machine had successfully sucked up Gaia's ocean, and its tentacles were now burrowing into the planet's surface, seeking mineral deposits as it had done on Akka. I watched with a heavy heart as it ripped apart my home, as it destroyed the only home I had ever known, or ever wanted. As I watched, more tendrils moved down and others returned. Questions began to surface.

Who built the Horror? Why did they build it? Why was it so big? Where had it come from?

These questions reminded me of the far smaller device that I had buried in the ground on Gaia. In particular, I recalled the one-sided monologue I had with it; that it wasn't good or evil – it simply was. It'd been built with certain capabilities, but the harm or benefit it caused all came down to the operator that commanded it and told it what to do.

"Is that what you are?" I whispered. "Are you just a machine that's been told to do bad things?"

The Horror continued with its destruction, completely oblivious to my questions.

As I watched it work, I couldn't imagine what good use case it could possibly have, but maybe, just maybe, whatever aliens designed and built this device had intended it for some altruistic purpose, and maybe it just fell into the wrong hands after the fact.

"Not that it matters … you are destined to be destroyed. Not here, not today, but one day. We will outlast you and build weapons capable of ripping you apart. Maybe all this death is your fault, maybe it isn't – but your demise will be a consequence of your capability."

I noticed a sudden flash of light to my left and instinctively turned my head towards it. There was a large chunk of wreckage, probably from one of the large capital ships, that was coming around from the left on its recently acquired orbit. As the object twisted and turned, its torn and jagged edges reflected the light of the stars across the night sky.

I watched as it travelled along its course and suddenly realised that, by chance, it was on a collision course with the Horror.

"Now, this will be interesting."

The ship wasn't as heavy or as large as the asteroid we'd thrown at the Horror, but the Horror was busy devouring a planet, whereas before its undivided attention had been on the incoming attack. I watched as the wreckage crossed my field of view, passed in front of the trinary stars. I looked over at the Horror – there was no change in behaviour.

Is it really oblivious to the incoming threat?

"Come on … hit the fucker!" I said, willing the wreckage on.

Moments later, the wreckage collided with the Horror, punching a hole straight into its side.

"Whoa!" I yelled, slapping the glass in front of me in celebration.

Paying attention to what was taking place, I realised light was radiating from the hole in the Horror, whose swarm had veered from its world-consuming mission to search the surrounding area for its unseen aggressor.

"What the fuck?" I gasped as I watched the light coming out of the already healing hole.

Suddenly, I recalled something that had been said during our first encounter with the Horror – one of the crew had said the Horror was outputting 342 yottawatts of power. I remembered thinking how that wasn't much less power than what Sol put out.

"It's a fucking Dyson sphere!" I exclaimed.

Now the Horror's size made sense, and to a degree, so did its capabilities. This machine had access to more power than all of humanity had ever used. I felt a novel respect for the technology before me, knowing it had access to a level of power unparalleled in human history. As the gap sealed and extinguished the light emanating from within, the door to the observation lounge opened up behind me.

"Everything alright in here, mate?"

I turned around to face Arty.

"Yeah … yeah – I just realised that thing is … incredible."

Arty raised an eyebrow. "The planet-destroying machine is incredible?"

"I mean … it's terribly incredible … or ah … incredibly terrible, I should say."

"Un hun."

"You know what, let's just forget this chat happened."

"That works for me, mate."

We both nodded awkwardly for a few moments, and then I asked. "So … you came in for something?"

"Yeah, right. We've ah, made a bit of a plan, mate, and wanted you to come and join us so we can run it past you."

"Gotcha. Lead the way."

As Arty turned and headed out of the room, I followed, taking one last glance at the Horror over my shoulder as I walked.

Incredible.

\\(∨)∥

As it happened, the plan was much simpler than I'd anticipated. The Insurgency would split into two groups; the first group, and the larger of the two, would stay onboard the current vessel. They would observe and, if possible, follow the Horror should it move, acting as a beacon for when the second team returned with the prototype conversion device.

The second, smaller team would board what was essentially a warp-capable dropship, which sounded very dodgy, but who was I to argue? This ship would make the eight-month journey to Erebus, land on the planet, hopefully undetected, and enable the strike team onboard to infiltrate the Empire's facility. This all sounded great except for one key detail.

"What do you mean I'm not on either team?" I exclaimed.

"I thought it kinda obvious, laddie," Doug replied drily. "Yer missing a fuckin' arm!"

"I will have you know that I am still rather capable, even if I am short a limb!"

"I dinna say ye were incapable. I'm just sayin' yer not capable enough to be on a team!"

"That's bullshit, and you know it! Put me on the strike team. You know my appearance is an asset. Well, at least the facial part of my appearance is. Bring me along – you know it'll come in handy."

"If I put ye on the team as ye are, you'll be a cripple. We dinna have the resource to make ye an arm, and we dinna have the time to go get one."

"I know, it's fine – getting a new arm can wait. The mission comes first."

Doug scowled. I knew he knew I was right. He just didn't want to admit it.

"Come on, mate. The lad speaks the truth, and he knows the risks. Let him on the team," Arty interjected.

"Fine. But if it goes sideways because the laddie doesn't have an arm, I'll be tellin' ye I told yer so!"

"I'll take those terms, mate. Raith, you're on the strike team with six other fellas and me. They'll compliment us with various tactical and technical abilities."

"Great, thank you. When are we leaving?"

"Right now, laddie," Doug said, pointing across the hanger to a ship. "That wee bucket o' bolts is gonna ferry you right into the heart of enemy territory."

The group started walking towards the ship, and I quickly followed suit, eyeing the vessel wearily as we got closer. Its worn exterior was tired, its paint long ago burned away by interstellar travel.

"That one's yours, laddie," Doug pointed at a cryopod as we stepped into the ship's cargo hold. "And that one's yours," he added, tapping Arty on the shoulder.

As we walked towards the pods, I turned to Arty.

"Are you sure this ship is, well, operational? Safe? Secure?"

"Definitely, mate."

I nodded as I stopped in front of my pod. The icons and letters had faded off all the buttons; the fact that it even had buttons meant that these pods were ancient, relatively speaking.

"Arty … these are archaic. Are these safe to use?"

"Yeah mate. Used them just the other day. Still right as rain."

I scowled and gingerly climbed into the pod. As I settled in, I could now look out and see the other Insurgency members already being frozen. With the power draw on the ship increasing, the vessel groaned, and the lighting flickered.

I leaned forward and glanced over at Arty's pod.

"You are absolutely, unequivocally, one hundred percent sure this ship is safe?"

"For the hundredth time, mate – fucking yes! It's safe! I helped put it together myself."

"That … are you a mechanic?"

"Well, not technically speakin'," Arty replied.

"Are you a warp engineer? Or a ship builder? Or anything remotely related to putting ships together?"

"Well … no."

"Then saying that you helped put it together doesn't reassure me!" I snapped.

"Alright, mate – calm your horses! Look at it this way, if I didn't trust this ship, I wouldn't be getting onto it, okay?"

That, admittedly, was somewhat reassuring.

"Okay, okay. This is fine."

"Just lie back, relax, okay? We're gonna be just fine."

The door to the cryopod closed, and immediately, the temperature dropped. The oral ingestion mask lowered itself onto my mouth and the extremely sour liquid poured into me, streaming down my throat and into my lungs.

As my eyes grew heavy, I made one last plea to the universe for safe passage and slipped into that dark, dreamless sleep.

❧

As I spewed up a lungful of cryofluid, I mused on how much I hated this part of the experience. I was never sure which was worse – the beginning when it felt like you were drowning in the cryofluid, or the end when you had to expel all the liquid you'd previously ingested. I usually thought that whatever was happening at the time was the worse one, and as more fluid came up, I stayed consistent, concluding that it was the worst situation.

"How're you doing, mate?"

I looked over to see Arty wiping fluid from his mouth.

"Just peachy," I mumbled, hurling once more. "Just fucking peachy."

Arty chuckled quietly.

"I'm sorry to say it never really gets better, mate. You'd think they could at least make the liquid taste nice, but no – apparently that's too hard."

I nodded, sitting back and taking a few deep breaths, the feeling of nausea finally passing.

"I assume we made it to Erebus?"

I watched as Arty slowly got to his feet and walked over to the ship's cockpit.

"It would certainly seem so, mate. And I told you the ship would be fine, didn't I?"

"Yes … yes, you did."

I got up and walked over to the cockpit as well, where Arty and the pilot were sitting.

"Eva, right?"

The pilot glanced over her shoulder at me. "Yeah, that's right."

"Did you have any trouble landing? Did you detect any signs that we might've been detected?"

"No trouble at all. Not a fuckin' peep out of anything. It's like they never thought anyone other than themselves would ever come here."

I smiled. If only she knew that's exactly what the Empire had thought.

"Excellent. Are you both happy with our position here?"

"Yeah, mate," Arty replied. "Go get the others ready, and we'll keep watch as planned."

"Copy that."

\\ \ \ v J JJ

The surface of Erebus was extremely barren; respirators were required to traverse its surface. In a landscape of rock and dust, the metallic, illuminated structures of the Empire base stood out like a sore thumb, only adding to Eva's comment from earlier. Our target was a bright red emergency exit hatch. Three of the strike team members were already at work on it, illuminated by the bright blue light of the plasma torch as they cut their way through the metal.

"How're we looking, Watchdogs?" I said into my intercom.

"Knock it off, mate. I fuckin' told you, we weren't gonna use callsigns," Arty snapped.

"Ah come on! Using callsigns actually makes it feel like a spy mission!"

"Why does it need to feel like a spy mission? And besides, mate, there isn't even anything to hide from. We haven't seen any sign of foot patrols, drones, or any other automated security, for that matter. In fact, the locked door is the most secure thing we've encountered yet!"

"Yeah but ... callsigns?"

"No!"

"Okay, fine," I sighed. "Raith out."

I turned toward the squad and asked, "How are we looking?" just as a circular section of the hatch fell inward.

"Pretty good I'd say, Raith," said the cutter – a tall, dark-skinned Martian named Volker.

"Nice work, team. Let's get inside."

One by one, the squad members jumped down into the hatch, the sound of their landings echoing off the walls, until I was all that remained.

"Ah, well. Here goes nothing," I said, stepping into the void.

I dropped about two metres, landing in a dim concrete corridor.

"Are you okay?" asked Jesse, a short, Terran woman.

"Yeah, I'm good thanks, Jesse. Is everyone else okay?"

I glanced around and got five thumbs up.

"Excellent. Alright, let's move out."

We followed the corridor for a few minutes until it opened out into a large underground hangar. We were met with the sight of a dozen completed frigates and the hum of machinery from another four under construction. It was hot and dry inside the hangar, and the air smelled of hot metal, oil, and sweat.

"Blimey," Volker breathed.

I shuddered at the sight. I had witnessed, far too closely, what three Empire frigates were capable of, never mind an entire fleet of them. And who was to say there weren't more hangars, also filled with frigates, or perhaps bigger ships, like cruisers?

"We should keep moving," Jesse urged. "We can't afford to get spotted here."

"Agreed. Do we know which way to head?" I asked.

"I think we should head this way," Volker said, pointing down the right side of the hangar.

"Okay ... lead on!"

\\ \ v) \\

The hanger eventually connected with the central complex, and one storeroom full of unconscious loyalists later, we were walking inconspicuously through the hallways. We'd tucked the left sleeve into the left pocket of the uniform to hide my missing limb, and it seemed to do the job, judging by the number of folks we had passed by without raising suspicions. Between the abundant signage, our ah ... *borrowed* uniforms, and access cards, we were quickly closing in on locations where the prototype could be.

"There's an R&D centre and laboratory up ahead," Keller, the squad's technical expert, commented as he accessed a console.

"How far up?"

"Maybe ... two hundred metres?"

"Okay, let's go."

We kept walking and, as expected, we saw the doorway to the lab. Volker walked up to the access panel and swiped the highest clearance card we had – the panel flashed red and let out an angry beep.

"Damn it!" Volker growled. "It's a secured work area!"

"Keller – can you bypass it?"

"Possibly. Let me take a look and I'll try to provide an ETA. Cover me!"

As Keller got to work prying open the security console, the rest of the squad grouped around behind him, hopefully obscuring him from view. And for the first five minutes it seemed to work, with several loyalists passing by without question. Then along came a commanding officer.

"What are you all doing here?" He asked as he came closer.

"Nothing, sir. We're just hanging out, chatting, you know how it goes!" Jesse replied.

The officer raised an eyebrow. "Surely, you've something better to be doing than just 'hanging out'?"

"Well, you know if we'd been given those increased break times that the union has been asking for, we wouldn't need to just hang out, if you catch my drift."

"What union?" the officer asked.

"We don't have a union? Oh dear, that's a problem," Jesse said, now somewhat lost for words.

The officer glanced past Jesse now and noticed Keller engrossed in his bypass.

"And you, what are you doing back there with the security panel?"

"It doesn't concern you," I said as I turned towards the officer.

"Your Grace!" he said, immediately dipping his head. "I didn't realise you were here!"

Moments later, his rationality overtook his conditioning, and he looked up at me, his eyes taking in the scar wrapping around my forehead and the wrinkles on my skin.

"You aren't —" he started to exclaim before Volker drove a blade into his chest.

The officer gasped, looking at Volker in shock as the life quickly faded from his eyes. Volker prevented him from collapsing by taking his weight, making it seem like he was still standing with us.

"How're we looking, Keller?" I asked.

"It's hard to say — I'm not very familiar with this Empire tech."

"What authentication does the panel require?"

"Ah … biometric – either retinal or handprint."

I turned towards Volker, who was already moving the dead officer over to the panel. Keller closed the panel and Volker placed the officer's hand on the scanner. A light appeared behind the scanner's screen, moving up and down as it captured the details of the officer's hand. After a few moments, the panel turned green, and the laboratory doors opened.

"Come on, let's go – move, move, move!" I said, ushering the team through the doors.

"Raith?"

I instantly recognised the voice and spun around to see Ichirō standing there.

"Son!"

Ichirō averted his gaze, appearing to be embarrassed.

I looked over my shoulder and saw the team standing in the laboratory, illuminated by the fluorescent lights.

"Go – I'll catch up with you!"

The team members all gave a nod and promptly started looking for the device. I turned back around to face Ichirō. It had been ten months since our last encounter, and he looked as if the life had been drained from him; his skin was ashen and his eyes sunken – he was a mere shadow of the young man he had once been.

"Are you alright?"

"Is that all you have to say to me?" Ichirō asked, returning my gaze.

"Yes. Why? What else would I say?"

"Aren't you angry at me? Don't you want to lecture me on my actions or something?"

I shook my head.

"Do you remember what I told you on Gaia?"

Ichirō shrugged sullenly.

"I told you that you can always come back to me. I love you and the door is always open – and I meant what I said. So … I'm not angry at you, Ichirō … I'm disappointed but not angry. Your actions, they're your actions, and right or wrong, you have to live with those choices. Do I think you could have or should have made different decisions … sure – but those are my thoughts, not yours. All I care about is that you're okay. That you're healthy and safe. Are you?"

Ichirō's eyes brimmed with tears. "I'm not sure."

"Is Tynan hurting you?"

"No … I mean … sort of … but not really. I don't know."

"Okay …" I said soothingly, trying to calm him.

Tynan had his claws in Ichirō, that much was clear. The question now was could I free Ichirō from Tynan's grasp?

"Listen, son, I know you probably don't want to hear this, but Tynan is not a good man. He is selfish and cruel, full of anger and hatred – he's –"

"Shut up! You don't know what he's really like because you didn't know him from before …"

"Before I rewrote everyone's minds?"

Ichirō nodded, tears now running down his face. I didn't have the time, nor the words, to eloquently explain to my son that I knew what Tynan was like before everything changed. If only he knew how I'd shared my mind with Tynan for years, and the nightly torment I'd experienced at the mercy of my former self. And if only he knew that the man he was presently loyal to was but a shadow of the real Tynan.

"I get it, you know. I understand."

"How could you possibly understand?" Ichirō yelled. "You know nothing of the truth!"

"Nothing of the truth, aye? You mean how you weren't affected by the mass conversion?"

Ichirō went to respond automatically and then stopped, realisation dawning on his face.

"Yeah, that's right. I know you remember everything – how it was beforehand, what the Empire was like, what Tynan was like, the power you had as heir to the throne. I can only imagine what it was like to see everyone around you transformed, suddenly not giving a shit about the Empire, Tynan, or you. I know you've been pretending these last couple of years that you were like everyone else, and I'm sorry – I should've spoken to you about this long ago. But ... I didn't know how to. And for that, I am ... I am so, so sorry. Truly, I am."

"Why didn't it work on me? Why can I remember?"

"I don't know the specifics, but I know Tynan experimented on you. We believe that while he was developing the conversion technology, he was also attempting to safeguard himself from it – just in case anyone ever used it against him."

Ichirō's face twitched, and it was a twitch I knew well – an angry twitch – the first sign of anger brewing within my son.

"Come and join me," I said as I spread my arms. "You can escape Tynan now and leave be –"

"Fuck! Are you missing an arm?"

I glanced to the left and realised that in making my gesture, the empty sleeve had become dislodged from my pocket and was now forlornly hanging off my amputated arm.

"Oh ... ah, yeah. You can thank Tynan for that loss as well."

Without uttering another word, Ichirō spun around and bolted, quickly vanishing from view as he fled. The clock was ticking now; the countdown had started.

I opened the laboratory doors again and stepped inside, quickly taking stock of my new surroundings. I instantly recognised the room – this was where they had cut open my head for a second time. The team wasn't present, but as I scanned the room, I noticed "R&D Storage" written above another doorway. That sounded like a promising place to go. I walked over to the doorway and the doors opened automatically as I approached. I stepped through and found myself in a large storage room with shelving stacked end to end with devices. The majority of it looked to be quite recent, likely crafted within the last couple of years, yet there was a decent amount of stuff that appeared to be older – technology taken from Earth after the fall of the Empire, like the mass conversion device?

The group was heading down a nearby aisle, walking towards me.

"We've found it," Jesse called out as they approached. "This is it, right?" she asked as she neared, holding up a very familiar-looking device.

"Yep, that's it! Nice find, Jesse."

"A nice find it may be, but nowhere near as nice of a find as all of you are," drawled a familiar voice.

We spun around to see Tynan standing in the doorway, flanked by soldiers. We quickly turned the other way, only to see soldiers appear on our other side as well.

"Come now … we've got some catching up to do, methinks."

Chapter 14
Perhaps We Are More Alike

2161, Common Era – Planet Erebus, Frontier Space, Tynan Empire

We were shoved and prodded with rifles as we were escorted to Tynan's throne room and forced to bow, just as I had been during my first experience on Erebus.

"I'll admit," said Tynan, as he sat down on his throne. "I was genuinely surprised to find you here. Not only because I was fairly certain you were dead but also because I didn't think anyone would be stupid enough to break in here."

I looked up, ready to respond to Tynan, but stopped as I saw Ichirō sitting beside Tynan on a smaller throne. Ichirō's eyes were red and puffy, and a bruise was present on the left side of his face.

Did Tynan hit him?

"Well, don't stop on his account," Tynan snapped as he noticed the direction of my gaze.

"Did you hit him?" I asked, directing a glare towards Tynan.

"Junior here still has much to learn. I simply … taught him a lesson," Tynan replied snidely.

"That's not a lesson – that's abuse," I said curtly.

Tynan grimaced. "Feeling bold, are we? Perhaps you need a reminder of your place?"

"I know my place, which is to be a thorn in your side!"

A wry smile crept across Tynan's face, and then just as quickly disappeared, as if he couldn't help but be amused, only to realise his own amusement and regret it.

"But let's just skip the small talk," I said, not wanting to give Tynan a chance to refocus.

"I've no time for your games, so why don't you just tell us what is to become of us?"

Tynan shook his head and tutted. "Where would the fun be in that, Raith? I'd be skipping all the juicy psychological torture I can inflict upon you."

The faces of my mother, father, and daughters flashed through my mind, safely far away from here. Amorina and Emma's faces appeared next, but Tynan couldn't touch them in the afterlife – if there was one. Ichirō was about as safe as he could be, sat at Tynan's side, and I hadn't seen Zavis – hopefully he was still safely hidden somewhere within the complex.

I chuckled. "What do you have left to torment me with?"

"Oh, I don't know … your fellow Insurgents. Aren't they enough?" Tynan asked, pointing to the other Insurgency squad members.

I looked to my right, at the faces of the Insurgents who'd broken into this base with me – Volker, Jesse, Keller, Zanna, and Wong. We all knew that Arty and Eva were still out in Erebus's barren wastelands, yet none of us had snitched on them – and none of us would. We all knew the mission, and we knew the risks. There was always a chance we wouldn't make it out.

"They mean nothing to me," I replied, hoping Tynan wouldn't want to put that statement to the test.

"Kill that one," Tynan said as he pointed to someone on my right.

Bang!

I shuddered at the near instant gunshot, shocked at how quickly a soldier had carried out Tynan's command. I heard a thud and glanced to my right where Keller was now slumped on the ground, blood pooling beneath him.

I returned my gaze to Tynan, locking eyes with him, staring insolently.

"Oh alright, I believe you," Tynan said, breaking the stare. "Perhaps you'll care about your friend more, then?"

A door to my right opened, and two soldiers dragged a broken, bloodied Zavis in and unceremoniously dumped him a few metres away from me. My stomach twisted at the sight of his wounds, once again feeling responsible for the harm that had transpired.

"Zavis! Are you okay?" I gasped, desperately hoping he wasn't dead.

My old friend slowly raised his head to look at me, giving a subtle nod as bloody spit drooled from his mouth. Wheeling in behind him came Phobus and Lorcan, looking particularly smug and evil. I could only imagine how much joy they'd felt seeing their old colleague being beaten and broken for his perceived transgressions.

I glared at Tynan, opening my mouth as I prepared to say something, but he interjected.

"And if that's not enough," he continued. "I also have your family!"

This time, a door to my left opened, and a posse of soldiers entered, carrying a woman and a young girl between them. The woman lifted her head, and I gasped.

It can't be!

She looked just like Amorina. The young girl also lifted her head, and my heart skipped a beat – she looked just like Emma!

They're dead. This is a trick. It can't be real!

"How *dare* you!" I snarled as I leapt to my feet.

Two soldiers rushed up from behind to restrain me, but missing an arm proved to be useful. The soldier on my left grabbed nothing but air, and when the other soldier made to grab me, I wrenched my arm out of reach.

They moved forward for another attempt but then stopped. I glanced back at Tynan and saw he'd raised his hand to stop them.

"How dare I what?" he drawled.

"How *dare* you impersonate my wife and child when you damn well know you killed them!"

Tynan's face twitched, and then the corners of his mouth curled upward. A wheezy snicker escaped his lips as his face split into a wicked grin.

"What's so funny?" I demanded.

Tynan clapped his hands together, threw his head back and unleashed a loud, joyous cackle. He then doubled over, still laughing wildly, tears running down his face. The laughter was cruel and mocking, and it echoed around the throne room, reverberating and intensifying. Others – like Phobus, Lorcan, and some soldiers – joined in, adding their own snickers and snorts to the fray. I felt my face flushing and growing hot, as if I'd done something wrong, like I deserved to be laughed at and mocked.

"What is so funny?" I yelled over the cacophony of laughter as it continued to grow.

Tynan fell forward off his throne, still howling with laughter, slapping the ground repeatedly. Finally, Tynan's cackles lessened, slowly diminishing until there was just the odd giggle. He pulled himself back up onto his throne and wiped the tears off his face.

"Oh," my doppelgänger said. "You thought they were dead, didn't you?" he asked mockingly.

I glanced over at Amorina and Emma.

Were they real? Could they be real? Could they have survived the attack?

"Even now, you can't quite believe it, can you? You really thought they'd died, and it did a number on you, didn't it?" Tynan said gleefully, letting out another cruel chuckle.

When I glanced at the girls again, I felt a spark of hope ignite in my chest. I didn't want to fan it though – what if this was another of Tynan's manipulations.

"How?" I asked, turning back to Tynan.

"Well, as it turns out, the engineering core is one of a ship's strongest and safest parts. After my Firecrackers tore the Republic fleet apart, my dropships quickly flew through the debris, collecting as many survivors as possible. Your wife and child just happened to be some of the lucky ones."

Some of the lucky ones?

"There were other survivors?"

Tynan nodded. "Quite a few actually. As it would turn out, Firecrackers are *definitely* more effective when fired side on or front on to a ship. Still, I've been able to extract some very cathartic revenge out of the survivors, including that bitch, Knox."

"Raith ..."

I looked over at my family to see Amorina looking at me.

"It's us, Raith. We're real."

My heart skipped a beat, and I knew, beyond a shadow of a doubt, that they were alive.

They are alive!

I dashed across the room, the sound of my footsteps echoing as I dropped to my knees and slid across the last few metres into the embrace of my wife and daughter. Tears of joy streamed down my cheeks, and when I pulled back, I could see Amorina's face also glistening with tears.

"I thought I'd lost you both," I sobbed.

"We thought we'd lost you too!" Amorina sobbed back.

When I looked down at Emma, I could see her cheeks glistening with tears as well.

"I missed you, Daddy," she whispered.

"I missed you too, sweetie pie!"

I pulled them both back into an embrace and enjoyed the relief that flowed through me, comforted by their presence.

"What do you have left to torment me with?"

My eyes snapped open as the echo of my previous bravado played inside my head.

"And if that's not enough, I also have your family!"

As Tynan's retort echoed through my mind, debilitating concern replaced my exhilarated joy. My family was alive, but that was little comfort when Tynan was around – they were in imminent danger because of his mere presence. Any and all threats to their lives were possible and plausible. I had to come up with a plan to keep them safe, and quickly!

"All right, that's enough. Pull them apart and bring Raith back over here!" Tynan ordered.

The soldiers acted quickly; they roughly shoved me away from my family and toward the centre of the room. I walked the rest of the way without further prompts as I desperately tried to think of a way to control the narrative.

How do I get out of this and keep everyone alive?

I turned towards my doppelgänger and looked him in the eye. "So, what do you want, Tynan?"

"For a start, answers. Why were you trying to get that?" Tynan asked, pointing to the prototype mass conversion device.

Tynan understood hierarchy and dominance. That had to be my way out of this situation.

If any of us were to have a chance of getting out of here, I'd need to take control.

Well, here goes nothing ...

"We wanted that so we could try to stop the Horror – you know, the thing that's set to destroy all of humankind if we don't stop it? You would've wanted to do the same if you had any shred of humanity within you."

Tynan narrowed his eyes. "I have humanity."

"Oh really? Tell me, where was your humanity when you betrayed your allies, attacking them from behind while they tried to fight the Horror?"

"That wasn't a matter of humanity, or lack thereof. That was strategy, Raith," Tynan scoffed. "It's just good business, something you should try sometime."

"It was cowardice. Because that's what you – wait, strategy?"

Tynan smiled slyly.

Fuck! I've just conceded ground to him.

He enjoyed this, knowing that he was in command of the conversation – hell, he was in command of the entire fucking situation – and he loved it. I needed to wrangle back control of the conversation, and to do that, I had to figure out what Tynan had meant by strategy.

What game was he playing?

"Second of all," Tynan said, "I am not a coward, and firstly, I do care about humanity, okay? The difference is, I care about a humanity that's united under me and my ideals."

I raised an eyebrow at Tynan's reversal of order, and he seemed to realise his mistake moments later. As realisation spread across his face, his right hand began to tremor and shake, and he quickly tucked it beneath his robes.

Curious.

"How can you say that with a straight face? Do you know how many people you killed in that Republic fleet? The fleet which, by the way, you were supposed to be part of – a fleet that was our only realistic defence against the Horror. But you don't care, do you? You don't feel anything for all the souls you silenced – by backstabbing no less."

Tynan's face twitched, just like Ichirō's face would when he was getting mad. I had to make a conscious effort to not smile. I was getting under Tynan's skin, syphoning away his control.

"Not only that, but you claim it was in the name of strategy. You're right, it was strategy. The strategy of a fucking coward."

Tynan clenched his fists and opened his mouth, ready to say something.

"What!" I yelled, stepping forward and cutting him off. "What are you going to threaten me with, you fucking cowardly cunt!"

I strode forward as soldiers rushed towards me in an effort to intercept. If they caught me, I'd lose the upper hand ... could I make Tynan stop them?

"And if you weren't such a coward, you wouldn't hide behind your soldiers!" I continued, pointing at Tynan.

In response, he stood up and held up a hand as he shouted, "Stop!"

The approaching soldiers stopped but didn't retreat – they were ready to complete their charge if Tynan changed his mind.

"There, see – not a coward," Tynan said defiantly.

"Still a fucking coward."

"I am not a –" Tynan started to yell, but he caught himself, wagging his finger as he grimaced. "Don't think I don't know what you're doing, Raith. It was ... it is, strategy, okay?

When the Horror has finished eliminating the current dregs of humanity, my fleet of multirole vessels will disperse across the stars, terraforming, colonizing, and safeguarding the worlds – the Empire's worlds. Humanity will flourish under my rule, and I will have more power than any other human before me. This new Empire will be *unassailable*, its rule *unquestioned*, and my power *undiminishable!*"

"You would rather set humanity alight, step back and watch it burn, just so you could rebuild it in your image ... over saving billions of lives? And you're not even brave enough to do it yourself – you're letting that mechanical monstrosity do the dirty work for you!"

Tynan opened his mouth to counter my statement, but I cut him off before he could speak.

"No, no – let me guess. It's just good business, right? Fuck me ... you're crazy and a coward."

This pre-emptive retort seemed to suck the air out of Tynan's sails, and he took a moment to gather his thoughts. "Still not a coward, and definitely not crazy, Raith – just misunderstood. That is the fate of all geniuses, is it not?"

"You think this strategy of yours is a stroke of genius? Cause it's really not. It's cruel. It's cowardly. It's –"

"I am not a coward!" Tynan snapped. "You are just too stupid to understand! All of you! You're all idiots – incapable of seeing *my* grand vision for humanity! But don't worry – I will drag most of you into the new age, even if it's kicking and screaming all the way!"

"And that ... is where you are wrong," murmured a faint voice.

Tynan looked past me, and I turned around to see Zavis standing, albeit unstably.

"Most of us see a truth you cannot, Tynan. Autocratic empires, such as your own, will *never* be successful, regardless of when they exist. It doesn't matter if it's the old Empire, the new Empire, an empire from the past, or an empire from the future – if it is an autocracy, it will always fail. That is the fate of all autocracies."

I looked back at Tynan, who looked rather bemused.

"I don't understand your logic, Zavis. Explain to me why an autocratic empire will fail?"

"An autocracy, by definition, is a state or society governed by one person with absolute power," Zavis explained.

"So?" Tynan shrugged.

"So, people think that power corrupts the wielder, but it isn't power that corrupts, rather it's the fear," I concluded.

"Fear of what? If one holds absolute power, what is there to fear?"

"The loss of power. That is why dictators rule with an iron fist – they attempt to snuff out any deviant thinkers and silence any rebellious voices. However, the tighter they squeeze their subjects, the more people slip through their fingers," Zavis said.

"That's why they fail," I added. "That is why *you* will fail."

Tynan's eyes shifted between me and Zavis, his previous bemusement gone. He looked down at Zavis. "Anything else you want to get off your chest?"

"As a matter of fact, yes," Zavis replied, straightening up as he puffed out his chest and held his head high.

"It's time I finally say what I should have said a long time ago," he said slowly and firmly. "It's not fucking about you!"

Tynan's face contorted in shock and his brow furrowed as he heard Zavis's comment.

"You and your self-serving, self-centred, narcissistic world view is flawed as fuck, Tynan! You want power, you want control, but they are unearned!" Zavis spoke with a commanding presence, his voice resonating with the wisdom of a man who'd grappled with power and control and knew what it took to have them. "You demand to have them, but you've no reason to. And even then, even when you have power, it's not some carefree force that you can just control. It's a burden, because it comes with responsibility – a duty of care to use that power to look after all of those less powerful than you!"

Tynan's face twitched, seemingly uncontrollably.

"The two of you think you're cute, don't you?" he sneered. "Acting all high and mighty, but guess what? I'm the one up here! Not either of you!"

"We're not high and mighty, Tynan – we don't need to be. We're just two men who can both see the reality you can't," Zavis retorted.

"Yeah? Well, take a look at this reality. Shoot him!" Tynan said, pointing at Zavis.

Three shots echoed throughout the room as Zavis's body jolted; he looked down in shock at the red stains blossoming around the bullet holes in his robes.

"Zavis!" I shouted, running towards my friend as he collapsed.

I dropped to the floor beside him and pressed my hand against what appeared to be the worst of his wounds. As I felt the warmth of his blood seeping through my fingers, my heart sank.

He's losing too much blood!

"Medic! Get a medic! Now!" I yelled out as the rest of the room remained motionless.

"It's … too late for that … my boy," Zavis wheezed.

I looked down at my old friend. "No, no – stay with me! Hold on, okay? You can make it!"

Zavis shook his head.

"No, Raith … I can't. And we both … know it."

I looked around the room frantically, but everyone I locked eyes with simply looked away.

"Really? Nobody?" I shouted. "Not a single one of you will get a medic? Fuck you all!"

Zavis's wet hand grabbed my face and pulled it downward.

"Listen to me … please, Raith. I don't have … much time."

I let go of Zavis's wound and instead pulled his head up and onto my lap, cradling it so that he could look up at me.

"I'm here, I'm listening," I said as tears rolled down my cheeks.

"I'll admit … this was not … how I planned to … leave this mortal coil," Zavis said with a coy smile.

I chuckled. "I know, right? A few years of retirement somewhere quiet would've been nice, aye?"

Zavis nodded weakly. "Yes … yes, that was … that was the dream."

His hand, which was resting on the side of my neck, clenched tighter as his eyes welled with tears.

"There are two things … I need to tell you."

"I'm listening."

"The Horror – don't fear it," Zavis said as he weakly shook his head. "Fear what … the weapon … was built to kill."

Fear what the weapon was built to kill?

That was a statement with a lot to think about.

"And I am so … proud … of you," Zavis said as tears ran down his face through his wrinkles. "So proud … of who you've … become. And this –" Zavis glanced at Tynan, "– this imposter … is but a … pale … imitation."

I could feel Zavis's breath growing increasingly shallow, and I knew it wouldn't be long before he was gone. He gripped my neck tighter and pulled my head closer to his face.

"Show him … what a … real … monster … looks … lik–"

Zavis's hand slipped from my neck and flopped to the ground, his eyes now devoid of life.

"Goodbye … my friend."

I gently lowered his head off my lap and closed his eyes.

Show him what a real monster looks like …

In the maroon liquid that we both sat in, I could see my pale skin in stark contrast to the angry, red scar that wrapped around my head and the smudged, crimson handprint on my cheek and neck. Within me, there was darkness, there was pain and anger and a past I'd tried so hard to suppress. I was afraid of that part of me … but so was Tynan. He was afraid of being subpar, of being an inferior copy. What if I played on that fear? What if I let the darkness out to play?

Show him what a real monster looks like!

I'd have to dive headfirst into my darkness and embrace it fully. To let it out would be a complete contradiction of the values I'd tried so hard to live by. But if I was going to compromise myself, at least it would be my choice to do so.

"My choices affect others, so choose how those choices affect them," I whispered to my reflection.

It was time to put my faith in Zavis one last time. It was time to show Tynan what an actual monster was.

I knew what a monster looked like – I'd started off every morning at home looking at one. I liked to tell myself that it was easy to see Raith in the mirror – Raith the farmer, the father, the husband – but in truth, I had to tell myself that that's what I was seeing. What I actually saw every day was what everyone else saw: Tynan Khidar, the merciless, self-centred emperor.

"I've got you, Zavis. I've got your monster right here," I whispered as a last tear rolled down my face.

"I prepared it earlier, in fact. Spent years cooking this one up … and now, I think it's ready."

All I had to do was summon the darkness I'd spent so much time suppressing.

❈

"Well, well, well. Isn't this … interesting," I said slowly and clearly, my voice projecting out into the silence of the room.

I turned my head to the right, audibly clicking my neck, then turned it to the left and clicked it again. I looked down at the stump of my left arm and wiggled it around.

"That's new … certainly not how *I* left things."

"Raith?" asked a familiar voice from behind.

I stood slowly, the blood on my saturated trousers now running down my legs, and calmly turned around. There I was, or rather, there was another me.

"Who's Raith?" I asked. "More importantly … who are *you*?"

The doppelgänger upon his elevated throne looked confused and his eyes darted about, seemingly to search for an explanation.

He uttered his name cautiously, "Ah … I-I'm Tynan."

"You can't be," I drawled, "because I'm Tynan."

The menacing tone of my voice made Tynan visibly shudder. The unease only lasted a moment before Tynan regained his composure.

"Ah, I see the confusion now. We had to initiate Project Phoenix and the Reclamation Protocols, so ... yeah," he said with an almost apologetic shrug at the end.

"The Reclamation Protocols ... so you lost the Empire?"

The last comment rattled Tynan's composure once more. "What? No, I'm the product of Project Phoenix — I literally rose from the Empire's ashes. It burned down long before I got here."

"So, who failed the Empire?"

Tynan chuckled. "Well, yo —" he cut his sentence short when his gaze met my own.

"Surely ... you aren't suggesting that *I* —" I pointed at my chest, slowly beginning to move towards Tynan, "— am responsible for the fall of my own Empire?"

The blood drained from Tynan's face. "I ... uh ... no, no! Of course not! I-I was merely saying ... that ... I ... I was just saying —" he spluttered, his panicked eyes darting around the room. "It was them!"

I turned to look where Tynan was pointing and saw Phobus and Lorcan.

"Ah — two more of my trusted advisors. Slightly worse for wear these days as well, I see."

"Yes, Your Grace, we are," the advisors said in unison.

Tynan made an indignant grunt. "You don't address anyone else as 'Your Grace' — only me!"

I whipped my head around to look at Tynan. "Silence, fool!" I commanded, and he promptly sat down and lowered his gaze.

I turned my head back towards the advisors. "Pray you can give a more succinct answer than this idiot. Who failed the Empire?"

"Zavis did, Your Grace," said Lorcan.

"He created and spent years running an insurgency to overthrow you and your Empire, Your Grace," Phobus continued.

"And it was us and a handful of loyalists that initiated the Reclamation Protocols, and set about your return," Lorcan added.

I turned to look at Tynan. "And this fool was the best you could do?"

I watched Tynan's face twitch, but before either Advisor could answer, Tynan had leapt to his feet and descended from his elevated platform.

"How dare you!" he snarled as he strode across the room towards me. "I am everything you are, only better! I am younger, stronger, and I have both my arms!"

As Tynan came into reach, I drew back my arm and slapped Tynan in the face, knocking him to the ground. Everyone in the room audibly gasped.

"Even with one arm, I am twice the man you are."

Tynan looked up at me, clutching his reddening cheek, his eyes wide with shock.

"You ... you ... you'll pay for this! Nobody lays a hand on me and gets away with it!"

"Wrong," I intoned. "I can lay my hand on you as much as I like."

"Oh yeah? What gives you the right to do that, huh?" Tynan demanded.

"Because in the Empire, you command what you own. You should know that."

As Tynan processed my statement, his expression changed from puzzlement to comprehension and then, as the truth dawned on him, dread.

"Okay!" Tynan said, shuffling backwards. "You've made your point, Raith! I get it, okay? You can stop now!"

As Tynan moved backwards, I walked forwards, and he quickly rolled over, climbed to his feet and stumbled away from me until there were a few metres between us.

"I'm serious, Raith! Fucking cut it out!" Tynan snapped.

"You keep using that name. Who the fuck is Raith?"

"You are!" Tynan screamed.

"No," I replied in a deep, guttural growl. "My name is Tynan Khidar, the one true emperor, as my father, Emperor Nicolas, was before me, and as my grandfather, Emperor Frith, was before him. Any empire, old or new, is my birthright! What can you lay claim to?"

Tynan's face was ashen, the bright red handprint on the side was the only colour. His breathing was quick and laboured as his panic intensified.

"But ... I ... I'm ... Tynan Khidar," he whispered with fear filled eyes. "I'm ... I'm the ... you aren't ... the one true emperor."

"You're pathetic. Look at yourself!" I roared. "Standing there, snivelling like a child! Babbling away. Blubbering through barely coherent sentences. You're weak. You aren't fit to bear my name!"

"That's not true! I you am! You me are!" Tynan garbled, his right arm shaking violently. "We same two side of a different coin!"

His expression shifted uneasily between confusion and frustration as he gripped his shaking arm.

"You're falling apart. You've got bad wiring or bad programming, or hell, maybe both!"

"Don't say it," Tynan beseeched.

"You're nothing but a pale imitation. Just an inferior copy."

"I'm nart! I'm nart a badly copy!" Tynan slurred.

"Alright. Convince me. Explain to me how you're *not* inferior."

Tynan appeared startled, as if unsure of how to take this sudden olive branch. He moved back up onto his platform – back to the high ground – and his arm stopped shaking. I'd given him a metaphorical length of rope, so now he once again felt like he had command of the room. Now I just had to make him hang himself.

"I ..." he cleared his throat. "I am you. I came ... from you. If you're saying I'm a bad copy ... it's because you've got bad data."

"Why would I have bad data?"

"Because the Insurgency used the conversion device on you. It ... it must've scrambled your brain."

"I see. Scrambled my brain, you say. Surely you would've had protection against that?"

"Well, I did attempt to build a defence against that – the SANE program – but I only got to experiment with it on Ichirō here," Tynan said as he indicated to his side with a slight jerk of his thumb.

Ichirō, who had paid very close attention to the unfolding conversation, turned and glared at Tynan. The stool had been positioned – now I just needed Tynan to climb onto it.

"You experimented on my only son?"

Ichirō and Tynan's faces twitched at the same time.

"Yeah, like I just sai –" Tynan's words stopped abruptly as he realised the trap he'd walked into, but it was already too late. "No, wait! It was –"

"What the hell, arsehole!" Ichirō snapped as he stood up. "What did you do to me?"

"It's not like that! I didn't … I wasn't … it wasn't me … hang on."

Tighten that noose, Tynan.

"What did you do to me?" Ichirō demanded.

"Come on, Tynan. Answer the boy."

Tynan glanced between me and Ichirō, looking like a cornered animal.

"Please … he's tricking us … I wasn't the one … it wasn't me!"

Tynan's arm trembled once more as he looked at Ichirō with desperate eyes.

"Tell me what you did to me!"

"Fine!" Tynan snapped. "I ran an experimental conversion profile on you! One that was intended to alter your mind and protect it from further alterations. That's what it was called after all – SANE – short for Sanctuary Against Neural Encoding."

"So, it was your fault," Ichirō growled. "Because of you I have been in a living hell for the past several years! While everyone around me forgot you, forgot the Empire, forgot everything – I remembered – I remembered all of it! In fact, I couldn't forget. The world that everyone else moved on from was permanently seared into my brain!"

The corners of my mouth curled up slightly. Now the metaphorical noose was tight around Tynan's neck. He just needed one final push to kick the chair out from under him.

"I bet it was easy for you to carry out such an experiment on your own child."

Tynan and Ichirō both turned to look at me.

"What?" Tynan asked, his voice cracking.

"When you experimented on Ichirō. I bet you didn't feel a thing. You just wanted results. And now, look at all the anguish it caused him … but you don't care, do you? It doesn't weigh you down at all."

Tynan's breathing quickened again, and I slowly approached him.

"The quickening of one's heart as you struggle for air. Feeling hot and flustered as you notice all the pressure sitting atop of you, compressing your chest. I mean, you couldn't even begin to imagine what that feels like."

Sweat had broken out across Tynan's forehead, and his breathing had grown quicker still.

"To be … *guiltless* … completely unashamed of your actions and the consequences. It's a joy, isn't it. Makes it so much easier to run an empire, doesn't it? You can make the hard calls, give the tough orders, and still sleep soundly at night."

Tynan's hands shook as he clasped and unclasped them. His flight-or-fight response frantically searched for danger as adrenaline flooded through his body.

"I mean, can you *imagine* all the things you could do … and live with afterwards? Experimenting on people, torturing them for months on end, destroying entire fleets of ships and murdering the thousands of crew onboard … and that's probably just scratching the surface."

Tynan reached up and grasped his head between his hands, squeezing his head between them.

"Stop … please … stop!"

"And just as well you couldn't feel remorse for all those actions, because if you did, there'd be no getting rid of it. Imagine spending every single day of your life living with the burden of those actions … that would be so hard."

Tynan's heart-wrenching wail echoed throughout the chamber as he toppled from his throne, curling up into a foetal position on the ground. I walked up the steps and stood over Tynan's diminutive form.

"If you could see yourself right now," I said, shaking my head. "I asked you to explain to me how you're not inferior. Consider me unconvinced. These feelings … they are your weakness. They make you guilty of being imperfect."

"I'm sorry …"

"You're sorry, aye?" I said, kneeling down. "Tell me, how does it feel to be at the mercy of another?"

Tynan only loosed a whimper and shrunk tighter into himself.

I reached out, grabbed a handful of Tynan's hair, pulled his head back, and leaned close to his ear. The stool had been kicked out.

"I told you the darkness was asleep within me," I whispered for only Tynan to hear. "I warned you … push me far enough, hurt those I love, and I would let that darkness out to play."

Tynan looked at me out of the corner of his eye. His face was ashen and dripping with sweat. He closed his eyes and let his head slump, defeated.

I let go of Tynan's head, letting it hit the floor with a satisfying thud. A short drop and a sudden stop. I stood back up, knowing that my work here was done.

❦

"Tynan?" I asked, looking down at my doppelgänger. "How did I get here?"

Tynan's eyes shot open, and he twisted his head to stare up at me. "Raith?" he breathed; the word barely audible.

"Yeah. Who else would I be?" I said with a shrug.

His eyes widened and I could read the emotional turmoil rushing through him. Fear that it wasn't real, confusion at what had passed, worry that it would happen again, and relief that I seemed to be Raith again.

"Oh, thank fuck," Tynan replied. "You're back!"

"I went somewhere?"

"Yeah. The other guy came out."

"The other … oh – oh! Shit … um, is everyone okay?"

"Yeah," Tynan muttered as he stumbled to his feet.

"What happened?"

Tynan glared at me as his eyes searched my face, looking for something. "We had a … conversation."

"Okay. What about? What was the outcome?"

"You really don't remember anything?"

I shook my head. "Nope … the last thing I remember was watching Zavis die … then I was here."

Tynan scowled and returned to his throne, giving his still red cheek a rub.

"You've got a little … mark … just here," I said, pointing to my cheek.

"Shut the fuck up," Tynan snapped.

I raised my hand in an apologetic gesture. "Sorry."

No one said a word – the only sound was the collective breath held by everyone in the room, processing what they had all just witnessed. I glanced around the room, wondering if everyone else was thinking the same thing as me: What was Tynan going to do next? After a full fifteen minutes of silence, Tynan finally spoke up, his voice breaking the stillness of the room.

"You and I, Raith – perhaps we are more alike than I previously thought. Neither of us is an original. You, of course, are the usurper – a parasitic personality that took over its host. I am … a lesser version of both you and Tynan."

"That's ... certainly one way of looking at things."

"Shush — I wasn't finished," Tynan snapped again, holding up his left hand. "As I was saying ... we are not Tynan. We are not the real deal. So, neither of us has a full claim to the Empire."

"I mean ..."

Tynan's jaw clenched and his eyes squinted at me, warning me to keep quiet.

"So, I believe it's only reasonable for a decision to be made regarding who the Empire should be given to, and how our fate will be determined accordingly afterwards."

Tynan watched me as if waiting for an acknowledgement. I nodded and he continued.

"Here's the choice and outcome I propose. If you get chosen, I will cede the Empire and all its power, resources — everything — to you, including this device," Tynan explained, pointing to the prototype mass conversion machine. "And if I get chosen, I will maintain control of the Empire and its riches. You and your allies will be prisoners, kept alive and forced to watch as I burn down humanity and then rebuild it from the ashes. I may not be the original, but you can be *damn* sure I'll keep Tynan's Empire alive and well and pass it down to the next generation in due course. Do you agree with these outcomes?"

"I'm not sure — who is going to make the choice?"

"Doesn't matter — do you agree to the outcomes?"

"Well, it matters because —"

"Nope — doesn't matter. Do you agree?"

"I'm not agreeing to anything until —"

"You have to answer — yes or no?"

"I told you I'm not —"

"Give me an answer now or you will automatically forfeit the futures of you and everyone you care about!"

All traces of fear had fled Tynan now. Now his nostrils were flared, and his breath was coming out in snorts. His speech was coming through increasingly clenched teeth.

I sighed. After the breakdown I had forced on him, I didn't know what would happen if I pushed his leniency too far.

"Fine. I agree with those outcomes."

"Excellent!" Tynan said with an exaggerated grin, his eyes gleefully wide. "The person who will decide which outcome prevails – which reality will come to pass – is you!" Tynan said, turning to his right and pointing to Ichirō.

"Me?" Ichirō exclaimed. "Why me?"

"Yes, you, boy! As for why you, isn't it obvious?"

Ichirō shook his head.

Tynan sighed. "Because you and you alone have the closest connection to the real Tynan. Not only are you his son, but you remember him the best – your recollection of him is, after all, unaltered and untarnished."

Ichirō glanced between me and Tynan. It was almost an impossible choice, and Tynan knew it. He, of course, represented the closest thing to Tynan's actual personality, and me ... well, I hoped that my love for Ichirō counted for something.

"Well, come on! Don't keep us waiting!" Tynan barked.

"Perhaps," I said, taking a step forward. "Perhaps we can each make a statement – to champion our respective outcomes – and help Ichirō make the choice? Say ... thirty seconds each?"

Tynan looked at me with a scowl, and then his expression turned contemplative.

"That's a good idea," he said with a gleam in his eye. "I'll go first!"

"By all means," I replied, motioning towards Ichirō.

"Boy – choose me! Together, we will build the new Empire bigger, better, and stronger than it was before! We will rule, side by side – no ambition will be too grand, no luxury too expensive. We will dine on the galaxy's best food, and we will lie with the most beautiful women – every desire, every wish, every fantasy – we shall have it all! We shall go down in history; our names will be synonymous with the likes of Caesar and Churchi –"

"And that's time, sorry – hate to cut you off."

"No, it's fine." Tynan waved away my sarcasm. "I said what needed to be said. Now, it's your turn."

"Yes … yes, it is."

I inhaled and focused. I had one opportunity to convince Ichirō that Tynan was not worth it. I looked down and realised my palm was clammy and wiped it on my shirt.

Let's do this.

"Son – this … hell of a choice, rightly or wrongly, is yours to make. And I know what it's like to be given an impossible choice, to make a decision, and then live with the consequences. Whatever choice you make, I'll respect it. But I hope that you and I, Amorina and your sisters, my mum and dad … that we'll all be able to find a new home and just live the good life in our own little slice of paradise."

Tynan turned towards me and sneered. "Wow … that was pathetic. Oh, making hard choices, let's go be a nuclear family. What kind of argument is tha –"

"I choose Raith."

Tynan swung back around to face Ichirō.

"What did you say?" he asked slowly.

"I said," Ichirō replied, standing up and leaning over Tynan. "I *choose* Raith!"

"But … but … why? You're giving up everything! All your potential! All that power!"

"You asked me to choose. I chose. Deal with it … arsehole."

Tynan shoved Ichirō, sending him stumbling backwards.

"No! I do not accept this!" he shouted and then turned to me. "You did something! You've rigged this! Or … or … you tricked me!"

"It's over, Tynan. By your own rules, you've been removed from power. Now move – you're sitting in my seat."

"It's my throne!" Tynan snapped. "I declare Ichiro's decision void! Both he and Raith are traitors to the Empire. Seize them immediately! Take them away and lock them up!"

The room remained motionless and silent.

"That overconfidence is a *bitch*, isn't it?" I mused.

"What?" Tynan asked.

"That overconfidence … or, specifically, *your* overconfidence, is a bitch."

Tynan stared at me with a perplexed look on his face.

"You know that thing that occurs when one's belief in one's ability exceeds reali-"

"I know what fucking overconfidence is!" Tynan snapped. "I just don't understand why the fuck you're talking about it!"

"I thought it was obvious – you were *so* confident in the bet that you gambled … *everything*."

The confused expression returned to Tynan's face. "What are you going on about?"

"Well, the bet was for Ichirō to decide who the Empire should be given to. If you got chosen, the Empire was yours, and if I got chosen, then the Empire was mine."

Tynan rolled his eyes. "Yes, and I declared Ichiro's decision void, remember. And in *my* Empire, my word is law!"

He glanced around the room at the soldiers.

"Come on! What are you waiting for? I said seize them!"

As the room remained motionless, I nodded. "Except for one little detail."

"What detail?" Tynan demanded.

"Your words were, and I quote, 'If you get chosen, I will cede the Empire and all its power, resources – everything – to you.' That's what you said *when* your word was law."

"And I voided those terms!" Tynan snapped.

I shook my head. "Except it doesn't work like that."

I turned and glanced around the room.

"Would you all do a spin for me, please?"

All at once, the clones in the room spun around, and a few of the loyalists attempted to follow suit, albeit not as seamlessly. I turned back and faced Tynan.

"Your voiding of the terms means nothing if you've already ceded your power."

Tynan's face fell as he looked around the room where every person he locked eyes with gave him a defiant glare.

"No ... no ... no, no, no!" Tynan growled.

"*I am* the emperor! And *I said* take them away! Lock them up!" he screamed desperately, but still, not a soul moved.

"Please escort Tynan to an isolated cell so that he can think about his choices."

A dozen soldiers immediately moved forward, making a beeline for Tynan, who looked at me in sheer and utter shock. I smiled, baring my teeth slightly.

Gotcha, bitch.

Ichirō and I took a step back, and in that same moment, Tynan lunged forward and snatched two of the soldier's weapons from their holsters. Shots rang out as Tynan started shooting and before the soldiers could react, their bodies jerked and fell, unmoving, to the floor. Shots continued to echo through the room. A few soldiers realised what was happening and attempted to flee, but Tynan had them in his line of fire.

"This is my throne! This is *my* Empire!" Tynan yelled and shot them in the back.

His eyes were wide, and his motions frenzied, covered in blood splatter, surrounded by the fallen soldiers. Satisfied that no one else was going to apprehend him, Tynan levelled his guns at Ichirō and I.

"No one and nothing is going to take tha –"
Bang!

A gun fired from somewhere behind us; a bullet tore through Tynan's right calf, and with a pained grunt, he crumpled to the ground, one of the guns flying from his hand. As he fell, he twisted to see who had had the audacity to shoot him. Almost all the other heads in the room swivelled as well, just as interested to see who the assailant was.

"Phobus?" Tynan asked, betrayal evident in his pained tone. "Why?"

Phobus let the gun he held drop to the floor, his head raised defiantly. "You're a failed science experiment ... *not* an emperor."

Tynan pushed himself up and lent against his throne, wincing at the pain he must have felt pulsing through his leg.

"It took me a while to realise as much – too long, perhaps. But I've realised that you are toxic.

Your imperfections have been poisoning the Empire, your loyalists, and –" Phobus looked at Lorcan beside him "– your advisors as well."

Phobus glanced towards me, then turned back to look at Tynan. "I realised it was time to administer the cure."

Tynan scowled. "Cure this, you maggot!"

He lifted the gun still held in his grasp and fired two rounds into Phobus. Phobus slumped over in his wheelchair, his white advisor robes quickly turning red. Tynan slowly turned his gun towards Lorcan, struggling to hold the gun up.

"No, Your Grace – I had nothing to do with this – please, have mercy!" Lorcan cried.

"This is my mercy!"

Two more shots rang out and Lorcan slumped forward. Tynan's grip on the gun loosened and it fell to the floor. Instantly, several soldiers saw their opportunity and raced forward to capture their former leader.

Finally, the Empire was no more.

Chapter 15
When Guilt Leads to Good

2161, Common Era – Planet Erebus, Frontier Space, Tynan Empire

The transition of power can be chaotic and an unpredictable process, and that was certainly true for the Empire. All eyes were on me, and everyone expected me to provide answers for every question, even if I didn't have the answers myself. I couldn't go five metres without being accosted by Empire loyalists and Insurgency members alike. They swamped me whenever I left my temporary accommodation, which I would go to any chance I got.

I would steal away a few minutes in the apartment just to find Amorina and hold her. Each time I'd ask myself is there a sweeter hug than embracing someone you thought dead and gone? I didn't want to answer my question, fearful of the circumstances that would lead to a sweeter hug. With each embrace, I was afraid to let go, foolishly believing that if I did so, she would disappear – perhaps irrevocably so. But for now, I was thankful for each embrace I shared with my wife. After all, it was only a few days ago when I'd believed I'd never feel her warmth again.

"You can let go of me now."

I pulled myself out of my thoughts and let go of Amorina, stepping away and averting my gaze, my fingers absent-mindedly massaging the back of my neck.

"Sorry. I was just … you know, thinking about –"

"I know!" Amorina huffed. "You don't have to explain every time – just give me shorter hugs, okay? You're beginning to make me feel smothered."

"Yeah, okay. Sorry – again."

Amorina held up a hand and glared at me.

I nodded and watched as she went and sat down in the bay window of the apartment; the sun casting her in a golden glow. Ever since the events in the throne room, I'd sensed a divide between us, but I couldn't grasp the cause of our disconnect. As she gazed out the windows at the bleak scenery of Erebus, I knew she wasn't there to take in the sights – it was just to avoid me.

"Daddy! Daddy!" I turned around to grab a hold of Emma as she raced up behind me.

"Hey there, sweetie pie! What've you been up to?" I asked as I picked her up and rested her on my hip.

"Mummy and I played hide and seek, and then Ichirō joined us as well! Now you can play with us too!"

I saw Ichirō entering the room, and I gave him a warm smile and nod. It delighted me when my son returned the nod; his demeanour had really improved since the throne room events and was getting better each day. He'd been unburdened of the weight he'd carried for the last several years, a feeling I knew all too well. He'd figured out why he remembered everything and had freed himself from Tynan's shadow. Ichirō was now gesturing toward Amorina, and as I looked over towards my wife, I knew a family game of hide and seek would have to wait.

"I would love to play with you, darling – but I can't right now, okay? Daddy needs to tend to some things, but Ichirō will play with you."

"Okay ..." Emma said, her voice heavy with disappointment.

"Ah, come on, sis! We can have fun while we wait for Mum and Dad to join us, yeah?"

As Emma nodded, I heard Amorina's sharp intake of breath when Ichirō called her mum – a moment that brought warmth to my heart.

I put Emma down, and she ran over to her brother, and with another nod in my direction, Ichirō led her into the other room.

I turned and slowly walked over to Amorina, sat down beside her, and stared at the dry, dusty world outside.

"What is it?" I asked.

"What is what?" Her tone was flat.

"What is the issue between us?"

"I don't know wh –"

"Don't –" I said, cutting Amorina off. "Don't pretend like you don't know what I'm talking about. Ever since the other day, in the throne room, you've been … I don't know – cagey? Distant?"

Amorina continued to stare out the window, but her lip quivered, and her eyes moistened.

"Was it real?"

I had to lean forward to capture her quiet words.

Was what real?

I shook my head in bewilderment. "Was what real?"

"The darkness – Tynan!" she snapped, finally turning towards me. "When he … when he emerged from you! Was that fucking real?"

"Pfft, no – of course not," I said dismissively. "Why would you think it was?"

I'd assumed Amorina would know it had been an act, but as she glared at me, I knew I'd miscalculated.

"Why would I think that?" Amorina said in her the-answer-should-be-fucking-obvious voice.

"Why would I think that?" she repeated as she got to her feet. "Let's go through why I might fucking think that, Raith!"

I momentarily considered telling her to calm down, but could only see that making things worse, and so, as Amorina paced back and forth, her onslaught began.

"When I first met you, Tynan's fucking voice was inside your head, tormenting you day and night." Amorina's voice quivered with rage as she spoke. "Sometimes ... sometimes he would even take control of your body, verbally and physically hurting those around you!"

"But that —"

"I wasn't finished!" she snapped. "In theory, we killed that part of you, but how sure can we be that he's really gone? Then you pull a stunt like the other day — what the hell was I supposed to think?"

Tears were now running down Amorina's face, and I shrugged helplessly.

"I don't know what to tell you ... except that it wasn't real."

"You say it wasn't real, but it was so goddamn convincing!" she sobbed. "How am I supposed to tell if you're playing pretend or if he's really back?"

"He's not back, okay! Trust —"

"Trust you?" Amorina exclaimed in an incredulous tone. "I don't even know which 'you' I'd be trusting!"

Amorina's words were like a thousand tiny claws latching onto my soul and ripping it apart. I know I'd intended my act to be convincing, but the last thing I expected was for it to shatter the bond between us. After all, the trust between us as husband and wife was meant to be the strongest bond between any two people in the universe.

And we don't even have that?

"Amorina ... please!" I pleaded, my heart breaking. "It's me, Raith!"

"And let's not forget the discoveries we made over the last two days," Amorina continued, ignoring my plea. "The fact that you experimented on your own son to save your own skin."

"How can you say all that?" I said as I leapt to my feet. "That was before I became Raith!"

"Or what about the halls full of artificial wombs, churning out clones? Or the mind-altering rooms that turn those clones into loyal soldiers? You did all of those things, you invented all of those technologies!"

This exchange had transformed from a rant to air grievances into a personal attack. Amorina knew my past and understood the difference between the life I'd lived as Tynan and the life I lived as Raith. I felt a sharp stab of betrayal in my chest, and a dull throbbing pain took up residence.

"You know damn well I personally had nothing to do with any of those – that was all Tynan's doing!"

"And that's my point! Where does Tynan end and Raith begin?"

Silence filled the room as we stood there staring at each other.

Did she really believe that?

"I can't believe you just said that ..." My voice came out in a harsh whisper.

"You can't believe that?" Amorina whispered back. "Do you have *any* idea how terrified you made me in that throne room?" she screamed as her body shook. "I couldn't tell that it wasn't real! I thought Tynan had awakened and taken you over, and that *horrified* me!"

Tears streamed down her face that was twisted into a melding of anger, terror, and concern.

"I'm sorry ... I wasn't trying to scare you – I was trying to break Tynan."

Amorina sniffed and wiped the tears from her face.

"We've learnt that Tynan's foresight was ... obsessive. He looked forward, saw the possibility of his own demise and engineered many a failsafe to counter those futures.

The Empire loyalists enacted those plans, giving rise to the new Tynan. A clone who attacked and kidnapped us, who killed thousands of people and destroyed hundreds of ships. He was content to watch humanity burn if it meant he could rebuild it in his image!" Amorina said in a hushed, venomous tone.

Where is she going with this?

"Then I look at you and I see the same obsessiveness … I see the fire glowing in your eyes. That terrifies me, Raith. You think you're different from Tynan … but I'm not so sure."

"You think you're different from Tynan … but I'm not so sure."

My world shattered.

"You think you're different from Tynan …"

My fears had come true. To defeat a monster, I'd become a monster – to the point where my wife, the one person left in this universe who knew me best, couldn't tell the difference between man and beast.

"I see the fire glowing in your eyes."

Ever since discovering my clone, I'd known this was a possibility; the chance that I'd become something my family couldn't recognise as I paid the high price of freedom.

I nodded and turned away, heading for the apartment exit.

"Where are you going?" Amorina called after me.

"I need … time to think."

𝄞 𝄢 ♥ 𝄐 𝄇

I stepped out of the apartment to a cacophony of voices and questions, the crowd eager for direction.

I wished Knox could deal with all of this, but the Empire clones and loyalists wouldn't listen to her, and the Insurgency members – well, they simply chose not to. Aside from the suite, there was one other place I could go where the mob wouldn't tread. I answered questions as I walked, but intentionally set a fast pace, aiming for my location of solitude.

As I made my way further into the depths of the facility, more and more of the surrounding pack realised where I was headed and dispersed. The final people slipped away, and the atmosphere shifted to a peaceful silence, with the only sound being faint background static and my footsteps. I came up to a bulkhead door, and its integrated security system spoke up.

"Restricted area. Two-factor biometric authentication required to verify authorisation."

I stepped forward and placed my head up against a scanner, waiting while it scanned my eye. With the scan complete, I took a step back and spoke.

"Raith."

After a moment, the system spoke again.

"Tynan: successfully authenticated and authorised. Proceed."

A shiver ran down my spine. Amorina couldn't tell where I ended and where Tynan began – and neither could this security machine it seemed.

With a metallic clang, the bulkhead doors split and slid apart. Once the gap was wide enough, I stepped through into the prison. In here, the sound of someone sobbing replaced the silence. As I headed towards the only occupied cell, my steps echoed throughout the hall and its vacant cages, heralding my arrival.

"Who – who's there? Who's coming?" came the prisoner's strained, exhausted question.

I remained silent.

"Can you let me out? Please?" the prisoner begged. "I can't stay here – it's driving me crazy! It's so quiet … all I can hear are my own thoughts – do you know what that's like?"

I stepped into view of the cell. "Yes, yes I do."

"Oh," came the disheartened response. "It's you."

Tynan looked terrible. He was sitting on the ground, slumped against the wall. His face was gaunter than before, his eyes swollen and red with dark circles beneath them. He was a sorry sight with his soiled clothes, tangled hair, and leg tightly wound in bandages.

So, this is what a broken man looks like.

"Well, let's be honest," I intoned. "No one else is in a hurry to come and see you."

Tynan shifted his eyes away from me, focusing on the floor of his cage.

"Question is …" he replied as he picked at a spot on the floor. "Why *have* you come to see me?"

"Well, for one, I came to check on you. And for another, it's quiet down here … and I needed some quiet."

Tynan looked up at me and smiled, the result creepier than usual curtesy of his sunken eyes and gaunt cheeks. "Not so easy running an empire, is it?"

"Not so easy being locked up in isolation, is it?" I immediately fired back.

Tynan's momentary glee evaporated, and he returned his gaze to the floor. It felt powerful to be standing over him, in complete control of his fate. It was my prerogative to show him mercy or to make him suffer.

"Speaking of your isolation, how *is* it going in here?"

Tynan's face twitched, and he shook his head. "I'm not talking to you."

"Okay."

The prison was silent once more, and I watched Tynan as he attempted to conceal the movement of his eyes as they flicked between me and the spot on the floor. But he remained silent, bar the growling of his stomach, so I shrugged and turned away, beginning the walk back to the prison entrance.

"Wait!" Tynan screeched. "Don't leave me!"

I turned back towards the cell. "Are you going to talk to me?"

Again, Tynan's eyes flicked between me and the spot on the floor.

"I'll have an extra meal brought down to you."

"Okay, fine! Yes! Yes, I'll talk. But bring the food down now, okay?"

"Okay, I will. Hey Bitsy?"

My faithful Arachnobot sprung to life as it transformed from its watch form to its arachnid form.

Hello Raith! How can I help?

"Can you please go to the kitchens and get them to send down a roast meal please?"

Of course.

Bitsy scurried down my body to the floor and then scuttled off down the length of the hall to place the food order.

"Why did you send that thing? It's going to take ages to get to the kitchen and back!"

"Because that's how long you'll talk to me for. When the food gets here, I'll leave."

Tynan gave a small nod, his lips pressed together in a thin line, as if he was begrudgingly accepting this.

"So, start talking. How's it going down here?"

My doppelgänger remained silent, continuing to focus on his cell floor.

"You know, I'll happily eat the roast meal when it arrives." I smacked my lips. "The crunch of those golden roasted potatoes and the crackling on the pork. The juicy, lightly salted carrots, peas, and soft roasted pumpkin. And let's not forget the rich gravy and applesauce."

Tynan's stomach erupted into a flurry of gurgles and grumbles. "Stop! I'll talk!"

"Good. Let's hear it."

"You want to know what it's like down here? It's hell, okay? When there's no movement, the lights go out, and it's so fucking quiet in here." Tynan's voice cracked as he spoke. "I'm always hungry, and always isolated. I don't even know how much time has passed – it feels like I've been here for weeks!"

"It's been four – almost five days."

"Only five days?" Tynan exclaimed, his eyes wide with disbelief. "I am literally going insane!"

"Probably not. Anyway, continue."

"What do you want me to say, Raith? That I know what it's like now, that I can understand what I put you through?"

"What you put me through?" I asked, bewildered.

"This is nothing like what you put me through. Your lunatics performed open brain surgery on me, without anaesthetic. Then post-surgery, you locked me in a pitch black, soundproof cell, with no toilet, for eight months – not five days – *eight fucking months*. All without proper medical care or nutrition to allow my body to heal. It's a fucking miracle I survived, to be honest."

"Yeah, I get it," Tynan said.

"I really don't think you do. Because you locked me in the same cell for another few months, once again surrounded by darkness and waste, my heartbeat pounding away in my ears, day in, day out. For goddamn months!

And you think you're doing it tough in here after five days, with your motion-activated lights, your toilet, and your shower?"

Tynan looked away, avoiding my gaze "Don't look at me like that."

"Look at you like what?" I snarled.

"Don't look at me with that look of disgust on your face."

"Why not, Tynan? Why shouldn't I be disgusted with you? You are breaking down after only one week in your 'luxurious' confinement, when you have made others suffer far worse."

"Because it makes me feel more pathetic than I already feel!"

I frowned, surprised by his comment. "You feel … pathetic?"

"Yes!" Tynan wailed. "The real Tynan showed me … what I really am – a fraud! A poor imitation of the real deal!"

Tears streamed down my doppelgänger's face as he continued.

"I wasn't him. I could never be *him*. Those bloody advisors and their janky technology – it took a bad copy! I was *meant* to be *just* like the original. Instead, I am this … this … fake!" He waved his hands up and down indicating himself.

I almost felt bad watching Tynan blubber away, but whilst being hard to watch, it was also satisfying – he had finally begun to pay his dues.

"These flaws … all of this corruption … that the scans took from you. It's made me … it's made me a … a coward! And … and I just feel so … so guilty! All the time! All the goddamn time!"

I knelt down, bringing myself closer to Tynan's level.

"What do you feel guilty for?" I inquired.

Could he be feeling remorseful?

"All of it! How I treated you … how I treated Ichirō … the ships I destroyed, and the people onboard … that I killed … oh god – I killed so many!"

"There's more to it than that, though, isn't there?"

Tynan looked up, meeting my gaze once more. "Please … please don't add to the burden that's weighing down on me. I don't know how much more I can take!"

"Good – that means you're already cracking under the weight of your guilt. Let's see how much it takes to break you, aye?"

"What?" Tynan asked, a flash of fear crossing his face.

I doubted he'd felt much fear during his brief existence, but I wanted him to feel it. I wanted him to experience what he'd put so many through. As the memory of Tynan's hands wrapped around my throat surfaced, I knew exactly what words to use.

"I want you to live the rest of your life struggling to breathe, feeling trapped, suffocated, frantically searching for air, and never finding any. And just when you lose hope, I'll let you take a breath."

Tynan blinked at me and whispered, "Tynan?"

"What?" I demanded. "No, you fucking idiot. Why would you think that?"

"I couldn't tell who was speaking. I thought he had arisen again."

I felt a pang of guilt, and Amorina's words echoed through my mind.

"I see the fire glowing in your eyes. You think you're different from Tynan but I'm not so sure."

Tynan couldn't tell if he was talking to Raith or Tynan. Amorina couldn't tell.

As I continued to kneel before my doppelgänger, I realised the dark tone I'd been imparting … and I liked it. I could understand Tynan's confusion and his difficulty in knowing who he was speaking to. Should I tone it back?

Ah fuck it. In for a penny, in for a pound, right?

"You need to take it," I said as I refocused. "You need to own the consequences of your actions."

"Am I not already?" Tynan implored. "What other actions could there possibly be for me to own?"

I smiled, and Tynan's face shifted into an apprehensive expression.

"Imagine this," I said, wanting to paint a picture in Tynan's mind. "Zavis comes to you one day with a report. A signal has been discovered, coming from deep space."

Tynan froze, the blood draining from his already pale skin, leaving him looking deathly.

"A signal from deep space," I repeated as I continued. "That's kinda cool, you think – it piques your interest. You ponder this mysterious signal, trying to understand what it is."

"Stop," Tynan croaked.

"The report says … this signal is a radio transmission containing a binaural beat."

"You shouldn't remember this," Tynan said as he began to rock back and forth. "Stop. Don't say any more."

"You researched what these binaural beats were and learned that when the brain processes them, they induce theta waves. And so, you research theta waves … and that research gives you some ideas, doesn't it?"

"I said stop!" Tynan said more insistently as he got onto his hands and knees.

"You invent designs and build machinery that is capable of rewriting people's minds.

It takes a few tries, but you finally build a machine that can do the job, one person at a time. You also get new reports during this time, detailing how the exploration vessels sent to find the source of the signal have stopped transmitting. You knew your vessels were capable machines – for them to stop broadcasting – they must've been destroyed. That means whatever is out there is either a weapon or a thing with great offensive capability."

Tynan was crawling towards me now. "I fucking said stop!"

"You design a device capable of mass conversion. It will work by blasting out theta waves and rewriting millions of people's minds simultaneously. Of course, your own mind is overwritten by your more primitive machine before you can see this plan realised, but your advisors carry on your hard work."

Tynan lunged forward, reaching through the bars and grabbing a hold of my shirt. He tries to pull me in towards him but lacks the strength to do so.

"Please," he begs, his eyes moist and his lips quivering. "Stop!"

I lock eyes with my doppelgänger. "You didn't know what was on the other end of that signal, but you built a dinner bell, and you rang it anyway, anticipating that it would bring the source to us. And it worked."

I paused and watched Tynan's face.

He knew there was one last line to say, his expression begging for it not to be said.

"But you don't have to imagine ... do you?"

"You've made your point! For the love of all that is good, please stop!"

"I haven't finished," I snarled. "Do you know how many people were on Akka? Ten thousand."

Tynan let go of my shirt and clutched the bars of his cell, pulling himself closer.

"Please … I'm begging you! Stop!"

"Do you know how many people were on Gaia?"

"Please!" Tynan whispered.

"Four hundred thousand people. And every one of them is dead because of you. Because of your choices. So, when you're looping through all the actions you feel guilty for … make sure you include all of those people. Cause that's all on you, too."

Tynan let out an almost inhuman wail and sobbed against the cell bars. I quickly stood and moved away, shivering as a chill ran down my spine, triggered by his screams as they echoed through the hall.

"Tell me!" Tynan yelled. "T-t-tell me … how to g-get rid of t-these feelings!"

"You can't get rid of them!" I snarled.

Tynan's body trembled as he fell silent, as if trying to fight back the tears.

"There has to be … s-some way of … getting r-redemption?"

I shook my head. "Honestly, Tynan … I don't know that you ever can. With everything you've done – I think you're irredeemable. The salvation you're looking for – I don't think it exists for people like you."

Tynan's body went limp, and I couldn't help but think this was the moment of critical failure. I'd crushed his spirit and broken his soul. There was no absolution for his sins, no way to undo his deeds.

The bulkhead doors opened, and a man walked in with a plate of fresh, hot food.

"The plate of food you ordered, sir," he said as he neared, handing over the dish.

It seemed that Bitsy had hitched a ride on the man and took the opportunity to jump off and scuttle back over to me.

"Thank you," I said as I took the plate.

As Bitsy settled back onto my right wrist, I watched the man leave the hall. Once he'd gone, I slid the food into Tynan's cell. But rather than immediately grabbing the plate and devouring its contents, as I'd expected he'd do, Tynan just sat there, staring at it forlornly. A calmness seemed to have fallen over him.

The calm after the emotional storm, perhaps?

"So, tell me," he whispered as he wiped his eyes dry. "What's happening up above? What plans are in motion to clean up my mess?"

Odd questions to pivot too.

"It's like I told you a few days ago – we're going to take the mass conversion device and try to lead the Horror away."

"How?"

I narrowed my eyes. What information was Tynan seeking?

"We'll attach the device to a ship, setting it to trigger periodically, with the ship being piloted to just keep ahead of the Horror. With any luck, it'll follow the theta blasts and we can lead it back into deep space."

I noticed a gleam in Tynan's eye.

"A person would pilot the vessel?" Tynan asked as he glanced up at me.

I nodded.

"Surely that would harm them," he uttered. "Being so close to the device and repeatedly exposed to so many blasts?"

I nodded again. "We don't know what effect it will have for sure – the blasts won't be applying any kind of profile. It'd more be like white noise, but we don't anticipate it positively affecting the individual. The crazy thing is we've had no shortage of volunteers for the piloting role."

Tynan picked up a roast potato from the plate, placing it in his mouth whole, and I smiled as it gave a satisfying crunch. After he'd chewed and swallowed, he looked over at me.

"Let me do it."

I studied him with narrowed eyes. "Do what?"

"Let me pilot the ship."

My eyes shot wide. "Ah … absolutely not!"

"I know … I know I'm irredeemable, but surely – surely if I do this, it must count for something, right? Let me be the one to get fucked over by the theta blasts. That has to be a worthy punishment, right?"

I narrowed my eyes again, suspicious of Tynan's motives. Was this a genuine act of self-sacrifice, or a ploy to escape?

"If you're playing an angle, it won't work. Volunteering for this mission isn't some … get out of jail free card."

"I know."

"If you think you can use the device bearing ship as an escape vessel, you can't. It's going to be a hunk of junk, only just capable of staying ahead of the Horror – no warp capability. If you think you can deviate from the course we set, to lead the Horror back towards civilisation, we will vent the ship remotely. You will die a sad death, alone in the void of space. If you think you can tamper with the conversion device, you can't – it'll be mounted to the ship's exterior. You'll not be provided with a space suit."

"I mean what I'm saying. Let me be that person – let me be that pilot. I don't want to run. I want to atone. Let this be my penance. Please!"

I watched as Tynan pleaded. It really seemed like he was being genuine.

Could he really be willing to sacrifice himself like this?

If he meant what he said, this would be a win-win – get rid of Tynan and spare an innocent person from suffering a terrible fate in the service of humanity.

"I will … consult with others about your offer. I'll let you know in due course what we've decided. For now, enjoy your roast before it gets cold."

I turned and began the walk back towards the bulkhead doors. Uncertainty and doubt swirled through my mind. Offering himself up like that was a very Raith-like action. My cruelness during the conversation had been very Tynan-like. The encounter with "the real Tynan" in the throne room had really done a number on us both.

Who even am I anymore?

❦

There had been a surprising appetite for Tynan's offer to pilot the vessel. Thanks to the Insurgency's monitoring of the Horror, we knew where the monstrosity had gone. The Chupacabra was equipped with fabrication equipment, materials, and the ship that would be the MCD bearing vessel – it would be prepared for its mission on the way. After loading the passengers into cryosleep, including Amorina and Tynan, we set off for our rendezvous with the Horror. I opted out of cryosleep, choosing instead to oversee the MCD vessel's preparations and construct a new arm for myself. I also wanted time to be alone and reflect on who I was. Who I wanted to be.

Every day I would go to the observation deck, sit down cross-legged on the floor and meditate under the hazy blue light cone of warp travel. I sat close enough to the window to see my faint reflection in the glass.

Who am I?

I stared at my face – my tired, scarred, aging face. A face that was too old, too bent and broken for the time that I had used it.

What am I?

I am alone in the universe. There is no one else like me, and if I had my way, there would be no one else like me either. One body that had played host to two very different lives. One lived cruelly and cowardly, serving only the self. The other lived kind and courageously, serving all but the self.

Which am I?

But which was which and which was I? One was born from the other, like a phoenix, rising from the ashes of the previous. But this new life, its skin was stained by those ashes – a discoloration that could never be scrubbed off or erased.

Which do I want to be?

I looked down at my left arm, reborn out of oil and steel. It was more than just an appendage now – it was a tool, like a hammer. I closed my metallic fingers, curling them into a fist. Now I could wield it like a weapon, capable of demolishing, bending, and breaking. I opened my fist, spreading my fingers out flat and wide. Now I could wield it like a tool, capable of building, mending, and making.

You are what you choose to be.

Good or bad. Tool or weapon. That was the question. I was capable of both. Tynan and Raith lived inside me, their personalities and traits present in my neurons and genes.

"My choices affect others ... so *choose* ... choose how those choices affect them."

❧

One year later, I stood in the hangar bay control room. There was a monitor to my left with a live video of what was left of Ares, the Horror almost complete in its destruction of the planet. Amorina was standing beside me, and we watched as a group of Insurgency members led Tynan into the hangar bay. As they undid his restraints, he slowly raised his head and fixed his gaze upon me. I hadn't spoken to him since that day in the prison, but with a subtle nod, Tynan conveyed all that needed to be said – thank you. Thank you for the opportunity to try and redeem himself. I nodded back in acknowledgment and watched as they pushed Tynan into the vessel, and the door closed behind him. The Insurgency members quickly left the hangar, and I reached out and activated the depressurization process.

As we waited for the process to complete, I turned towards Amorina. "You know when we last talked?" I said, referring to the argument that had happened only a few days ago for her but a year ago for me.

"Yeah?"

"You said you didn't know where I ended and where Tynan began."

"I remember," Amorina said curtly.

"I couldn't answer that," I said, pausing as I considered how to proceed. "And that man down there ... he couldn't answer it, either."

"What's your point?"

"My point is that he wanted to be Tynan but couldn't be – there was too much Raith in him. He couldn't separate what was Tynan and what was Raith.

If it wasn't for that part of me inside him, he wouldn't have felt remorse, and without that guilt, we couldn't have beaten him — not like we did. Nor would he have volunteered to do this."

Amorina shrugged. "What are you getting at, Raith?"

"That I can tell the difference. I know where the line is. In myself, but also in Tynan. I knew how to manipulate him because I understood, intimately so, the guilt that he was feeling because that's the guilt that I feel."

"Hanger depressurised," announced the control console.

I pressed a few more buttons on the console, opening the hangar bay doors. As they slid apart, Ares and the Horror came into view, the planet looking tiny and helpless compared to the bulk of its captor. The ship below powered up, rose off the floor of the hanger, and slowly eased itself out into space. Once it was clear of the doors, I initiated the closing sequence and focused on the exterior view of the ship. Tynan's vessel flew to its designated coordinates and a 30 second timer appeared on screen.

"Tynan's willingness to sacrifice himself is a product of both the guilt and the empathy inside of him. Those are both attributes they mistakenly copied from me. You want to know where one personality ends and the other begins? That's the dividing line."

The timer reached zero and on-screen we could see a pulse blasting away from Tynan's vessel. The Horror reacted immediately, its great swarming tendrils retreating from Ares and moving towards the ship instead. On-screen the timer had started again, and Tynan had begun to move the ship, keeping it ahead of the Horror's arms.

"That may be true," Amorina said slowly. "But the fact that there's a line at all means that there are traits of Tynan's that you will always have ..."

I nodded. "Yes, but I control those darker impulses – I have been doing so for years."

"Is that enough, though? Enough to keep the darkness inside you suppressed?"

"I have to believe so," I said as another pulse emitted from Tynan's ship. "I didn't think witnessing what we're seeing right now was possible. That my doppelgänger would not only volunteer for but follow through on an offer to self-sacrifice and lead a civilisation killing threat away from ... well, civilisation. Even the impossible can happen when guilt leads to good."

"Why are you telling me this?"

"Because I did a lot of soul searching over the last year. Trying to understand what I am, who I want to be ... that kind of thing. The first step is admitting you have a problem, right? I acknowledge that there are elements of Tynan within me ... and there always will be. But I am the master of my fate – by my actions and choices alone – I determine who and what I am."

Amorina looked at me with a concerned, teary gaze. "Don't make me a promise you can't keep," she whispered.

"Good or bad. Tool or weapon. I am capable of being either. You are what you choose to be, and I choose to build, not demolish. I choose to mend and make, not bend and break. This is my promise – to never be cruel or cowardly."

"For both our sakes ... I hope so."

I nodded.

I hope so too.

"Can you forgive me? For all the pain I've caused you?"

Tears rolled down Amorina's face. "You have already been forgiven, my dear. The problem is your actions have not been forgotten."

I nodded again. It made sense. It was in her nature to forgive, but to forget, well ... very rarely was that a choice – for anybody.

"Do you think we can move past this? That you could trust me again?"

Amorina shrugged sadly. "I don't know," she whispered. "I can't promise you that a year or two will pass and that things will magically be as they were before. But I will try ... to move past this. To trust you again. But ... there're no guarantees."

I smiled. It wasn't a solution, or a promise ... but it was a willingness to try, and I would take what I could get.

"Thank you," I whispered as my own tears fell.

Amorina chuckled and wiped off her wet cheeks.

"Look at the pair of us, aye? Bawling our eyes out."

I chuckled. "It's good, right? Good to let it all out."

"Yeah." Amorina smiled sadly. "Come on, bring it in and give me a hug!"

I didn't need to be told twice and immediately stepped forward. I pulled Amorina into an embrace and lifted her off the ground.

"Ooh!" she exclaimed in surprise.

"I've missed you. I've missed this!" I whispered, burying my face in her neck and breathing in her scent deeply.

"I missed you too," she whispered back.

Everything will be okay ... right?

Chapter 16
All's Well That Ends Well

2163, Common Era – Earth, Inner Rim, the Republic of Humanity

"Raith, do you have any last statements to make before this council delivers its verdict?"

The great hall of the Republic Council was filled to capacity, and as I looked out at the sea of representatives, the air was filled with the sound of shuffling papers and murmurs. I scanned over the faces of the people who had grilled me for the last seven days. The delegation consisted of councillors from Machina Station in the Mid Rim, representatives from the Inner Rim worlds of Earth, Mars, Terranova, and Astarte, and a lone governor from the Frontier world of Akka.

Their lines of questioning were thorough and intense – and rightly so.

When did I become aware of Tynan's existence? Had I taken appropriate steps to alert the Republic of the Empire's resurrection? When did I become aware of the Horror's existence? Why did I work with Tynan to attack the Horror? Why did I convince President Knox to work with Tynan rather than arresting or destroying him?

On and on the questioning went, grilling every action, every choice, every move and thought I'd made over the last few years – though it didn't feel that long to me.

I surveyed the crowd and considered the many questions asked, searching for a final statement that could sway the council's decision in my favour.

"No, I have no further statement to make, councillors," I answered with a shake of my head.

"Very well then," said the speaker of the house. "The council representatives will now give their final votes."

The sound of clicking buttons filled the room as each member leaned forward to cast their final votes on the desk panels in front of them. After a few moments, the speaker's panel lit up, and they viewed the results.

The speaker cleared his throat, then began his address. "The Republic Council's verdict is as follows … on the charge of private correspondence with a foreign government, the council finds you … guilty."

Amidst the crowd, I was able to pick out President Knox. I'd discovered that she was the one who had made the bulk of the accusations against me, resulting in this week-long inquiry and the charges I now faced. Right now, she was smiling, but I hoped the further verdicts would erase her grin.

"On the charge of using weapons of mass destruction, the council finds you … guilty."

I noticed the anxiety on the faces of Amorina, Ichirō, Emma, Adanna, Winona, and my father as they waited for the verdicts from the spectator seating. Already their faces were falling, twisting with despair at the two guilty verdicts.

"On the charge of assisting or instigating the escape of a fugitive, the council finds you … guilty."

Tears flowed as my family's reactions worsened. This wasn't how we'd expected events would go. As painful as it was to lose my mother to her illness, I couldn't help but feel grateful that she was spared the heartache of seeing these verdicts.

"On the charge of destruction of Republic property, the council finds you … innocent."

I glanced over at Knox just in time to see her smug smile fade a little. I knew her accusations had been an act of self-preservation – an attempt to shift the spotlight and the blame away from herself.

Every innocent verdict I got would be an extra area of scrutiny placed on her in her own up-and-coming trial.

"On the charge of treason, the council finds you … innocent."

As Knox's smile disappeared a bit more, I could feel my mouth curve upward at the corners.

"On the charge of mass murder, the council finds you … innocent."

I really had to focus to not smile after that announcement – it probably wouldn't be a good look to smile after they've said you didn't commit mass murder.

"And on the charge of crimes against humanity, the council finds you … innocent."

With a sigh of relief, I felt the tension leave my body. That was by far the worst charge that had been brought against me, and now it posed no threat. Knox's smile had disappeared completely now, and I finally allowed myself to crack a slight grin.

"That gives us three guilty verdicts and four innocent verdicts. Before we move forward, the council wants to recognise that while you have been found guilty on certain charges, the circumstances that led to your actions were beyond your control. They wish it to be noted that the final decision takes into account the extenuating circumstances."

I gave a quick nod of confirmation to the speaker. I knew that they'd designed the trial to be a show, to some extent, to prove to the Republic that those involved in the crisis would face consequences. Still, I was glad for that clarity – whilst they'd deemed me guilty, the sentence was going to be a soft ruling rather than a harsh one.

"The council wishes to offer you a choice of sentence regarding the atonement you must face for these guilty verdicts.

You can either endure three years of imprisonment, or five years as commander of Project RESTORE – the Restoration of Extrasolar Stella Territories, Organic and Residential Environments."

The speaker's last statement caught me off guard; the idea of giving a convict a choice of sentence was unprecedented. I'd also never heard of Project RESTORE before.

"Can I please get clarification of what this Project RESTORE is?"

"Of course. Republic surveyors have evaluated Akka, Gaia, Ares, and Erebus and confirmed their terraformability. And thanks to the confiscated Empire vessels, we have a fleet of ships capable of being deployed to those worlds and carrying out the terraforming work. The ships are there, and we have provisioned the crews – all that remains is for someone to lead the project and ensure its successful delivery. Since you inadvertently played a hand in discovering or decimating those worlds, it seems only fair to offer you a chance to rebuild them."

Seeking guidance, I turned to my family, knowing that whatever I decided would have consequences for all of us. As I watched them, they focused on Amorina, waiting for her to make the initial choice. She held up two fingers, making the peace sign, and the family followed suit one by one – each holding up two fingers as well.

"Thank you, councillors, for your leniency in this matter. I appreciate being given the choice of sentence and I gratefully accept the role of commander for Project RESTORE."

The speaker smiled and nodded. "And this council thanks you, Raith, for your actions in the face of insurmountable odds."

As the councillors rose to their feet and gave a round of applause, I smiled. This was a victory.

Stepping out of the council building's side entrance, the bright sunlight washed over me, and I couldn't help but close my eyes and take a deep breath. Every world had its own unique air, a complex mixture of gases and smells, shaped by their elemental composition, the local flora and fauna, and the activities of its inhabitants. The air in the city, especially in the government district, was almost sterile, devoid of any natural or industrial scents. But I kind of liked it anyway, if only to appreciate its uniqueness, and that today it smelt like freedom.

"Daddy!"

My heart leapt at the sound of my youngest's voice, and I opened my eyes just in time to see Emma racing towards me from my left, with the rest of the family trailing behind.

"Hey there, sweetie pie! How you doin'?" I asked as I knelt down, and my daughter raced into my arms.

"I'm good, Daddy. Are you okay?" she replied, radiating joy.

Seeing her smile was one of the few things that brought me true happiness, and I grinned in return. "Yes … yes I am."

It was a rare moment of genuine happiness that I savoured with every fibre of my being. Parents must often reassure their children that all is well, even when it isn't, because adult issues are not for children to bear. Thus, it made it all the more satisfying when we could actually, and honestly, say things are good.

"Well done, son," my father said as the family caught up to us.

I let go of Emma and stood up, then my father pulled me into a hug.

"I'm proud of you," he whispered in my ear.

As Father let go and stepped back, Adanna and Winona stepped forward and hugged me simultaneously.

"Hey Dad!" they both said.

"Hello my dears! I've missed you both so much!"

The weight of lost time hit me as I held them, and I felt my eyes moistening with tears. It'd been almost three years since I'd seen them last. I'd already missed so much of their lives, and now I'd lost even more time with them.

"We've missed you as well!" Winona replied, her voice wavering as she spoke.

We let go of each other and I held them at arm's length, taking a moment to gaze at my daughters' faces. They looked a little older, a little wiser, but it filled my heart with happiness that they both appeared to be healthy and happy.

"You both look … fantastic! I look forward to hearing all about your adventures!"

"We can't wait to hear about *your* adventures!" Adanna replied with a grin.

I chuckled. "There'll be time for that as well!"

I turned towards Amorina, who smiled and gave a subtle nod. "Well done, Raith. It was a good outcome," she said quietly. I nodded in reply and swept my gaze over all of my family.

"Well, I just want to say thanks to all of you!" I said gratefully. "Your support meant the world to me."

"Ah, we didn't do anything," said Ichirō with a dismissive wave of his hand. "In fact, we couldn't do anything. It's been … really hard watching them grill you and not being able to interact with you until the trial was over."

I nodded, appreciative of my son's honesty. "I know it's been hard – and you were all amazing. Even if you felt like you were powerless to help, your presence was everything! Looking over and seeing you all there and, more importantly, knowing that you were all safe – that gave me the strength to keep going."

Ichirō nodded, but his furrowed brow and shifting gaze betrayed his unease.

"What's on your mind, son?"

"What if … what if they work out you lied?"

Father, Adanna, and Winona exchanged confused looks, and I motioned for Ichirō to follow.

"Give us a minute, guys," I said to the others, and they all nodded in understanding.

After walking a few metres away with Ichirō, I turned and placed a hand on his shoulder.

"Listen … the system can be very black and white. Either you're good or you're bad. Either you're right or you're wrong. Sometimes that system works … but often, it doesn't because it can't account for all the grey complexities of the real-world."

"Yeah, I get that but –"

"Let me finish, please," I said, cutting Ichirō off.

He nodded, and I continued.

"There isn't a single person on that council who can understand what it's like to be in your shoes. They don't know and will never know what it's like to remember whilst everyone else forgets. Nor can they understand the complexity that that would add to one's decision making. As such, if they knew that you'd joined Tynan for a time – that you'd worked alongside him – odds are, they'd simply paint you as a criminal, and they'd punish you like one too."

A tear ran down Ichirō's face and he nodded.

"But we both know that at your core you're a good kid. I know I didn't know her very well, but your mother, Alyssa, did a good job raising you."

"But what happened with Tynan …"

"Sure – you made mistakes. And look, I get it – that man demanded devotion from everyone around him. A devotion that was drummed into you since you were a child, and as we know, it's a devotion that you still remember all too well. If I thought my father had been reborn, a father I was loyal to, I probably would've stood by his side as well."

"Really?"

"Yeah, mate. Listen: I covered that up, first of all because, like I said, they wouldn't have understood the situation, and second of all, you deserve a second chance. But I need to make something very clear.
Just because I swept this under the rug doesn't mean you're off the hook."

"I know," Ichirō nodded solemnly.

"Do you? That path – Tynan's path – it's a very dark road to walk down. It's very easy to lose your way and potentially never find your way back. Like me, I think you'll need to work on that dark side of yourself each and every day. To look in the mirror and remind yourself which path you should walk down. And if you choose the darkness – if you choose to make evil choices – I will not protect you. You would have to face your own consequences then. Do you understand?"

"Yes," Ichirō replied, wiping the tears off his cheeks. "Thank you."

"What for?"

"For believing in me and showing me … kindness, compassion … and love. For giving me a second chance."

"Of course. You're my son," I said as I pulled him into a hug.

I let him go, and we turned back towards the family together. "Come on – let's re-join the others."

We walked back over to the family, and I gave a subtle nod to the others – a reassurance that all was well.

"Thanks for waiting, guys. Alright, let's find somewhere to dine and celebrate our victory and reunion! Then tomorrow, we depart for Gaia!"

I watched as Father, Adanna, and Winona exchanged a glance.

"What's going on?"

"The girls have something to tell you," Father said.

"Okay," I said with a shrug. "Fire away!"

"Well, when we arrived on Earth it was with the refugees," Adanna said, "and it's been almost two years since then."

I nodded, although I wondered where they were going with this.

"Earth is very different to Gaia – there's so many more people here, so many more things to do," said Winona.

Clarity dawned on me.

"And we've reconnected with old friends and made new friends, and Winona's even got a boyfriend!" Adanna added.

Winona's face immediately turned bright red, and as she looked away, I understood the point they were trying to make.

They want to stay.

They'd had lives here prior to us taking them to Gaia, and from the sounds of things, they'd picked up right where they'd left off. Earth, understandably, felt like home to them.

"Anyway," Winona huffed. "We've also both been looking at going to university. We've found courses we like, they'll let us in, and Grandpa was able to talk to the government, and because of who you are, they'll pay for our tuition."

"And before you ask," said Father, now chipping in as well. "I'll stay here and keep an eye on them. There's nothing for me on Gaia anymore, not with the planet decimated and your mother gone. Plus, I'm tired and damn near too old to go gallivanting back across the stars – you can only go into cryo so many times before you're sick of that shit they pump into you."

"Additionally, our mothers are here as well – they got evacuated from Gaia too. So, between them and Grandpa, we won't be alone or left without support close on hand," Adanna added.

I smiled sadly, knowing I didn't really have a choice in the matter. They were adults now, and they had their own lives to live – their own stories to write. "Well, it sounds like all of you have this planned out."

"I mean, we do, but we kinda wanted to make sure that you and Ma were okay with us staying."

I looked over at Amorina, who smiled sadly as well. "You girls ... gosh, we can't really call you that anymore," she said with a chuckle. "You're both young women now."

"Intelligent, kind, and compassionate young women," I added.

"Exactly. And your father and I are very proud of you, and we're sorry we've not been around for a few years."

"It's okay. We understand you were surviving a tyrant and saving humanity while you were at it," said Adanna.

"Be that as it may, we're still sorry. Of course, you can both stay on Earth. But I expect regular updates on how life is going – like, at least once a fortnight!" said Amorina.

"Of course!" Winona replied.

"And we're thrilled that you're going to study as well. Do you know what courses you're going to do?" I asked.

"I'm going to do a degree in warp engineering," Adanna said.

"And I'll be doing a science degree, double majoring in cryogenics and cellular biology," replied Winona.

"Those sound like fantastic areas of study!" Amorina exclaimed, spreading her arms for an embrace.

As mother and daughters hugged, Emma included – least she missed out on a family hug – I turned towards Ichirō.

"What would you like to do, son?"

"I want to come with you," Ichirō replied without missing a beat.

"And I want to come with you too!" Emma cried.

The group laughed, much to Emma's indignation. "I'm serious!" she insisted.

"We know you are, sweetie pie. Of course you're coming with us – we'd miss you too much otherwise!"

This seemed to appease my youngest, and I looked around my family. We were an odd bunch, that was for sure. Some bound by blood, others not, but we'd all found each other for a reason – a father needing a child, and sons needing a father. A man and woman who needed each other, and the daughter born of their love. Daughters born of past affairs in a previous life. No matter the circumstances of the relationship, each one was as valid as any other. But it was time to part ways.

"Okay, okay! Enough standing around – bring it in – group hug!"

As everyone gathered in the middle, and warmth and laughter surrounded me, I revelled in the feeling of togetherness.

Emma bemoaned being squished, which drew forth a round of laughter. I knew I had to make the most of this because part of me believed I would not get to experience this again. The distances between worlds, while not insurmountable, were still great, and I knew time could pass all too quickly. Tears rolled down my face when the embrace finally ended and everyone had taken a step back. A feeling of nostalgia hit me, that longing for simpler times, and I knew I was really going to miss everyone.

\\\V)\\

I opened my eyes, and the first thing I saw was the dark metallic ceiling looming above me. In the room's quiet, the sound of my mechanical arm was the only thing that broke the silence. I raised that arm and Bitsy's display lit up, showing me the time. I still had a few minutes before I would have to get up and begin my new daily routine.

"Morning, buddy," I said.

I had had my arm modified so that there was a hollow for Bitsy to tuck into, instead of being wrapped around my wrist, as it was designed to do. The space came with a charging port to help compensate for the reducing efficiency of the Arachnobot's batteries.

Good morning, Raith! How can I help?

"Can you please get the morning reports ready? I want to hit the ground running today – make a good impression, you know?"

I don't know, but I will get the reports ready for you!

As the Arachnobot lifted itself out of its hollow and scurried away, I returned my gaze to the ceiling. They say you go through life blindly if you don't think about the consequences of your decisions, usually causing more harm than good.

If life had taught me anything over these last few years, it was that I, more than anyone, needed to reflect on my life and choices I was making. The consequences of my actions always seemed to be particularly ... impactful.

Abruptly the room illuminated to its maximum brightness, and the ship's local radio station buzzed through the rooms built-in speakers.

"Dim the lights and turn off the radio!" I snapped.

The lights immediately dimmed, and the room fell silent.

Those settings clearly need to be adjusted!

With a sigh, I pulled the covers back, swung my legs out and over the edge of the bed, and got to my feet. My bones clicked and tired muscles protested at being used after a year in cryosleep. More and more, it seemed I needed longer for my body to recover from the effects of long-haul space travel.

I slowly made my way to the bathroom and stopped in front of the mirror, taking in my body's current state. I was still thin – I hadn't yet had the chance to regain the weight I'd lost during misadventures. My hairline had receded further, and my recreated head scar was still vivid and pink. My new arm, which I'd chosen to forgo having artificial skin on, was still silver and shiny, not yet having had the chance to become dull, scuffed and scratched. Many had queried why I'd chosen to have it uncovered.

"A reminder," I whispered.

A reminder to myself, more than anything, of the ramification's choices can have. Plus, if Tynan ever showed up again, I wanted a really obvious way to tell the two of us apart. I leaned in closer to the mirror, staring into the depths of my eyes – the windows into my soul.

I'd come to accept that the darkness inside was a part of who I was and that I'd always have the potential to become a monster. But I knew who I was and who I wanted to be.

I knew which wolf I'd be feeding every day. I just hoped that those around me – the people I loved and cared about – would see the man and not the monster.

The shower turned on beside me and I knew that the day was steadily marching onward. Balancing the restoration of four planets, raising a son and daughter, loving a wife, and making time for myself was going to be no easy feat.

"Alright, come on, you old sod. There are things to do," I told my reflection.

With a hot shower awaiting, I turned away from the mirror and focused on the day ahead.

❨❨❨❱❩❩❩

Being the mission commander had its benefits, including the luxurious penthouse suite, split over two levels. Due to the wrap-around observational window, you were greeted by a stunning view from both the upper-floor bedrooms and the open-plan living and dining area below. It displayed an unobstructed view of the ship and stars beyond, and presently, Gaia's brown, scarred surface sat before us as well, a reminder of the work that lay ahead.

Tynan had clearly designed this space with himself as the focus; what better room for an emperor than one that evokes a feeling of power, with a full view of your domain?

I peered down into the living area where Emma diligently did her schoolwork and Ichirō was quietly sketching – a hobby I didn't know he possessed until recently.

Amorina stood by the window, gazing down at Gaia, watching the different terraforming modules being transported to its surface.

I walked around the landing and down the stairs, heading over to Amorina, where I placed an arm around her shoulders. I noticed her flinch at my touch and immediately withdrew my arm.

"It's okay, you can put your arm back," she said, "sorry, my flinch was just … automatic."

"That's alright," I replied, and I slowly put an arm around her once more.

She leaned into my embrace and nestled her head against my chest. There was still a lot of distance between us, and I knew it would take time to come right. All I could do was be understanding and put the work in.

But even then, there is definitely a lot of work ahead of us.

"Good morning, by the way," I said cheerfully.

"Yes … good morning," Amorina replied softly.

I glanced behind me at Emma and Ichirō, happily absorbed in their respective activities. All things considered, this was nice.

It's certainly better than a jail cell for three years!

I knew Amorina wasn't entirely happy at the moment, but I hoped that, with time, her wounds would heal, and she would find happiness once again.

"You have already been forgiven, my dear. The problem is your actions have not been forgotten."

As her words echoed through my thoughts, I knew that her happiness depended on whether or not she could move on from her memories, and I really hoped she'd be able to. I missed the Amorina that didn't flinch at my touch and spoke with enthusiasm and confidence, instead of hushed tones and doubt.

Positive thoughts, Raith … positive thoughts.

For now, my daughters were happy, my son was happy, and I was happy – my mind was free of obsessive thoughts, nightmares, and dark inner voices. As I gazed down at Gaia, I couldn't help but smile at the sight of the terraforming process finally beginning, glad that we'd all started down the road to recovery. I knew there was a lot of work to do … but surely, all's well that ends well.

Right?

Epilogue
Fear What the Weapon Was Built to Kill

2164, Common Era – Space, Beyond Frontier Space

In the centre of an interstellar graveyard, there lay a great void where once an ancient and powerful construct had slumbered. But that great horror had been awoken and had headed out into the stars, to chase its newfound prey. What neither it nor the prey had realised was that the location of this floating cemetery was no accident. It sat in front of the only entrance to a region of space surrounded by black holes. And now, that passageway was unguarded.

A large, ancient ship dropped out of warp into the middle of the graveyard's void, soon followed by another ship, and then another, until hundreds of thousands of vessels were occupying the space. This was the fleet of an ancient, interstellar empire, now cut off from the galaxy no more.

The first of the ships to arrive was the command vessel, its archaic form battered and battle-scarred, but still strong, still capable and deadly. Thousands of creatures awoke from a millennia-long slumber inside its cold, dark halls.

Their pale skin glistened in the blue lighting of the ship, and their pitch-black eyes seemed to both absorb and mirror the world around them. This was a primordial race, one that had grown dark and corrupt over the eons of their species' existence. Their lives were long, and their memories longer still. They did not forget, and they did not forgive.

They did not know whether their aggressors were still around, but they'd be sure to pay if they were still alive.

But revenge was not the most pressing issue in the minds of this race's leaders. No, they were far more interested in the species that had inadvertently freed them from their centuries long imprisonment. The leaders called out their technology, spread throughout the galaxy, hoping that it was still there, and in working order. Sure enough, the network responded. It was patchy, and in a terrible state of disrepair, but there was enough functionality for the leaders to achieve what they needed.

They reached out through their interstellar web, spreading their shadow far and wide, searching for their rescuers. Before long, their telepathic probe found a human vessel, and with ease, they reached inside the minds of the crew onboard. Through their memories, the leaders lived vicariously, seeing all the humans had seen, all they had heard and smelt, touched and tasted.

The leaders saw their colonies and star ships, their trials and tribulations. And once they were done, they fed their knowledge back into the heads of these humans, filling them, overwhelming them, until their brains could take no more, and they haemorrhaged to death.

The will of the leaders was absolute, and their race obeyed all commands without question. They issued a decree: Spread the fleet out in all directions. Waste no time in reclaiming control of the galaxy. Mend the ships. Upgrade them if there is any worthy technology. Save the conquering of humanity until last.

Within minutes of the decree being issued, ships warped away, traversing paths among the stars that had long since been untrod. Soon, the galaxy would be held in their iron grasp again. Soon, they would restore the natural order.

The great void lay empty once more as the last ship flashed away. There were no witnesses to the emergence that had just happened, except for the carcases of machine and creature. Alas, the dead can tell no tales, and so this interstellar graveyard would keep its secrets. But it wouldn't matter – for as a new day arose upon the galaxy, its inhabitants would awaken to a horrific new reality, and soon they would all remember an evil long forgotten … ·

The Forgotten Saga Continues ...

Corrupted Race is coming in 2024 – join Quill's newsletter to keep up with the latest preorder and launch updates!

Sign Up for Quill's Newsletter

Join Quill Holland's mailing list today, and you'll get not one but two free eBooks direct to your inbox!

Be among the first to learn about Quill's new releases & receive exclusive content, including sneak peeks, discounts, and giveaways! You'll be emailed once or twice a month, and you can unsubscribe anytime.

Sign up at www.quillholland.nz

Acknowledgements

A book is never just the product of one person's time and energy – it takes many hands to shape and refine a story into its finished form.

So, a big thank you to my alpha readers, Jonathan and Ashley, who helped mould the story during its infancy.

Thank you to Cailey and Cherie for your development edits – you helped the story overcome its shortcomings as it grew and matured.

Many thanks to my beta readers, Evan, Amy, Rachael, and Kevin; as my test audience, you really helped complete the final draft.

A huge thank you to my editor, Cherie, for all her brilliant work editing and proofing – her efforts make the story shine!

Last but not least, thank you to Dewi Hargreaves for once again charting the universe of the Forgotten Saga, and a big shout out to David from Cover Creator for another stellar cover design!

Also by Quill Holland

The Forgotten Saga

Book 1: Forgotten Evil
Book 2: Awakened Horror

Short Stories

The Last of Her Kind
What Mattered Most

Pilgrimage of the Amalgamal
As featured in Lost Boys Press's 2023 Anthology,
Empire of Beasts

About the Author

A programmer by day and a writer by night, Quill Holland is a young New Zealand author who is always creating content. Ever since he was young, Quill could be found with his nose in a book or watching the latest science-fiction movie. As a result, he's developed an imagination that never stops, and naturally, sci-fi and fantasy are the domains that Quill's work inhabits.

A creative writing graduate from the New Zealand Institute of Business Studies and a member of the New Zealand Society of Authors, Quill has several self-published stories. When he's not debugging code or creating worlds, Quill likes to dabble in illustration and photography, as well as exploring the natural beauty of New Zealand with his partner.

Connect with Quill on:

Website: www.quillholland.nz
Twitter: @quill_holland
Facebook: @QuillHolland
Instagram: @quillholland
Goodreads: @quillholland

www.ingramcontent.com/pod-product-compliance
Lightning Source LLC
Chambersburg PA
CBHW021231060726
47590CB00005B/1720